The Bureau of
Second Chances

The Bureau of
Second Chances

Sheena Kalayil

Polygon

First published in Great Britain in 2017 by
Polygon, an imprint of Birlinn Ltd.

Birlinn Ltd
West Newington House
10 Newington Road
Edinburgh
EH9 1QS

www.polygonbooks.co.uk

ISBN 978 1 84697 392 5
eBook ISBN 978 0 85790 926 8

British Library Cataloguing-in-Publication Data
A catalogue record for this book is available
on request from the British Library.

Typeset by Biblichor Ltd, Edinburgh

For James

I

A FEW months after the death of his wife, Thomas made the decision to return to India. From that moment of resolve, it took less than half a year to arrange his affairs. He handed in his notice at the optician's where he had worked for nearly twenty-five years, deflecting his colleagues' enquiries and accepting their best wishes. At the end of the requisite three months, he was given a send-off dinner and presented with a gift voucher for a large department store. 'We had no idea what you'd need to take back with you,' one of his colleagues confessed.

He spent some weeks with a solicitor, transferring the deeds of the house – the unremarkable 1930s semi that he and Nimmy had bought after their marriage – to his daughter, Nina. He had numerous phone calls with Mariamma, who attended to the other house – the house that he and Nimmy had built in Cherai, facing the Arabian Sea – making sure that the water-pump was in good order, the generator running; it was three years since he had last been. When he could avoid it no longer, he turned to his wife's last effects. She had been scrupulous during the last year of her life, insisting she had no wish that he be lumbered with the burden of trawling through her clothes and trinkets after her death. She had already given a neatly wrapped parcel of her most special saris and wedding jewellery to Nina. Another parcel of saris had gone to the women's community group that ran a centre for victims of domestic abuse, and the box of old trousers and jumpers that she wore around the house had been deposited at the charity shop on the high street.

But even so, she had not been able to erase all remnants of her life. And these occasionally surfaced: aide-memoires of his wife. He found some undergarments that had come out of the wash and which he had, months ago, automatically put back in the chest of drawers in their old bedroom. The loose tracksuit bottoms and chunky sweaters, their pockets stuffed with the gloves and woolly hats she had worn in her last weeks, when she had complained of being perennially chilled: these he found pushed into the depths of their wardrobe. There were the vests that were still nearly brand new: he had bought them just days before she had died, when he had felt that if he could do nothing, he could keep her warm at least. And there were her toiletries, left behind when she spent her last two weeks in the hospice: her talcum powder, her face cream, the coconut oil she rubbed into her hair after her bath. He had stood for some minutes with that small bottle of oil in the palm of his hand. He remembered that when she was having her treatment, her hair falling out in clumps, she had been so upset at the sight of the oil, a reminder of her thick wavy hair, that he had hidden it among his shaving paraphernalia in the medicine cabinet in the bathroom. It was only after her hair had grown back to a becoming cap that she had asked after her oil and he had returned it to her. All these bottles and pots were as she had left them, in the top drawer of their dressing table.

He left the very last clear-out for Nina's visit. She flew over from France the week before he left for India. He let her spend time in her mother's bedroom on her own. He no longer thought of it as 'his' bedroom; he had been sleeping in the box room for more than a year. When she emerged, red-eyed, holding a small cardboard box containing everything she wished to keep, he silently took her in his arms and held her, stroked her hair, with a certainty he had not felt for years that that was what she wanted. When she was a little girl, comforting her had been simple and natural: she had always run into his arms when she scraped her knees, when she came off her bike, when she had suffered a slight. He had many, vague, memories of holding her to his chest, unable to stop himself from chuckling at her anguish while she heaved and sobbed into his shirt.

Now, however, his daughter was a woman of nearly thirty. He could not say that she confided in him; she had not sought solace from him for years. And when he held her he could feel that she was taller than her mother, her head brushing against his cheekbone. She felt substantial, with long limbs, shoulders, hips, elbows. He held her for longer than she needed to be held: he was enjoying her warmth and closeness. Then they separated. She had flashed an awkward smile, lowering her eyes, and had gone back into the room. He joined her after a few minutes and together they filled some plastic bags with items that he would take to the charity shop.

When they went back downstairs, after he had given her the details of the estate agents, the letting fee, their commission, after she had answered his queries over her job and her life in Paris with her usual perfunctory brevity, her eyes clouding over with secrecy, they sat in silence.

'Are you sure this is what you want to do, Pa?' she asked eventually. 'You're not very old. It will be a really long retirement.'

'I don't see it as retirement,' he replied.

'But will you be able to adjust? You've lived here so long.'

'Your mother and I went back nearly every year before she got ill.'

'But what will you do?' Her voice was steady, but there was an expression in her eyes that he could not read.

He thought for a few moments.

'After settling in, I'll look around,' he said. 'I might even see if there's a need for a teacher or a teaching assistant somewhere.'

She raised her eyebrows, then splayed her fingers, studied her nails. It was a familiar ploy: one she had used with much success as an adolescent, designed to feign a disregard for what was happening in her immediate environs. He reached across the dining table, took her hand. It lay in his passively, until, as if as an afterthought, he felt a small pressure, a squeeze.

'Now that you are no longer living in London,' he said, his eyes on her but hers still cast down, 'there is no one keeping me here. I'll enjoy the change. And you'll visit, won't you?'

She did not ask much more. He was not an elderly, frail parent; he had only just turned fifty-six, was in good health. He could, she knew, always return; no decision was irreversible.

But that night, as he made up her bed in her old room, empty now except for bed and wardrobe, he felt his decision was gathering a sense of permanence. His eyes swept over the house with a sense of detachment, as if he had left already and was inspecting his work of the last few years. He had painted the walls a few weeks ago, and there was still a faint smell of newness. He would do the same with the big bedroom and box room once Nina had gone back to France.

She climbed into her sleeping bag, her hair falling over her face, and he let himself gaze at her, drinking her in. She was a young woman, full of ambitions and desires he had no knowledge of, born of he and Nimmy, but individual, a person with a soul not of their making. Although she had seldom come and stayed in the years since leaving home and before Nimmy's diagnosis, at that moment he felt tremendously close to her – this adult-child – and tremendously distant, a feeling that was disturbing in its familiarity. He kissed her goodnight and then lay for what seemed many hours in the dark of the box room, the curtains undrawn, so the streetlight and the lights of the passing cars cast shadows on the wall. He hoped he would hear her call for him, as she had done when she was a small child, but he heard no more from her and presumed she had fallen asleep.

He remembered the first night that he and Nimmy had spent in the house, lying on a mat on the floor of the big bedroom, dizzy with excitement at being householders after three years of saving, Nimmy's stomach already a mound. The first night they had spent with the baby wrapped in a white blanket lying between them on their bed, marvelling at her curled-up fists, her rosebud lips, her shock of black hair. Helping Nina paint her bedroom aged fourteen; Nina arriving back in the summers during her university years to clump around her bedroom behind a closed door.

But I don't need to be here to have memories, he thought. In that small room he felt like he was speaking to his wife, that she was lying in the dark beside him, her body encased in the long house dresses she favoured. He could picture her face: the thick eyebrows, the cusp of her lips. She had looked younger the closer she had grown to death, her face the triangular shape of her youth, rather than the rounder womanly shape of motherhood and her middle years. Her short hair, grown back after the chemo, curling around her ears and revealing the smoothness of the back of her neck, harked back to the styles worn by the fashionable, wealthier girls in her year at college, who had styled their hair into chic gamine cuts, foregoing the traditional long plait. Her wrists, her ankles, towards the end were all impossibly thin and fragile. The last time he had held her he had thought of her as a girl, not his wife of more than thirty years.

He drove his daughter to the airport a few days later, and then straight on to the used-car dealer who had made him a reasonable offer. He took the bus back to the house, looked out at the familiar streets as they passed by. The grey pavements, the flurry of people of all hues, the shops and bars of Tooting Broadway: all far removed from the slender state hugging the coast in the south of India. Could he do it? he thought. Could he slip back into the rhythms dictated by the swell of the sea and the cycle of the moon? The question preoccupied him over the last hectic days, but by the time the plane landed, by the time the taxi he had hired pulled up at the house, the only thing he could think of was how he felt like he was breathing anew. And how sweet, how heavy was the air.

The house occupied him for his first weeks. It was not in disrepair but felt careworn, unloved. The water pump and generator were, however, in perfect working order – unsurprising, given that they were less than a year old – and every evening he enjoyed a shower, after which, wearing only a mundu tied around his waist, he stood on the balcony, where the warm breeze cooled and then dried him. He spent the first days dusting and cleaning the house out; Mariamma from next door sent her son to help. The shutter for the window in the second bedroom had suffered during a storm and was now swinging off its hinges. All the rooms had a thin, sticky film on every surface. Ants had taken over the ground floor: a family, a village, a city. At first he took a certain pleasure in watching their industry, their endless repetitive toil. They marched along the skirting boards and then, for some insect reason, on reaching a door continued up and then over the arch sketching a black outline, as if a child had traced over the lines and angles of his house. After some days, however, he grew tired of having to step over their parades, stand on them in error and feel the little bites: not painful but plentiful. He and the boy spent a week laying down bicarbonate of soda, a remedy suggested by Mariamma, and then sweeping out the remnants, the mounds of tiny carcasses, in the mornings.

The backyard was an exposed square of land, sandy, hosting a trio of elegant coconut trees. He negotiated with the man down the road for a delivery of bamboo and other supplies, and then, after sketching some plans on a piece of paper, he constructed a canopy, a supporting frame: a gazebo. The physical work, the sun strong on his bare shoulders, woke him up to his new life but also reminded him of his upbringing in the hills. As a child, he had swum in the rivers and paddy fields that surrounded them, climbed trees; his muscles had been lean and taut from a young age. In London he had found a swimming baths near his work where he went nearly every day, the chlorine of the water a bitter contrast to the slippery warmth of the rivers of his childhood. One morning he stood on his balcony, gazed at the sea.

Then, he straightened up, went downstairs and crossed the road. On reaching the beach, he could see, further to his right, the fishermen still pulling in their boats. He continued across the sand and plunged into the sea.

The water embraced him, the waves resisted and then pulled him further in. He could feel nothing below his feet, just expanses of the warmth. The undertow was persistent, but he was a strong swimmer and it did not take him long to find a rhythm, find a way to use the wave to move forwards. He swam out, and when he opened his eyes he was surprised to see that the land was now far away. A panorama lay before him of the beach, the fringe of coconut trees. Behind him, the vastness of the ocean, the sky. He was not on the land any more but in limbo, wallowing in the warmth, as a baby in his mother's womb. He swam further along, through the waves, and found that when he was ready to turn back, the sea helped him, nudging him forwards and then spitting him out so that he landed ungracefully on the sand, his chest heaving with his exertions. He had faced the land and been thrust upon it, as if he were to be thrust into a new life. He felt reborn.

Just as he had never constructed anything in a backyard, he had never swum in the sea before. Since buying the small square of land a few years ago and then overseeing the construction of the house in fits and starts, he and Nimmy had found the visits to Cherai increasingly hectic: the backdrop was always her plaintive family, nagging, demanding their attention. A stroll on the beach had been the closest they had come to enjoying the sea. Now, having ploughed through the waves, the salt water swilling in his mouth and ears, he saw a new release. Rather than returning to the house that they had built to pick at a life that had been thwarted, he had been given a chance to create something new: a step towards the rest of his living years. He had felt when he was in the water, looking back at the land, as if he was only then making his decision to return: there and then. As if, if he chose, he could turn around and swim away, back to his life of the last decades.

Three weeks after his return, he made the long train journey to Calicut, where his elder sister was in a convent. There, he spent an enjoyable two days. He was given a room in the visitor wing and took his meals with the nuns. He and his sister took a walk every evening along the tracks winding through the hills. They reminisced about their younger days and about their parents, both buried in the church of their village, Vazhakulam, along with their elder brother, who had died in a bus accident nearly thirty years ago. When his sister asked after his daughter, Thomas replied with a smile and an air of resignation.

'She will visit,' he said.

'She must come here,' his sister said. 'I've not seen her since she was this high,' placing the flat of her hand at her breast.

Thomas smiled, not refuting her even though his sister was round, diminutive; his daughter had most likely been towering over her aunt when she had last visited India, aged sixteen.

When they turned their conversation to Nimmy, his sister spoke in hushed tones, slipped her arm through his. 'God moves in mysterious ways,' she said. 'Here I am at sixty-three, and nobody will really miss me.' She shushed his protests: 'It's true, I'm just an old nun. But Nimmy, a mother, taken at fifty-five . . .' She sighed and shook her head. 'It's not for us to understand, Thomasmon,' she said. 'We just need to accept.'

He had long eschewed the piety of his upbringing, but he took comfort, if not in his sister's words, in the whole encounter. His affectionate and mischievous older sister, whom he had adored when he was growing up. He had been bereft when she had joined the convent and left the family home; he was just fifteen years old. Her comedic appearance: her dark, masculine face in habit and veil. The pithiness of her Malayalam and the rendering of his childhood name: *Thomasmon*. He had not been called that for years. He left his sister with a full heart, promises to return and arrangements. He would visit again at Easter in a few months' time, and she would come and stay with him at Christmas.

On arriving back in Cherai, he walked for some hours up and down the beach, long after the sun had gone, while some youths hoping to have a quiet smoke of ganja loitered in the shadows. His next port of call required some preparation. Nimmy's mother was still alive, nearly ninety and suffering from dementia, a mother of nine and a grandmother to fourteen. She lived in Idukki district, not far from where Thomas himself had grown up, in the house of her eldest son, Thomas's brother-in-law. They would be welcoming, he knew. But full of questions: what were her last days like? Did she not get treatment? Why did she not visit before she died? And then: where was she buried? Who would attend her grave if he were here? Back in Tooting he had asked himself the same questions, effortlessly finding answers for each. These he could not now recall. He remembered that they had planned to come to India the year before the tumour was found, but something had forestalled their plans. By the time they were looking into flights, Nimmy was complaining of an ache in her stomach. After the chemo, she had then undergone radiotherapy. When she was pronounced terminal, she had spent all her energies in preparing him and their daughter for the eventuality. And, although the days had sometimes dragged by with tedium, with a feeling of suffocation, although he had sometimes sat alone in the evening, angry with everyone, even Nimmy for getting ill, sat alone in a time that seemed to slow down with a cruel relish, each second a drip feed towards the inevitable, in the end, the *end* had arrived with a rapid stealth. He had not really thought of the others: her aged mother, who admittedly had long said farewell, and Nimmy's five brothers and three sisters, all scattered over India and beyond.

Arriving in Idukki some weeks later, he found Nimmy's family had grown softer, less brash and abrasive. In truth, the distance established over space and time, over thousands of miles and more than thirty years, had not frayed bonds but rather calmed frayed tempers. All the arguments, the niggles of old – why did Thomaschayan not remit more money than he did, stingy miser; why did Nimmy not spend more time in her old home on their visits back to India – had themselves grown older, and remained in the shadows, like elderly aunts. The arguments had grown old and weary, Thomas thought, but Nimmy was not allowed to. He cast aside his momentary bitterness and tried to throw himself back into her family in a way he had never done when she was alive. They were, all of Nimmy's siblings, parents now, some were grandparents. They had broken up into small exclusive units dealing with their own quota of personal dramas. While Nimmy's mother did not recognise him, the rest seemed primarily concerned with Thomas's well-being. After the customary salutations, the questions he had expected arrived but were asked half-heartedly. Rather than dwell on Nimmy, the family preferred to probe after Nina. Photos were produced, she was exclaimed over: she looks like her mother, but she has your chin. Beautiful girl, she needs to marry, don't delay it too long. He could deflect the queries with ease, throw his hands up in mock exasperation at the lack of nuptials, playing the baffled father with panache.

It was only after a long and bountiful meal, where he was served delicacies that he had not tasted for years, that his brother-in-law took him aside, suggesting that he and Thomas go for a walk, to look over the old village. As they walked, just as the heat of the day was beginning its slow decline, his brother-in-law drew out a small business card from his breast pocket.

'When you are ready,' he said, 'get in touch with Jos. He told me to tell you to call. He needs someone to take over his business while he and his wife are away. They're going to the States for about six months to visit their first grandchild.'

On the bus back to Cherai, Thomas had stared at the small card, creased with sweat and crumpled at the edges: 'Jos Chacko, Optician, Chacko's Optical Store, Off MG Road, Opposite Boat Jetty, Ernakulam, Kochi, Kerala'.

The card stayed in his trouser pocket, and it was only when he was hanging up the washing some days later that he discovered the white fragments, soggy, impossible to reassemble. But he remembered the address; he suspected that he knew exactly where the store would be because there had been a well-known optician's, Panikkar's, on that street. Jos must have bought it and reopened it under his own name. He needn't ring, he decided. Jos would have found someone already, and, rather than put his friend in a quandary, it was better that he turn up at the shop on the pretence of passing by, dropping in. If his brother-in-law was in touch with Jos, then his friend would know about Nimmy. At least he would not have to have that awkward conversation.

He prevaricated a further five days; by now he had been back two months. He had developed a daily routine: waking up when the room became too hot, swimming in the sea, embracing the fresh morning air and walking across the backwaters to Junction. He could do the necessary shopping for the day and be back at the beach before the sun was at its highest. The afternoons, he spent reading. He had always enjoyed his own company and even as a father and a husband he had always kept a space for himself. He did not have any friends nearby, but he had developed an easy rapport with the cluster of autorickshaw drivers who stationed themselves at the turning from Cherai Beach to Junction. Most knew him already from the visits he had made when overseeing the build of the house; those who didn't would have been apprised of the news about Nimmy. They behaved with a consideration that touched him. He had no idea what troubles and trials had befallen them, but clearly, living in his own house, however modest its size, with no financial difficulties, placed him in a different tier. And yet, it seemed that they regarded his loss as momentous as any they had endured.

When he was drinking his coffee in the morning, he thought, today is the day. He would go into Ernakulam and look up his friend. He caught the bus into the city and during the journey enjoyed a few pleasant memories of his college days with Jos. By far the more flirtatious, Jos had never seemed short of a daring comment for the female students on their course. He came from a wealthy family who owned a pharmacy in Trivandrum, already earmarked as his inheritance. As young men, they had been close and had at one stage considered opening their own partnership together. But then Thomas had married Nimmy and moved to London. Later, he heard that Jos had also married and moved in turn to Houston. He had last seen Jos about seven years ago, when the two men had arranged to meet up with their wives in town. He remembered a small woman, Rose or Rosie?

The street was cleanly swept, tidy. The pavements were in not bad repair, and the street was narrow enough so that, at least at this time of day, there was a pleasant shade. The store was, as he had expected, in the premises of the old Panikkar's. He stood for some minutes on the other side of the street. Ahead, he could see people crossing over the main road towards him: passengers arriving at the boat jetty a few hundred yards away on ferries from the islands. To his left was a coffee shop which he had not seen before, with a freshly painted sign, Green Gardens. If Nimmy had been with him, they would probably have entered the café; they could have been among the passengers disembarking after visiting the islands, which they had done occasionally on their trips back. The thought occupied him, and he stood still for some moments before he noticed a movement in the window of the optician's. Someone was waving at him.

He crossed the street and opened the door. Inside, the cool air greeted him. The colours of the rugs and chairs were bright; a glass cabinet along one wall held an array of frames of different styles. Someone was holding the door open for him.

'Welcome, sir.' Her voice was brisk. 'Please come in.'

He stepped inside quickly, the door swung shut and they faced each other. She was young, smartly dressed: black trousers and white collared shirt, her hair arranged in a neat bun at the back of her head. He could detect, however, that her sober costume, rather than clothing her, was containing her; she was bristling with enthusiasm.

'Please. Sit.'

She motioned to the plump blue armchairs artfully arranged in pairs up against the far wall. He nodded and sat down. The young woman returned to her desk, smiling at him. Then, with a quick movement she stood up again and walked over, her arm outstretched.

'I am Rani, sir,' she said. They shook hands. 'Mr Jos will come out soon.'

She pointed at the door behind them, which had a small frosted-glass window.

'He is with a client in the testing room.'

'Thank you.' He cleared his throat. 'I'm . . .'

'Mr Thomas, sir,' she interrupted, smiling widely, revealing large white teeth.

She pronounced his name as he was called by all close to him: his family, his wife and friends. It had only been when he had arrived in London that he realised he was destined to be 'Tomus' to the rest of the world.

As if she could read his thoughts, she added, 'From London.'

It was often a sobriquet, but just as often said in one breath: Thomasfromlondon. He nodded and smiled back.

'How did you—'

'We've been expecting you. You will be joining us, I hope.'

'Well—'

'And Mr Jos said you were tall,' she continued. 'And I could tell from just looking at you!'

'I see.'

There was a slight pause while she continued to smile widely, then she clasped her hands in front of her.

'We are a nice business. Honest, professional.'

'I'm sure.'

'And you are so qualified. More than Mr Jos!' she giggled.

She was nervous: this accounted for the babble and the laughter. And indeed, so would he be in her position. He was well-enough known to his friend; he was as yet an unknown to this young woman, who, if he decided to take on the post, would have to work with him every day.

'Do you get very busy?' he asked, in an attempt to deflect the attention from himself.

'So-so,' she said. 'Some days, so busy. Some days not.'

She smiled again, nodded.

He smiled back, and they remained like this for some moments, until he saw a hint of unease creeping into her eyes. He stood up.

'Shall I wait in the café across the road?' he said. 'I don't want to disturb you.'

'Oh no, you are not disturbing!'

She looked aghast, her palms aloft, as if she had been entrusted with safeguarding his continued presence and could not allow him to leave.

The door to the street opened. A middle-aged woman entered, fanning herself with the end of her salwar. She looked from one to the other.

'Sorry, am I interrupting?'

'Madam.' Rani's hands dropped to her sides, then she turned back to Thomas. 'Please sit.' She threw the words at him and then darted across the office. As she started pulling several plastic boxes off the shelves, he resumed his seat. The atmosphere changed. Action stations: the description popped into his head. Rani was arranging several frames on the counter.

The woman gave Thomas a sidelong glance. 'So hot,' she said and then, sauntering to the counter, drew up to Rani. 'These are the frames?'

'These are from our usual suppliers, but we also have an international catalogue. Expect a week's wait at least.' She spoke quickly.

The woman stared at the dozens of frames being unloaded before her.

'I was thinking of . . .' she began.

'For a round face, square glasses are better, madam,' Rani said. 'They have a slimming effect.'

Her frankness amused him and did not seem to offend the client, who, in contrast to her earlier imperious manner, became meek, trying on the frames that Rani advised, deferring to Rani's pronouncements. Blue was unflattering to Madam's complexion; larger frames only emphasised her heavy eyebrows.

As the two women continued their discussions, he surveyed the store and, beyond, the street outside. It was pleasant, he found, to be somewhere which had a purpose. He had only worked for a few months in the country of his birth, after his graduation, as a teaching assistant at his old college, before joining his father in the rubber plantations in the hills. In those days, leaving India had seemed the only way to have any chance of a secure future. Not yet twenty-four, he had married Nimmy, a

17

nurse with a post to accept in London: it was one of the reasons his father had approached her parents, made the introductions. They had left soon after their marriage and had worked there ever since. He knew that, without a reason to do otherwise, he was in danger of secluding himself in Cherai. Perhaps he would settle into his new life better if, at least for the next few months, he had some company, had some interaction with the world beyond the fishing village.

By the time his old friend joined him from the testing room with his customary effusive welcome, slapping his back and proclaiming how well he looked, Thomas had already made his decision. The details were simple: Jos and his wife were expecting to stay in Houston for six months to help their daughter and son-in-law with their first child. A photo was brandished: a chubby baby, two proud smiling parents. Rather than leave the shop in the care of an acquaintance – Jos mentioned the manager of the café across the road – it would be altogether much more satisfactory to leave it in the hands of a professional and, what was more, a friend. Thomas would be doing a great service to give of his time to take over the duties for that period.

It was a generous offer, sensitively worded. And as Jos talked about logistics – contacting suppliers, the process of ordering frames, making the lenses – there began a stirring, as if, deep inside his midriff, a set of cogs had started turning again. The life that lay ahead, evoked by Jos's words, was appealing. The business was not his, and so he would feel no great responsibility. He would have to wake up early, in order to get the bus from Cherai Junction to Ernakulam, but he could get off at the High Courts and then walk the remainder of the way. The journey would take an hour – not dissimilar to his daily commute in

London. Rani would already have opened up the shop, and they would welcome their first clients from ten o'clock. He could be back in Cherai by six, after which he would feel that he had earned a quiet evening. The weekends would be his, to walk along the beach, to swim.

On the bus back that afternoon, with arrangements made for some days' overlap before Jos and his wife left for Texas, Thomas stared out of the window. This time a year ago, he thought, it was the middle of winter in London. The garden was bare of its leaves, and we were having problems with our boiler. Nimmy had the schedule for her chemotherapy, and we were making plans for her hospital visits. His mind floated back as, outside, the stalls and vendors of the city grew sparser, until they were on the road heading to the sea.

2

LATER, he would remember how surprised he was at the busy-ness he had inherited. He enjoyed having a reason to wake early, gulp his coffee, walk briskly to Junction to board a bus that jostled among the other vehicles on their way towards the city. At that time of the morning, the congestion that would clog the streets, transforming them into rivers of dirty, dusty, unmoving cargo, was yet to emerge. He began to recognise some of the other passengers who made the same journey, and where they alighted. By the time he arrived at the shop, Rani would already have been on the phone for at least half an hour, making appointments. His first clients of the day might be waiting for him, sitting on the blue armchairs, turning the pages of a magazine.

It was work that was familiar to him, but the setting and the clients were different enough so that he did not feel he had exchanged one job for its twin. There were fewer instruments, fewer tests, and he was treated with the deference that was more commonly afforded to a medical professional. There were scheduled appointments for two hours in the morning and afternoon each, but the rest of the time was kept free for arranging the prescriptions to be sent to the labs, and for accommodating any clients coming in off the street. Jos had been correct: as the road was the most convenient to use to cross from the boat jetty to the main artery, MG Road, passengers from the ferries would walk past and then often drop in. Many clearly just wanted a brief respite from the heat outside. After a perfunctory glance at the frames in the cabinets and the prices of the eye tests, they would leave. But others would linger, ad hoc arrangements for an eye test would be made.

On his first day as optician-in-charge, he had felt some trepidation as he opened the door and entered the store. He had been back a few times, when Jos had reviewed the procedures and equipment, but this would be his first real day of work. Jos and his wife had flown out the previous night. Rani was waiting for him and sprang to her feet on his arrival, ushering him in. She had laid out the instruments he needed on the desk in the testing room, and she showed him the bottles of water in the small fridge in the main room, the small restroom outside across the small backyard. She was chattering, and he could detect the same nervousness in her behaviour as when they had first met. It would be strange for her to have him around for the next six months. 'You will find us quite backward, Mr Thomas,' she had said, 'compared to London.'

She clearly felt the opposite, only pride in Chacko's Optical store, and he was quick to express his disagreement. And yet, he found out quickly, there *was* something quite old-fashioned about the workings of his friend's store. For one, there seemed an inordinate amount of paperwork considering the simplicity of the business. The small computer on Rani's desk seemed to be under-used: she made appointments in the ledger, kept details of payments, in duplicate, in a book of paying-in slips. In quiet times he would come out of the testing room, have a drink of water from the bottles they kept in the small fridge.

21

Rani would always be at the desk, poring over some documents. Thomas had no knowledge of the accounts and had no need for such: Jos had said that Rani's salary was paid into her bank account, and Rani dealt with any payments from clients. As far as he could tell, it was only the orders that were activated on the computer.

For this, he would sit at the computer, and she would move to the cabinets and tidy the frames. The orders were easily filled out, and he needed only a few minutes in her seat. At the end of each day, Rani locked the cabinets and the drawers of the desk, while he sprayed the testing room and the chair with antibacterial solution, wiped the eye visors and instruments. They stepped out on to the street together, and he would wait until she had locked the door before he turned away. Then they separated, with cordial goodbyes: he walked in the direction of the High Courts, she the opposite way along MG Road.

At lunchtimes, they had an hour of respite. Rani flipped over the sign on the door – *Closed for lunch break!* – then settled back at the desk. On his first day, he had approached the desk; she was laying out a paper napkin and pouring herself a glass of water. He smiled at her and said, 'I'm going out to stretch my legs.'

'Did you not bring a tiffin?' she asked.

He shook his head. 'If I'm hungry, I'll get a snack outside.' He paused at the door. 'Can I get you anything?'

She looked surprised at the offer and then smiled. 'No, I bring my own lunch, Mr Thomas.'

They made the same polite exchange the next few days as he left the store. He spent most of the lunch hour walking near the boat jetty across the road; he enjoyed the sun on his shoulders as he watched the ferries arrive and leave. The passengers disembarked and there was the usual rush to clamber on, grab the best seats at the front where the fumes from the engines would be lightest. Occasionally, a large tanker or cruise ship, moored further away in the water, would appear, just discernible through the heat haze, and as if to verify its presence, a group of seamen would climb off the ferries, their uniforms and caps attracting some interest from the small boys selling sweets and peanuts from trays. Towards the end of his hour, he would buy a snack from a vendor: that did for his lunch.

Before long, he was used to the daily routine. The mornings were the busiest: clients booked appointments before the heat of the day drove everyone indoors, seeking some relief under a fan. Afternoons mostly relied on footfall. In quiet periods he stayed in the testing room, with the door slightly ajar, reading at his desk; Rani would be at her post in the reception area. It was companionable, peaceful. From their positions at opposite ends of the office, they would occasionally glance up, catch each other's eye, exchange a brief smile.

At the end of his second week, as he was leaving for his lunch hour, he saw Rani returning from washing her hands in the restroom, patting them dry with a small handkerchief. She glanced at him and smiled, with a flash of her large front teeth.

'Going for your walk?' she asked.

He nodded, then said, 'And what do you do, Rani, while you're eating your lunch?'

'I read.' She patted her bag and then after a moment's pause drew out a book and laid it on the desk. He moved back into the room away from the door, walked over. She giggled nervously when he picked up the book. He stared at the cover and then looked up at her.

'Do you know it, Mr Thomas?' she asked, her eyes bright.

He nodded, his mind whirring.

'Of course,' he said finally. 'It was my favourite when I was a student. It's a surprise to see you reading it.'

'Thought it was too classic for me?' She was laughing now, her mouth stretched wide.

'No, not at all,' he lied. He fingered the cover. '*Chemmeen,*' he read out loud, then looked up and smiled. 'Have you finished it yet? Will I spoil it for you if I talk about it?'

'Mr Thomas, I must have read it about three times. Each time I have finished it I have started it again.'

He laughed. 'That's impressive.'

'And now I can imagine nothing more romantic than falling in love with a Muslim against my family's wishes!' She delivered the last words with a dramatic flourish that made him smile in response. She turned the pages, searching for a section, and then passed the book back to him. 'My favourite part.'

He looked at the pages and read the words; he had forgotten how lyrical Malayalam could be. He shook his head to clear his thoughts; revisiting the prose held a sweetness that took him unawares.

When he lifted his eyes, he saw that Rani was watching him.

'Truly,' he said, 'a beautiful book.'

'Yes,' she said.

For a few seconds they were quiet, enjoying the moment, then he cleared his throat. 'I'll let you have your lunch,' he said.

She smiled, reached into her bag again and pulled out a steel tin. He nodded, turned away and let himself out.

He walked across the main road, towards the jetty, and then along the street running parallel to the sea, where the large trees cast some shade. Whereas most days his eyes would be fixed on the water, the comings and goings of the ferry absorbing his attention, today the scenes before him were but a backdrop. His mind was elsewhere: restless, roaming. Suddenly, he understood why: the memories of the novel were entwined with memories of his younger days, before he left India. The book had been published in the late fifties, in the year of his birth, and by the time he had read it, it had already received the accolades and critical awards that would enshrine it in Kerala's literary history. He tried to recall the details of the plot: a tryst between a Hindu girl and a Muslim boy, made all the more unusual because the writer had set the story in the fishing community. Sections of the narrative were written in the particular dialect they used: a dialect so thick it was incomprehensible to most. A marriage of convenience for the girl to a local Hindu boy, a betrayal and then retribution from Kadalamma, the sea goddess. She had been merciless: the lovers dead, lying on the sand, the hapless husband killed by a shark.

When the film of the book had come out, he had gone to see it in a large gang of his fellow college students; he remembered that they had occupied one whole row in the cinema. Most of his peers were more interested in the large and shapely breasts of the lead actress, half-bursting from her wet sari blouse, than in the allegory that the writer had painted. He had joined in half-heartedly with the crude comments and the crass noises that his friends had made to accompany the chaste lovemaking scenes: all in an attempt to mask his own entrancement, his beating heart. Seeing his favourite book beautifully displayed on screen had moved him as never before. He had found the actress ravishing. Not only because she offered an earthiness, a seductiveness, which at the time was wholly out of his sphere of experience, but because she had perfectly embodied Karuthamma, the Hindu girl, with whom he had fallen in love, helplessly, on meeting her on the page.

When he brought himself back to the present, he looked around him and realised that he had walked further along the promenade than he usually did on his lunchtime excursions. As if the thoughts of his youth had directed his stride, he saw that he had arrived across the road from the bookshop he only vaguely remembered noticing a few days ago. He crossed the street and pushed open the door. The shop assistant he spoke to wore an earring.

'*Chemmeen?*' the youth repeated. 'Prawns? Have you seen our cookery section?' and before Thomas could respond, he had darted off, leaving him trailing behind.

As they were approaching a pile of large hardback cookbooks, he tried again. 'Actually, that's the name of the book. *Chemmeen.*'

The shop assistant stopped short and looked at him uncomprehendingly.

'It's a classic,' Thomas continued. 'They made it into a film. In the sixties.'

Finally, the expression on the young man's face cleared. 'That rings a bell. Not sure if we have it. I'll check,' he said, returning to the cash desk and tapping on the computer.

Thomas left the bookshop a few minutes later, an order placed, and a sense of something achieved beyond simply making a purchase. It was the first thing he had bought since his return that did not have practical value but, rather, contributed to a reacquaintance with his earlier pursuits, a re-emergence of his younger self. More than any other encounter he had had so far, holding those pages in his hands had reminded him that he had returned. He was walking the streets that he had walked as a young man, before he had married Nimmy, even before Nina was a little beating heart in his wife's belly. It was as if he had received some affirmation: he had lived here before, and he belonged here.

He felt an excitement at this thought, but, he reminded himself, he would have to be patient. The ticket he had been given showed that he had weeks to wait before the book would arrive. Given that the shop did not stock a copy of the book, he wondered where Rani had got hers: it had looked new, not a hand-me-down. On returning to his friend's store, he had wanted to share the news of his small adventure, but Rani was on the phone. It was only when they were locking up at the end of the day that he told her where he had been over the lunch hour.

She exclaimed with pleasure.

'Really? Because of me?' She seemed so pleased to have made an impression on him that he laughed.

'It's hard to get hold of,' he said. 'I had to order my copy. Where did you get yours?'

It was a throwaway question, but instead of answering she shrugged her shoulders and turned away: an action that was so uncharacteristic that he was momentarily taken aback. He inspected her surreptitiously: she was rummaging in her bag ineffectually. To his consternation, he could see that her face was red with distress. 'Somewhere in town,' she mumbled.

He turned away, not wanting to cause her more embarrassment.

'Where are my keys . . . ?' he said, patting his pockets in pretence. He removed himself to the testing room, where he waited a suitable while. When he returned, he saw with some relief, that she had regained her composure and was smiling, waiting at the door.

'See you on Monday,' she said as they parted.

'See you.'

The next day was a Saturday, and when he went out for his morning swim, he saw the fishermen again, pulling their boats in. They were now used to him: only one would wave. He could hear their voices, the harshness of their language. The dark sinewy bodies reminded him of fish themselves. He was tempted to walk across, speak to the youngest who watched him: Do you know *Chemmeen*? The book? The film?

But instead he swam out until he had the headland in his right-hand vision, then he turned on to his back, looked at the sky: blue-red with a dusting of clouds. He swivelled back on to his stomach and swam back, arriving on the sand panting, his arms and legs aching. He looked up and saw the house to one side, the grove of swaying coconut trees and the complex of thatched cottages belonging to the new beach resort. The sun was beginning to rise and the air held a hint of freshness. An empty promise: the day would be as hot and humid as any other. With the warmth of the sun drying his skin, he felt something inside: a contentment.

The weeks at Chacko's Optical Store elapsed at a pleasingly relaxed tempo. He avoided referring to the novel – he did not want to upset Rani again – and it was only a few days into his second month at the store, as he was nearing the door on his way for his lunchtime stroll, that she asked, 'Has your copy of *Chemmeen* arrived yet, Mr Thomas?'

He let go of the door handle, turned back to face her. 'No. It won't for a few more weeks. I was told they were getting one sent from Madras and it would take a while.'

'I'm happy to lend you mine.'

She had arranged her hair differently, he noticed, in a long plait, a pair of pink clips positioned quaintly on either side of her middle parting.

He smiled. 'That's kind of you, but I wouldn't want to deprive you.'

'I'm taking a break from it,' she said. 'Four times is enough. For some months at least!'

They smiled at each other.

'So, what are you reading today?' he asked.

He saw a flush rise to her cheeks as she slid out a magazine from under the ledger; he recognised the romantic serials that could be bought at most newsstands, the lurid cover. Not very highbrow.

'Not a classic,' she said, as if reading his thoughts.

He laughed. 'Nothing to be ashamed of. It's good to vary things.'

She nodded, still blushing, laid the magazine on the desk.

'Rani,' he said, on an impulse. 'Can I invite you for lunch?'

She stared at him, then motioned to her bag. 'I've brought something.'

'You could have it on your way home,' he said. 'I'm sure it will keep. Why don't we go and get something fresh at Green Gardens?'

She nodded, smiled, then stood up, patting her blouse and trousers. They left the shop, and he could discern some pride when she turned the small square over: *Closed for lunch break!*

There was a languor in the air: it was that moment in the day when time seemed to slow, too weighed down by the heat to tick away as normal. A man on a bicycle rode past, his wheels rattling, followed by an autorickshaw, whizzing past, bleating with irritation. Thomas instinctively reached for Rani's arm, as he would have done with Nimmy, remembered just in time. He glanced at Rani: she was shading her eyes with her hand and seemed not to have noticed his momentary relapse. He opened the door of the café for her, and she passed inside.

Was he imagining it or did the manager, the man whom Jos had introduced him to, stare at them for just a fraction too long, his eyes swivelling from one to the other with astonishment, before breaking into an uncertain smile. 'Mr Thomas! Welcome!' Was he imagining it or did Rani stiffen in response, give an imperceptible shake of her head?

He was filled with dismay. He must cut a desperate, lecherous figure, lunching with this young girl, even younger than his own daughter! He should have known that as a widower he would be subjected to a meticulous dissection of his actions; he wasn't old and people would be wondering how he could, as a man, look after himself. He turned to Rani with a thought to suggest they go somewhere else, but the manager had by then descended on them, now beaming, to shake Thomas's hand and pat Rani on the shoulder.

'I decided to encourage Rani to have a proper meal,' Thomas said, his cheeks warm.

'Good idea,' the manager replied, turning to Rani. 'She's such a hard-working girl. We'd all like to have a daughter like her.'

It was a forced comment – the manager was not very much older than Rani – and it rang out with a shrill tone of falsehood.

But the two men laughed heartily, hurriedly, then both stopped abruptly. There was a pause.

'Ah yes.' The manager sighed, as if recovering from a particularly strong bout of mirth, then bowed. 'Please, take a seat.'

He saw that Rani was no longer beside him, but had seated herself at a table near the window. She was perusing the menu with the same efficiency with which she perused the catalogues of frames.

'We should order the lunch special from the hot plate,' she said as he was sitting down. 'The masala dosa is made fresh every day.'

'You seem to be quite the expert,' he said, smiling. 'Perhaps you come here more often than I thought.'

To his chagrin her face crumpled, only for an instant, but long enough for her usual brisk manner to evaporate.

'Not really . . .' she began.

'Of course,' he said, in what he hoped was a soothing manner but which to his ears sounded smarmy, patronising. In an effort to regain some control of the atmosphere, he looked out the window.

This was all much more stressful than he had imagined. But he had, he supposed, fallen out of touch with the ways of his country. Perhaps it was indiscreet or inappropriate to invite his assistant to lunch. He was, to a certain extent, protected by his relatively advanced years, but he no longer had a wife as collateral. His intentions when inviting a young unmarried girl, no matter how innocent, could still be misconstrued. And it was not he who was the more vulnerable to censure: it was she.

A silence fell. He had thought that a conversation about the novel would be an easy fallback, but now he felt unsure of conferring over a great passion with the inexperienced young girl opposite him: his comments could be interpreted as titillating. The silence extended until he became afraid of the opposite: that she would think he found her an unworthy conversationalist.

'Rani . . .' he started, then stopped.

While she was staring out the window, he realised, her eyes were not on the street outside but on the manager's reflection, visible in the glass. He glanced across and saw that the manager was indeed watching them. When he saw Thomas looking at him, he broke into a wide smile, laughed insincerely and waved. Thomas turned back to Rani, but not before he saw her eyes fixed on the manager. She blinked and turned to him, gave a little whinny, then composed herself.

After an awkward silence, he started again.

'Rani. Tell me about yourself. Did you study? Where are your family from?'

'Oh, sir.' She laughed again, but looked much less strained. 'Well,' she began, smiling as if to temper her words, 'I am from an ordinary background, I can say. From Palakkad area. Do you know it?'

He shook his head. 'Not well.'

'My father is a cook for the railways,' she said. 'That is the only way he managed to send us all to school. Me and my three sisters. I got a scholarship here for college. Then I got the job with Mr Jos.'

It was a tidy résumé. But what she did not say was more revealing: her story was plain to him. He looked at her, sitting across from him. She belonged to just the right caste and class to blend so well into the multitudes as to become invisible. By truly belonging, she seeped into the flesh of the country,

32

became its veins, its tendons, silent below the surface, unseeable. It was only if you bent forwards and peered into Rani's face that you could see the brightness of her eyes, admire the set of her mouth, or the slenderness of her neck. It was possible that even her father had not examined her in that way. He might, instead, have welcomed the fact that Rani was fending for herself, relieving him of the burden of arranging her marriage.

He stopped his train of thoughts, unsettled by the ease with which he had painted a picture of Rani's life. I could be completely wrong, he told himself. She was pretty, smart. She could be the adored and cosseted clever daughter, the most vivacious. The darling of her father's eye, a father who did not want to rush and marry her off to any suitor. He found his eyes meeting Rani's and knew with a pang that his first picture was more likely to be the truer. He cleared his throat.

'Do you go back to Palakkad often?'

'More often than not my father visits me. I go three times a year at most. I see my father sometimes at the railway station.'

He nodded.

'And where do you stay here in Ernakulam?'

She smiled again, shaking her head with mock severity. 'Mr Thomas. You sound worried about me.'

He laughed. 'No, not really, Rani. You see, it's been so long since I lived here. I feel quite out of touch with daily life. When I was a student, most girls your age were still living with their parents.'

'Well,' she said, then sipped from her drink, 'I may be older than you think, Mr Thomas. I'm twenty-five. Nearly an old maid.' She raised her eyebrows, then grinned at his protests. 'In this modern India,' she continued dryly, her expression serious, 'girls like me often live away from their families.'

She folded her hands together, laid them on the table and then smiled. 'I live in a hostel in Konthuruthy, which is a nice area.'

He smiled back. 'That's good.'

'Yes.' She gave another wry smile. 'Curfew at ten p.m. No gentlemen visitors.'

'Glad to hear,' he ventured, and was pleased to see her laugh in response.

Their dosa arrived, and he took some relief in the distraction. They munched in companionable silence for some time.

'And you, Mr Thomas,' she asked, wiping her mouth on the napkin. 'Tell me about you.'

She had finished her food, her plate was empty and she pushed it to one side, tilted her head and waited for him to speak. He had asked the same of her and she had complied. Now, faced with the same question, he thought, where to begin?

'About five years ago, my wife and I decided we wanted to buy some land and build a house,' he said slowly. 'We always planned on retiring here. Well, I'm in that house now. In Cherai.'

He decided to do something that he rarely did: he pulled out his phone and showed her a picture. She looked intently and with great curiosity, asked him questions about the layout, the building project and seemed pleased with his patient answers: two bedrooms upstairs with a bathroom, a living and dining room with a kitchen downstairs. Nothing ostentatious, a comfortable home.

'I've been there,' she said when she finally leaned away from him, handing back his phone. 'It's a nice beach.'

He nodded.

'And your daughter, Mr Thomas?'

'Nina.' Again he swatted at his phone and showed her a photo: Nina and her mother the year before Nimmy got ill.

Rani stared at the photo for a long time, her eyes flickering over the tiny screen.

'I think she looks like her mother,' she said finally.

'Yes, most people say that.' He reached across, but she held on to his phone.

'She's very beautiful,' she said. Her tone was polite and wistful at the same time. He plucked the phone from her fingers, and she looked at him.

'She'll visit, and you'll meet her.' He glanced up. 'I'd like you to meet her,' he added.

'She grew up in London?'

He nodded.

'Oh, I would love to go,' she sighed.

There were a few minutes of silence when he could think of nothing to say in response. Of course she would love to go: which young girl did not dream of London? There was no point in drawing her attention to the details: the streets were not golden but grey. Not everyone lived in affluence but more often than not lived in modest comfort. For a girl like Rani, leaving India would hold an impossible allure: out of her reach and so forever to be yearned for.

He glanced up and saw again that she was watching him quietly.

'But no rush,' she said.

He felt a wave of gratitude. She was sensitive to his feelings, tactful; she did not want him to feel sorry for her, even though he had had a life that had evolved, by many standards, into some measure of success. His parents had been an anchor, had probably sheltered him because he was their youngest. His father had decided his life trajectory for him, chosen Nimmy to be his wife; he had had no anxieties or hardships. What could not have been ordained, however, was the more elusive gift that Nimmy and he had found in each other: companionship.

His limbs suddenly felt very heavy, lethargic. He was unused to eating a heavy meal at this time of day, he thought. Or perhaps the early mornings and long bus journeys in the heat were taking their toll.

He shifted in his seat and saw that Rani was watching him.

'Tell me about your wife.'

He gave a short laugh, shook his head, but he was shocked to feel sudden tears prick his eyelids. He cleared his throat and arranged his plate before him, dipped his fingers into the bowl of water between them. When he had run out of things to fiddle with, he finally met her gaze.

'Maybe another time,' he said quietly.

She did not say anything, but she inclined her head.

'Would you like anything else?' He pointed at the menu.

She seemed not to have heard him. 'There are many others,' she said suddenly.

'Others?'

'Like you,' she said. 'Well, not all like you. Not all widowed. Sorry,' she added quickly, waited for him to nod his acknowledgement then continued breathlessly, 'yes, many others. Married but now divorced, grown-up children. Alone again. But this time no parents to arrange a marriage, find a partner.'

How had the conversation ended? He couldn't remember on the bus home that day. They had both spotted, through the window, the two o'clock appointment, looking irritably at the sign. He remembered sending Rani ahead to open the office, remembered handling the bill. The manager was affable, clapping his shoulder, but Thomas sensed a relief that they were leaving. And the afternoon had been so busy that he had not had a chance to resume his conversation with Rani, who appeared by then, in fact, somewhat aloof, distant. He tried not to dwell on it, hoping that he had not offended her with his invitation.

But on the bus home, the sun setting, he and his fellow passengers tired from the day's events, he remembered that she had said something before their meal was curtailed, and he was sure that he had heard her correctly: 'But what if they want a second chance?'

3

I N the days that followed their lunch, he woke to the sound of the sea, the shouts from Mariamma's backyard. The trees that lined the sand: they swayed and whispered as before. All remained unchanged in Cherai. But there was a shift in the atmosphere in the optician's: a shift that he felt had happened after their conversation. There was nothing concrete, nothing he could put his finger on, but the sense that something had altered gnawed at him. Perhaps it was simply that in the first flush of working at his friend's store he had not taken heed of Rani, and he was now more observant. But as the days passed by the feeling persisted: it was as if she had been holding her breath, waiting to see if he would pass muster. Now that it appeared he had, she could breathe a sigh of relief, and resume. What exactly she was returning to he could not say. He had invited Rani to lunch on a whim but, reluctantly, he began to wonder whether she had engineered the invitation. He found himself returning to the words he believed he had heard her say: what had she meant?

He noticed that he heard her voice more often during the day: she would either be on the phone or conversing with someone in reception. Suddenly, she seemed to be unfeasibly occupied. Given that he was not attending to any more clients than before, he could not understand why that should be. But the most disconcerting observation was that she did not allow him to be involved in the workings of the store beyond the eye tests, preferring him to remain secluded in the testing room. He had not imagined her to be territorial, but what other explanation could there be for her behaviour? If the phone rang, Rani was always there to answer it. If ever he picked up any post left on the doorstep, Rani was quick to relieve him of the burden: 'Don't worry, Mr Thomas. I'll do that.' And more than once he got the impression that when he left the office for his lunchtime stroll, she had been biding her time, waiting for him to leave. The more he observed, the more he felt as if he were trespassing. If Rani was on the phone, he detected a slight change in her tone on his arrival. It was too much of a coincidence that nearly every time he walked into the reception she would appear to be tying up a conversation: 'Right, I'll call you back with the details.' She always used the formal 'you', so it was unlikely that she was making personal calls. Perhaps she felt uncomfortable dealing with clients in his earshot; he could tell she had been embarrassed when one customer had arrived and insisted on speaking in English. Her knowledge of the language was limited, and she had given Thomas a grateful look when he had gently steered the man to conducting the conversation in Malayalam.

Once, when he was sitting at the computer, Rani in the testing room finding some more forms of some kind, the phone rang. He picked it up.

'Chacko's Optical Store.'

There was a hesitation on the other end. He could hear someone breathing, until a woman's voice said, 'Is Rani there?'

He looked up and saw Rani at the doorway of the testing room, the expression on her face expectant. He passed the phone to her and, as he had suspected she would, she said she would ring back with the details. She avoided looking at him for the rest of the afternoon.

A few times when he went back into the reception area, he had seen the manager of Green Gardens leaving the store, pausing only to call back in jovial fashion, 'Mr Thomas!' So, she had a closer friendship with the man than he had imagined, which could explain his shifty behaviour the other day. And yet, there did not seem to be the spark of romance between them: there was more a sense of co-conspirators. That was it, Thomas decided one evening: it was like living in a conspiracy.

In many ways the workings of the store continued as before. There was clearly a loyal base of customers who were fond of Rani. He had, at first, found Rani's manner amusing, and then perturbing. The short entertainment he had witnessed on his first visit, between Rani and the middle-aged woman, had not been unusual. Rani was not a quiet, meek presence; she did not speak to the clients in muted, ingratiating tones, underlining her position of offering a service. She was not yet hectoring, but so enthusiastic as to be overwhelming. It was, he realised, a manifestation of the pride she took in the store.

'Those frames, sir, we are the only ones to stock them. The nearest outfitter is Bangalore.'

'Madam, we have more in the catalogue, the latest styles, from our suppliers in Mumbai.'

Rather than responding adversely to her interjections, the customers would murmur in reply and a discussion would ensue. She was a popular addition to Chacko's Optical stores, he could see. She was charming: he had learned this from their lunch together. Her enthusiasm was infectious to all who spoke

40

with her. She was genuine, with a self-deprecatory wit and an easy warmth. This was what clients found so beguiling, what made her presence in the shop appealing.

But, even so, given that spectacles were hardly a perishable purchase, it was odd that people kept reappearing. The man with red highlights in his hair, who had come the previous Tuesday: Thomas saw him again in the reception talking to Rani a week later. The lady-lawyer who had ordered three pairs of glasses in differing styles: ten days after Thomas had attended to her, she was back at the desk talking to Rani. There was the engineer who lived in Abu Dhabi and had told Thomas that he was back in Kerala for a couple of months sorting out his property: he returned within five days of ordering his frames. While Thomas was in the testing room most of the day, even from the quiet of his sanctum he could hear the buzz of the reception, the shop taking on an air of being a social hub.

His immediate worry was that she was siphoning off funds, but he dismissed that almost instantaneously. Jos had set up his accounts and methods of payments with a fastidiousness that would require real criminal intent to breach. Rani emanated a sense of goodness that could not be contrived. What was more likely, he decided, was that she was using the office amenities to further some personal endeavour. It was unlikely that she had access to a landline, a computer or a printer in her hostel in Konthuruthy. She was availing herself of the office; once Thomas had been vouched for, she had felt safe enough to resume her activities. Perhaps she was arranging something for her family?

He felt guilty over these musings. It was mean-spirited to begrudge her these privileges: most people would do as she, use the facilities at work to deal with domesticities. And he had no need to tar all their interactions with the brush of conspiracy: his invitation to lunch had followed his discovery of their shared love of a novel. She could not have planned his reaction.

When Jos rang a few weeks after the lunch at Green Gardens, he did not express his worries.

'How's the baby?'

'What?'

His friend sounded harried, as if it were him overseeing an unfamiliar business, rather than spending half a year at his son's pleasure. It was with some annoyance that Thomas repeated, 'The baby. Your grandson.'

'Oh, you know,' Jos muttered vaguely. Then spoke more clearly. 'Actually, I'm a little bored. We're looking after the baby now that Sita has gone back to work. We don't have a car, and so we're stuck in the suburbs in the house most of the time.' He sniffed. 'Rosie is doing most of it, I have to admit.'

Thomas chuckled. His irritation evaporated and he felt some sympathy.

'Tell me,' Jos was speaking again. 'Any problems?'

'No.' He hesitated. 'Rani is taking care of everything.'

'Yes, she's a real asset.' Jos seemed happy to expand. 'The clients love her. Which surprised me at first. She wasn't my first choice. I thought we would do better business if we had someone more decorative.'

'Mm,' Thomas dallied. 'Do you know if she has family nearby?'

'Her father works in the railways. She's from Palakkad, I know. Her mother died when she was young. Ten? She doesn't go back very often.'

A woman's voice called out in the background, and they ended their conversation.

So she had not lied about her origins, he thought. There was no mystery there. But she had not mentioned her mother, and he wondered if it had been out of sensitivity for his feelings. He felt guilty: she had not tried to tell him a sob story, or extract his sympathies. She was, in fact, irreproachable, and he needed to dismiss any suspicions he had.

He managed to distract himself over the next few days. It was Easter in a week, and he had promised his sister he would visit her in Calicut. During his lunch hour one day, he went over to the train station to make enquiries and book a ticket. On the way back, he was tempted to visit the YMCA, where as a young man he had played many games of pool in the recreation hall. He found it without much difficulty and spent nearly half an hour learning about the renovations that had been made from the elderly caretaker. He was late arriving back for his first afternoon appointment: the woman was already seated in the reception area.

Rani seemed particularly agitated by his timekeeping.

'You are late, Mr Thomas.'

'Yes, sorry—'

'Please go into the testing room, madam.' Thomas noticed that she was propelling the woman with a determination that bordered on rudeness.

'And Mr Thomas,' she said, turning and guiding him with a surprisingly sturdy hand on his back.

'Rani—'

She closed the door firmly, but he protested: he had left his pens on her desk. She was breathing noisily with flared nostrils as he remained in the reception area, lingered purposefully

43

while he tried to gather his thoughts. Eventually, he had no reason not to return to the testing room. As he was closing the door, he heard the front door open. Rani stood smiling in welcome at whoever had entered.

'Everything is arranged . . .' she began.

'Sir?' The woman behind him was already seated in the chair and was looking at him with irritation.

He had to shut the door, but not before he caught a glimpse of a red shirt, smart trousers. He was distracted during the examination: there was something about the way Rani had stood up and greeted the customer, a different manner from her demeanour as receptionist for Chacko's Optical Store. She had seemed doyenne-like, expansive. As if she was welcoming someone into her own parlour.

There was only one more appointment after the woman, and when the client left, he walked into the reception area. It was quiet for a change: there was no one there other than Rani. She had tidied the coffee table: the magazines were in neat piles. She had her head bent and was busily writing in their accounts ledger. She did not look up at him as he moved towards the door, stared out on to the street. Then she straightened up and threw a forced smile in his direction, moved towards the cabinets.

The phone rang. She turned back immediately but Thomas had reached forward and grabbed the handset.

'Chacko's Optical Store.'

Silence. Someone breathing on the other end, and then a click. He turned around and saw Rani staring at him. When their eyes met, she turned back to the cabinets, started pulling out drawers and closing them at random. He let her carry on and then she slowed down, as if aware of his eyes, until she opened the last drawer, closed it quietly.

'Rani,' he said, and he could hear his own voice as she would: a deep baritone of disapproval. 'What is going on?'

Her back stiffened, then she turned to face him. She opened her mouth as if to protest, but something in his expression quelled her words. He walked over to the door and flipped the sign over: *Closed!* Anyone standing outside would still be able to see them, so he twitched the blinds shut.

The room was now calm and dim. They remained in their positions, unmoving, until she stirred, took a key from the bunch at her waist and walked over to the desk, opened the bottom drawer. Instead of pulling out a plastic box of frames, she extracted a yellow folder, a ring binder, not bulging but nearly full. She placed it on the desk, then leaned back in her chair. He stared at her uncomprehendingly, then pulled a seat from the wall and placed it next to the desk. The file lay between them.

The minutes ticked by. Literally. He could hear the tick-tock of the wall clock behind him.

Then she spoke. 'Inside,' she said, 'are letters. From clients.'

She opened the file and, turning it so that he could see, flicked through it. There were several sheets in plastic wallets, a small photograph clipped neatly to the top right-hand corner, each page covered to varying extents with handwriting – some extending to the end of the page, others a mere paragraph.

'I ask them to write a letter telling me what they are looking for.'

He took the file from her hands and turned the pages, one by one.

I was married some ten years before I discovered . . .

I am a successful engineer with PR in Dubai . . .

My name is Meena and I was born in 1975 in Bangalore, although I grew up in Mumbai . . .

His eyes were drawn to the header on each page, which read: *Rani Vamadevan. Marriage Bureau Consultant.*

'What is all this?' He looked up, bewildered. 'Why are our clients writing to you?'

'They want a second chance, Mr Thomas,' she said simply. 'Their marriages have ended, but they still have a long life ahead. And they want to meet someone.'

Thomas stared at her. By now she had lost the startled expression and was looking composed, serene. She tucked a strand of hair behind her ear with a near nonchalance. She had crossed her legs and was raising her ankle up and down to a rhythm he could not hear. She looked to one side as if she could see far beyond the grey plastic Venetian blinds, then turned back to face him. Only a slight quiver at her mouth betrayed her.

'So I ask them to write to me,' she said, as if it were an addendum. 'And I see if I can find a match.'

Again, a long silence.

'So,' he said finally, 'you are running a dating agency.'

She made a little moue of disagreement.

'No. I call it a marriage bureau, Mr Thomas. These are serious people, looking for some . . . commitment.'

'Rani, you're running a dating agency from my friend's shop!'

She did not answer but remained still, her hands folded over each other.

'Why?' he spluttered. 'Why on earth . . . ? I'm sure Jos would raise your salary if—'

'I'm not doing this for money, Mr Thomas!' Her eyes were bright with indignation. She shook her head. 'Of course I wouldn't do such a thing for money. If anyone is making any money it's . . .'

She caught herself.

'Who? Who is with you in this?' Thomas stood up but then felt huge towering over the young girl and sat down again. 'I demand to know, Rani!'

She shook her head.

'No one else is involved with the . . . matching,' she said finally. 'But the couples get a special meal for their first date at Green Gardens.' The last was conveyed at a rapid pace.

He slumped back in disbelief. He remembered the manager's expression – what was his name, Vijay? The shared glances between him and Rani, the forced laughter and nervousness.

He fixed her with his most serious gaze. 'Does Jos know?'

She shook her head slowly.

'How long have you been doing this?'

Again a long silence during which she held his eyes.

'Three months,' she whispered finally, her voice quavering at the end, as if she were testing the veracity of her answer.

'And,' he began, then found he had to clear his throat and start again. 'And what do they write about when they write to you?'

She continued to stare at him, not allowing her eyes to leave his face, as if she could hypnotise him into slapping his knees and standing up, saying, right, that's all sorted then! But then she blinked and swallowed.

'I ask them to think about their first marriage.' She scanned her desk and found a piece of paper and placed it in front of her. 'And I tell them to make two columns.'

She picked up a pen and drew a vertical line.

'Then,' she continued, 'I tell them to reflect on their marriage. After going through a divorce, most of them tend to focus on the negatives. But I insist that they consider what they really liked about their partner and write that in the left-hand column.' Thomas watched, mesmerised, as she wrote: *He was very handsome.*

'And then,' she was gaining momentum, 'I tell them to avoid negativity. You know, like, "what I hated about my husband". But to think about what they would like to have changed, and put that down in the other column.'

He watched as her pen hovered over the page. To his relief, after some hesitation, she scribbled a series of dots and crosses.

'Then,' she turned to him, an element of triumph creeping into her voice, 'I ask them to use this as a basis for the letter they write to me about themselves—'

'Rani,' he interrupted her, 'you're playing with people's lives!'

'I'm not, Mr Thomas!' Her voice was startled.

He reached forward and pulled the sheet of paper towards him. 'This exercise? What can it tell you about them?'

'I can see what they are looking for! I can see what their hopes are! They could tell their parents all of this when they were young, but now they have no one to go to!'

She was gripping the pen with both hands now, her face flushed with agitation.

He put the paper down, smoothed it with his hands, his mind racing.

'Rani,' he said as gently as he could. 'You're not making sense. Parents know their children, or at least they know their children more than what you can learn from a letter or an application form!' His voice rose at the end, but she did not flinch.

They faced each other silently, then she spoke.

'You're imagining your daughter, Mr Thomas,' she said calmly. 'But I'm not talking about people like Nina. Of course she could rely on your advice. She would turn to you and respect your choices.'

He opened his mouth to correct her but closed it again: this was not the moment nor was it relevant. She placed her hands, palms down, in front of her on the desk; her back was ramrod straight.

'My clients come to me. I don't force them to do anything.'

Her face was clouded, her mouth set stubbornly, and then her body relaxed. She looked at him and said softly, 'It's their choice, Mr Thomas.'

He shook his head. 'I just can't see why they feel that *you* are the best person to make these decisions.'

She was quiet for some time.

'Perhaps, Mr Thomas,' she said eventually, 'perhaps, you are right. I may not be the *best* person. But I may be the *only* person offering this service in Ernakulam. Let me show you.'

Her fingers flew over the keyboard of the computer. She opened a search engine and typed some words into the search bar: *second marriage matrimonial agency Kerala*. Several hits arrived, and she clicked on the first: photos of smiling heads and shoulders, with a few cursory phrases assigned to each to the right. No names: the pictures were anonymous until registration.

'Rani . . .' he began, but could not stop himself scanning a few examples: *She is 31*, he read. *Status: Divorcee.*

He glanced down the page. For each smiling headshot, the same 'status' was replicated, even when Rani calmly clicked to the next page.

'You see, Mr Thomas,' she said. 'Hundreds, and just on this site.'

He cleared his throat.

'And what do you notice about them, Mr Thomas?'

He was quiet, reluctant to participate in her tutelage.

Finally, he said, 'They seem young to me.'

She nodded excitedly and turned to him. 'Exactly! It's not like the old days, Mr Thomas. People, especially women, are not prepared to stay in a boring marriage! They don't feel that it is their duty to please their parents. They might have expected romance and are disappointed with the routine of married life.'

He stared at her silently until she reddened slightly.

'Sometimes you sound much older than you are,' he said, unwilling to hurt her feelings but unable also to stop himself. 'Most marriages have their routine bits, but that's part of the package.'

She looked back, her lips pressed together.

'None of these internet agencies offer something different for an older client, Mr Thomas,' she said, her voice quiet. 'You are right in what you say about marriage, and of course you will have more experience than me. But after a five-year marriage, you might be happy to have your photo on such a website.' She gestured at the screen. 'After twenty years and some children, you might feel differently.'

He turned back: *She is 27. Status: Divorcee. She is 30. Status: Divorcee.* The words swam before his eyes.

'I offer them something completely different,' she continued, 'A service with a personal touch that is so lacking . . .' She waved her hand at the column of portraits.

She is 29. Status: Divorcee.

'My innovation is to go back to basics. No fees, no registration. No internet, no computer, no details. Just my folder.'

He looked down at the folder, open between them, and turned the pages. The faces stared back at him, unsmiling. Not the most flattering of images, an underwhelming gallery.

She reached forward and quietly pulled the folder away from him, returned it to the drawer and locked it.

'Tell me more, Rani,' he said quietly.

She didn't speak for a few moments. He watched her: she looked ridiculously young to him, ridiculously unqualified for her enterprise.

'When our parents arrange a marriage,' she said, her eyes on the desk, her voice steady and low, 'they think of caste and religion. Looks, skin colour, education.'

She raised her head to look at him. 'If you're a girl, your father may need to pay a dowry. But these things are not important for my clients. They've got children, most of them. They have careers. Sometimes they just want someone to go to the cinema with . . .'

He watched as she lowered her eyes again, so that her eyelashes cast a faint, feathery shadow on her cheek. Then she stood up and busied herself shuffling papers, moved back to the cabinets. The interrogation was over, was her message. But he could see that her hands were trembling: she was not immune to his censure and not as sure of herself as she was portraying.

'And have you had any successes?' He struggled to keep the sarcasm from his voice. 'Have there been the second marriages that these people seem to be looking for?'

'My involvement only extends so far,' she said primly. 'I arrange a first meeting, and the rest is up to them.'

She was half turned away when she continued, 'Some have come back. They want to try again.'

'Oh, Rani, Rani,' he groaned. He tried to dispel the unsavoury images that rushed into his head: of overweight middle-aged men seeking gratification, Rani their innocent conduit. He turned to watch her: she had her back to him and was ticking a list.

'How many people are we talking about?' he asked.

'Fifteen,' she said without turning around.

'Fifteen clients in three months,' he said. 'That sounds like a lot to me.'

She started to say something, stopped and then resumed. 'It's Vijay,' she said, turning around. 'If he sees a potential customer, he adds my card to their bill.' She walked back to her desk and extracted a card from her bag. *Rani Vamadevan: Consultant, Vamadevan Marriage Bureau, c/o Chacko's Optical Store.* Set side by side on the card, the two different services did not seem at odds: one helped you look for things, the other looked for you.

'I'm sure Mr Jos has benefitted from more people visiting his shop . . .' she said softly.

He brushed her words away, stood up so suddenly that she took a step back.

'I can't let you continue with this.'

'But . . .'

'You need to close down your . . .' he had trouble finding the right word, 'operations.'

'Mr Thomas!'

'Rani, there is no way—'

'Mr Thomas, please!'

Her eyes were filled with tears, her hand was at her throat, a picture of anguish. He pushed on: 'It's for your own good, Rani. Find another outlet for your ambitions.'

He regretted his choice of words instantly: paternalistic, dismissive. What could he know about her ambitions? She stood before him: still, a forlorn figure, looking at her feet.

'It's not fair,' he said after a long silence.

She did not respond, and he saw a tear splash off her chin.

'It's not fair to be using Jos's store without telling him.'

He cleared his throat, and after some time she raised her eyes to meet his.

'Do you agree with me on that at least?' he asked gently.

She nodded slowly. Then she reached forward and took her card from his fingers, turned it over and stared at the blank underside.

'Maybe,' he began, and her head snapped up, 'maybe you could continue if you don't try to grow your services. Until Jos returns. No more new clients.'

She beamed at him. 'Thank you, Mr Thomas!'

'And then when Jos comes back, we have to let him know.'

'Yes, of course.'

'So you have to let Vijay know. No more cards, etcetera.'

'OK, Mr Thomas.'

He sighed. 'I'm still not sure—'

'It is a good compromise, Mr Thomas. Like you said, no new clients. I'll just take care of my existing batch.' She was babbling now, her colour had returned to her face, she was patting her blouse down as if ready for business.

'Yes, but remember, Rani—'

'Of course, Mr Thomas. I'll speak to Vijay. It will all be as you say.'

She turned away and started ticking her list furiously.

The rest of the day passed quickly. Whenever he came into the reception area, she rewarded him with a wide smile as if to assuage his pride: you won, don't worry, Mr Thomas. It just may not feel like it. In the evening, they parted as usual at the door.

'Have a good evening, Mr Thomas!' she sang out, rushing towards the main road while he muttered a response.

That night he sat at the dining table long after he had finished the simple meal he had cooked for himself. Normally, he would have gone upstairs soon after: the breeze from the sea was more pleasant than the ceiling fan. But he sat and stared in the dim light, his mind not alighting on any one thing. Her enterprise had piqued his interest. The image of the website was sketched in his mind, the list of headshots. Finally, he glanced around: there was a notepad among the pile of papers on the side table. He pulled out a piece of paper, drew a vertical line, dividing the page in half.

What I liked about Nimmy, he wrote, *her kindness, her smile, her hair.* Then he found his pen had stopped writing. He looked at his words, and the three bullet points seemed generic and trivial, laughably paltry, scanty for more than thirty years of marriage. He closed his eyes and tried to think; he let his mind wander, tried to remember her voice and tried to imagine what she would have said if she were to find him sitting at the table writing a list of her virtues.

But when he opened his eyes, he wrote in the other column: *What I would change about Nimmy. How she never read any books, how she was never interested in the news, the way she chewed her food with her mouth open, how she was ashamed about sex.* He stared at the paper, appalled, then crossed the last words out feverishly. He leaped up, crumpling the paper into a ball which he cast to one side, and stacked up the plates, dumped them into the sink in the kitchen. He took the stairs two at a time and rushed through his bedroom to the balcony. It was dark all around: no one could see what he had written, know what he had written. But he found that his heart was thumping. He held the rail to steady himself, gulped in the night air. It was only after several minutes that he relaxed his hold on the balcony rail, slowly let out his breath.

He remembered that when they were first married – those first months when they had delighted in each other's bodies, spent evenings lying together, stroking, whispering – he had once begged Nimmy to stand before him, to let him see her completely naked. He had cajoled and pleaded. When, finally, she had relented, she had left the bed, stood before him and then made a slow pirouette. He had feasted his eyes on her, his voice somewhere deep in the pit of his stomach, before she clapped her hand to her mouth as if surprised at herself and dived under the sheets next to him. She had let his hands run over her smoothness, let him revel in her soft bits and her firm bits, her swells and hollows. He had prevailed on her to do the same again and again, each time with less cajoling needed: she enjoyed being looked at. After Nina was born, however, for months they did not have the bed to themselves, and Nimmy was reluctant to let him touch her, worried that they would disturb the baby with their love-making. Later, she became self-conscious of the weight she had put on and continued to put on and never managed to lose, no matter his protestations that he did not mind. Perhaps deep down she could intuit that he missed that slim, supple body he had gorged himself on those first years.

He closed his eyes. Where did all this come from? he asked himself. Why am I having such thoughts about her now? Rani's technique, it seemed, was effective: disgruntlements were brought to the surface. It was true that he had found Nimmy's prudishness frustrating. She often made excuses, leaving him over the ensuing years to surmise that she felt that his appetite for making love to her was unseemly. She never truly gave herself to him in the way that he did with her. He gripped the balcony rails again and leaned over, the sound of the sea before him, the night so dark it felt like he could plunge his hand into it, feel its sensuous warmth.

We were our first lovers, he thought. And our only lovers. Nimmy is the only woman I have seen naked, held naked. Perhaps that is what I would write in my letter to Rani, my application to the bureau: *I was born in Vazhakulam and am a trained optometrist. I would like to meet a woman with long beautiful legs, who must be willing to disrobe in my presence, unlike my bashful dead wife. This is a crucial point and one which will determine the success or failure of the match.* He tried to laugh but there was no one to hear him, so why pretend? Instead, he stared forward as the waves rose and fell, rose and fell, in their ceaseless rhythm.

4

H<small>E</small> tried to phone Nina when he got back home, late in the evenings, reaching her answer machine. Whenever he heard her voice message in French and then English – *Hi, you've reached Nina and Michel* – he felt a tremor of unease, hearing his daughter's voice, and hearing it blithely pronounce her name alongside Michel's. She had been in that small ménage for more than a year; she had told them of Michel on her first visit back to see Nimmy after the diagnosis. Neither Nimmy nor Thomas had had the energy then to query their daughter's lifestyle; neither had been enamoured with the idea that their daughter was living, unmarried, with a man they had not met. From her closed expression, however, it was clear that her domestic arrangements were not up for discussion.

He left messages on her answer machine, but each time as he was hanging up he had a strong feeling that she was there, listening to him, not picking up. She was avoiding him. If she had wanted to talk to him, she would have rung back. It had been months now since they had spoken. She didn't want to talk to him, and he was forced to deduce the reasons. She was a legal advisor for a large multinational and could be going through a stressful period at work. Or she and Michel could be making decisions about their future. He knew that Nina had expressed a desire to return to New York; Michel was keen to stay on in Paris.

The decisions they agonised over, the few conversations between them that had been in his hearing and then, further, in English, had confirmed the conclusion at which he and Nimmy had long arrived: their daughter was an alien. She had not been long in her teens when she had established that the way she wanted to live her life was not in tune with their vision of her future. She had kept them on tenterhooks, terrified of the path she would take. But after an adolescence peppered with phases of indolence and insolence, she had pleasantly surprised both of them by choosing to study law and graduating with an excellent degree. Their happiness at her success, however, had seemed only to annoy her further, as if it was testament to the narrow limitations of their approval. She had not drawn closer to them, but drifted further. To New York, then Paris, then into a relationship with a man Thomas had only met once.

They had raised their daughter far from where he and Nimmy had been formed, hoping that would lend her opportunities richer than she could expect in Kerala. But something they had not envisaged had transpired: they had raised a child who looked through a different lens, saw a different set of hues and shadows. She was forever impatient with them, expecting them to move along as fast as she, shedding traditions by the roadside, constantly reminding them that they had chosen to leave, chosen to stay. *This* is home now, had been her recurring mantra. And when Thomas had turned fifty, she had not missed the opportunity to point out that he had, by then, lived in London longer than he had lived in India.

By returning to Kerala, and re-immersing himself in the life of his younger days, he had only confirmed the gulf between them. He had never shared with his daughter his thoughts about a novel that he had devoured as a young man, in the language of his childhood and young adulthood. She was, despite being his child, more unreachable than someone like Rani. The question troubled him. If all that had resulted from his and Nimmy's ambitions for their child was a vast area of unmentionable, arid distance, if he was back here now anyway, had it ever been worth it, leaving?

He might have been distracted the next few days with his musings over his daughter, but Rani did not seem to notice. Even though they had reached a compromise, somehow it appeared that Rani had gained the upper hand. Perhaps she felt she could eventually chip away at his resistance and acquire him as a supporter. Perhaps, given that he had revealed his love of *Chemmeen*, a paean to forbidden love if ever there was one, she saw him as an accomplice in matters romantic. Perhaps she envisaged that she would eventually entice him into her bureau, that he would write a letter expounding his wishes for a future match.

The atmosphere in the optician's, as always seemingly dictated by her mood, was gay. One morning, however, there was an unusual hiatus: there were no appointments booked for the next hour and a half. He decided to go for his usual lunchtime walk a little earlier. If someone dropped in speculatively, they would have to wait or make an appointment for later in the afternoon. Rani was on the phone when he walked into the reception area.

'The best way,' she was saying, 'is to meet here. Then I can make sure there is no misunderstanding . . .'

She was clearly still enmeshed in the world of introductions, whether with new or existing clients was impossible to tell. She glanced up at Thomas as he moved across the room.

'Yes, I think I've made a good choice,' she was saying now, brazenly.

He shuffled to the door, feeling his lack of potency, uncertain whether she had heeded his warnings at all. When she glanced at him, the handset still at her ear, he motioned to her that he was going out, held up a finger to signal one hour. She broke into a smile, waggled her fingers. 'Yes, like I said. A dentist . . .'

He closed the door behind him with some relief and for a moment hesitated on the step. Should he go back inside, stand over her with a bemused expression until she hung up sheepishly?

But he had little volition to do so. His initial surprise at discovering her endeavours had faded; memories seeped back into his skin with stealth, so that what he queried one day could be explained the next. He had wondered why a girl like Rani, with a decent job and salary, would have either the energy or desire for another enterprise. But then he remembered that just as the land was used and populated assiduously, so it seemed that one's time should be used as meticulously as possible. He remembered that his father had, aside from working in the rubber plantations, grown flowers which were sent off at intervals during the year to hotels on the coast that they never went to; his mother was a seamstress, sewing into the night, alongside running their household. Rani was only following in that tradition, complementing her job at the optician's with another. The curiosity was that it was one from which she appeared not to make any financial gain.

He stepped off the pavement, on to the street. It was much too hot to be outside, the air was leaden, a thick fug through which even the sounds of traffic were muffled. Even the cars seemed lethargic, stunted by the heat. He was not hungry, more thirsty, and so crossed over to a kiosk where he bought a bottle of water from their chest-fridge. He walked towards the sea. Marine Drive was bright in the sunlight. The white stones sparkled, the water glittered beyond the low sea wall. If Jos's store had not been located in this part of the city, he doubted he would have agreed to help out. The promenade and the surrounding streets, the water, the ferries and the collection of islands were all linked symbiotically, lending a cohesiveness which dissipated a short distance beyond. A mile further inland, the city descended into a jumble of shabby buildings, tower blocks, fragile shacks, dusty criss-crossing streets and interminable traffic. Only near the water did it make an effort to cast off its backwater, backward reputation, try to match the more glittering urban centres in the further north of the country. He could not envisage swapping the peaceful beauty of Cherai to travel every morning into the spluttering, coughing heart of the city; perhaps Jos had known that before he called on him.

It was only after walking nearly halfway up the length of the promenade, the High Courts to his right and Bolgatty Island now visible in the distance, that he found a space on a bench. The only other occupant was a woman in sunglasses: the straw hat on her head and her manicured, painted toenails peeking through stylish leather sandals proclaiming her foreign-ness. He exchanged a polite nod as he sat down, and then, as if to confirm his assumptions, she called out, 'What time do you make it?' She was talking to a tall boy, leaning against the low wall, facing the sea. When he turned around, Thomas saw an oval face, wide-set green eyes.

'Half an hour more, I guess.'

Later, he wondered what had made him speak to the woman. Perhaps from some form of homesickness: if not for England, for English, a not unreasonable thought, given that for the last thirty years it had been the language he had communicated most in. Or perhaps it was simpler: Rani's exploits had sown a seed in his mind, reminded him how pleasant it was to sit next to an attractive woman, side by side on a bench, the sea before them.

'Are you visiting?' he asked.

Her immediate expression was frustration: a shadow flitted over her features. She would have been accosted with the usual litany of which-country-where-are-you-from interactions. But then she relaxed.

She nodded. 'From the States. Are you?'

'Not exactly. I used to live in London, but I live here now.' He pointed up the promenade. 'A few miles that way, in a small fishing village, Cherai.'

'Oh, right.' Her voice held a timbre of interest. He could just make out through her darkened lenses her eyes moving over him, before she turned away and gestured at the youth, still standing with his back towards them, facing the water.

'My son,' she said.

'A nice-looking boy.'

She smiled suddenly. 'Yes, he is, isn't he? Thanks.'

Then she added, as if in explanation, 'His dad is Italian, actually. My husband, I mean.'

He found himself feeling an instantaneous pang of disappointment at the words – *my husband*. He glanced at her hands and saw a gold wedding band.

'And you are . . .'

'Yes, Malayalee.' She smiled again. 'Born and bred New Yorker, though. Queens.'

'I've never been,' he said. 'But my daughter worked there for a year. She loved it.'

'I don't live in New York any more. We're out in the midwest now.' She took her sunglasses off and he saw large eyes, a fragile network of lines at the corners, neatly plucked eyebrows. Her hair was a silky sheet that framed the curve of her cheeks; her lips were full. It was hard, he found, to look away. He glanced at her legs, which as far as he could tell were long and lovely, encased in navy-blue capris, then cleared his throat and turned to look at the sea.

'Where did you live in London?' she asked.

'Tooting Broadway,' he said. 'Have you been?'

She nodded. 'A few times. I have a cousin in Croydon. I usually stay with her if I'm in London for business.'

He nodded.

'I'm supposed to be going at the end of the year,' she added. 'I'll have to look up Tooting Broadway.'

He laughed. 'It's not on the tourist trail,' he said, then paused. 'But it was home for more than thirty years.'

'Oh wow.' She did not attempt to hide the curiosity in her eyes. 'So why are you back here? No wait, let me guess.'

She crinkled her eyes and tilted her head to one side, her hair falling away from her face, the ends scraping her arms. 'You're not old enough to be retired, I wouldn't say. But I suppose anyone can take early retirement if they wanted to,' she said. 'It must have been that famous London weather. Although whenever I've been it's been glorious.'

He said nothing and she smiled. 'So? Was it the weather?'

'Well . . .' he was loth to continue, but what could he do? 'My wife died,' he said in as matter-of-fact a voice as he could muster. 'And I just thought . . .'

She had made a sharp intake of breath, raised her fingers to her lips for a moment before laying them on her lap.

'I'm so sorry,' she said. 'How clumsy of me . . .'

'Please don't worry,' he said, but she remained still, looking at her fingers.

'She died of cancer,' he decided to say. 'It's been nearly a year now.'

'I'm sorry,' she said, lifting her face to look at him.

'Please don't worry,' he repeated.

She was quiet, and he was regretful. He had not wished to curtail the conversation, but he could see that it was difficult to move on from where they had arrived. She was turning her sunglasses over and over in her hands, as if when she stopped she would know what to say.

He gestured to the boy. 'Is your son enjoying the holiday?'

She flashed him a grateful look. 'I *think* so.'

Thomas smiled. 'You're not sure?'

'He doesn't talk much,' she said, and something in her tone made him feel that he could laugh without causing offence, which he did. They sat watching the youth, who was now kicking his foot gently against the wall, his hands in the pockets of his knee-length shorts.

'A difficult age?'

'Well, he's thirteen. You can imagine. It wasn't his idea to come on holiday with his mother. His older brother stayed at home; he had too much going on . . .'

They fell silent again, then she said, 'D'you know what? I prefer having Hari on his own, actually. I can never think when

64

his brother is around.' She turned and smiled at him. 'I sound awful, don't I?'

He smiled back. 'I have only one daughter, grown up now. I can't say it was any easier raising a girl.'

'I'm sure you're right.'

A seagull landed on the wall near the boy.

He glanced at her. She was watching the bird and so he could let his eyes take her in: her hair tucked behind her ear, her slender neck. He turned back to see the boy reach out to the bird, and with a shriek the seagull took off, its wings a white arc against the haze.

'So . . .' he said

'So . . .' she said at the exact same time.

They laughed and he held out his hand: 'After you.'

She smiled again. 'I was going to ask,' she said, 'about what took you to London.'

'My wife was a nurse,' he replied. 'She got a job there, and her family wanted her to be married before moving so far away. I don't think either of us expected to stay so long. For the first ten years at least, we were so sure that we would be coming back the next year.'

'So what changed?'

He had her full attention: the straw hat was next to her on the bench, forgotten. Her sunglasses dangled from her fingers, her head was turned to his, her eyes moving over his features.

He shrugged. 'I can't remember one thing,' he said. 'I do remember that by then my daughter was in school. I think we were also so close to paying off our house and so we kept thinking, just a few more years. Then it just escaped our minds. Until five years ago. We bought some land in Cherai and built the house.'

'So you planned to come back after all.'

'Yes.' He smiled. 'And I have. Just on my own, rather than with her.'

She made a sympathetic noise, and he said again, perhaps needlessly, 'Please don't worry.'

They turned in unison to look at the sea.

'It's very interesting,' she said suddenly. She opened her mouth to say something then seemed to change her mind, shut it. But then she turned to him and spoke.

'Don't take this the wrong way,' she said. 'But you remind me of my father.'

He let himself collapse a little, theatrically, a hand on his heart, as if her words were an arrow. She burst out laughing, her eyes gleaming with delight, and touched his arm briefly. He grinned back, watching her laugh, not without some self-satisfaction: it was clear she was charmed by him.

'No, let me finish,' she was saying, still smiling. 'My dad went over to the States in 1962. He got a scholarship, and he studied at Columbia. Came back *here* halfway through his studies, married my mother and went back *there*.' Her hands flipped over to one side and then the other. 'My elder sister was born not long after. Then I came along.' She sighed, then said drily, 'And fifty years on, two kids, jobs and lives in the States, they still talk of India as *naatile*.'

The word was a pleasant punctuation mark, respectably pronounced.

He laughed. 'I might have done the same on occasion.'

She laughed with him. 'Yes, exactly.'

There was a movement ahead, and they turned to see the ferry suddenly emerge before them, as if it had been hiding behind the curtain of haze waiting for its cue. He felt his heart-beat quicken. She would be leaving soon – should he ask where she was staying?

But he said, 'So, may I ask why you are visiting Kerala?'

'God, why?' she repeated, as if she was allowing him the privilege of imagining that she had never been asked, or indeed asked herself, that question. 'Well, I tell everyone it's to let my son learn a bit about that side of his heritage. But then I've never brought my older son here. Nor my husband.' She smiled and looked at him, shading her eyes with one hand. 'I guess the real answer is that *I* want to feel a little more Indian than I actually do.'

'Mom, I think they're boarding.' The youth was standing in front of them, his body blocking the sun, so Thomas could not see his features clearly, just his long lanky outline.

'We're going to Bolgatty Island,' the woman said. 'Have you been?'

'Not for many years.'

She stood up and slung her bag over her shoulder, then held her hand out. 'Vishukumari,' she said. Thomas stood up and took her hand.

'And my son, Hari.'

'Hello,' he said to the boy.

'Hello.'

'I'm Thomas,' he said. 'It was a pleasure.'

He did not want her to go, but she smiled and then took her son's arm, turned away.

It was easy for her to break the spell and move away, leaving behind a trail of unanswered questions, unspoken invitations. He watched as they walked further up Marine Drive and joined the bustle of people queuing up. This was not what he had expected from his lunchtime walk: the sense of a missed opportunity. He wondered whether he should have mentioned Jos's shop, then immediately he pictured Rani's folder. The image troubled him: she did not belong in there. He was wistful when he turned away and started retracing his steps. Before he left Marine Drive, he let himself turn back. He couldn't even make out the boat jetty any more. She had been swallowed up by the mass of humanity, by the swarms of people that inhabited this city.

When he returned to the shop, Rani was not on the phone but diligently writing up the inventory, and he felt guilty for his mean thoughts earlier. The last client of the day was a woman with her twelve-year-old son, a bright boy but one who was clearly indulged. He was squeezed into trousers that were too tight for his podgy frame, and was wearing a khaki shirt with some kind of badge: a scout club of sorts.

'I'd like to be an ophthalmologist,' he said to Thomas as they were leaving the office. 'When I'm older.'

Thomas smiled. 'A fine career.'

'*Midukkun,*' the mother interjected. 'He's very clever. Very good grades in school.'

They chose a frame and left the shop. Rani wrote up the order, and Thomas stood at the window. The mother and son had crossed the road and entered Green Gardens, re-emerging with a large ice cream each.

He turned to Rani and saw she was also watching them from her position at her desk.

'People spoil their children nowadays,' she said. 'Did you see how fat he was? And only twelve.'

'You may be right.'

'They just give their children whatever they want. He was hardly starving, was he?'

Thomas glanced at her, amused by her vituperative tone. 'No. One couldn't describe him as starving,' he said mildly.

'And at the same time there are children living on the streets without anything in their bellies.'

He had nothing to say to that. Rani had turned back to the paperwork, but was making little stabbing gestures, then gathered a pile of folders and closed them in a drawer with a little bang.

'Are you OK?' he asked gently.

She lifted her eyes, and he saw that they were full of tears.

'Sometimes,' she said, 'I miss my mother.'

'Oh, Rani.'

She leaned over and pulled a handkerchief from her bag, blew her nose. Then she turned away, looked out of the window.

'She died when I was ten,' she said quietly. 'And quite simply, my life has never been the same since.'

Her words hung in the air.

Eventually, Thomas said, 'It must have been hard for your family. My mother died when I was twenty, and that was hard enough.'

'My father has four daughters.' She turned and smiled at him, but her eyes were sad. 'I think he felt lost for many years.'

He stayed silent for some time, then walked over and sat on the desk, reached over and patted her shoulder.

'Sometimes it makes me feel sad,' she said.

He nodded. 'Of course.'

'In many ways we were lucky,' she continued. 'My grand-mother lived with us and she looked after us. But it wasn't the same.'

'No,' he said.

He could see that the picture he had drawn of her life and of her father, when they had sat opposite each other at lunch in Green Gardens, was not so dissimilar to the truth. With four girls to marry off, her father would have felt hard done by; a daughter who was happy to leave home to forge her own life was both a blessing and an embarrassment. It was clear that Rani did not have an imminent proposal to consider. The best young men would have already chosen their brides. It was for someone like Rani to wait, perhaps find an older husband for whom a dowry would not be a priority.

Her marriage bureau, her wish to help others fend off loneli-ness: she had exposed her own self. At that moment, sitting on the desk, looking down at her, he felt that he could see directly into her heart. He was overwhelmed by a desire to take her hand from where it lay on the desk, squeeze it: you will find someone, Rani. I hope he takes care of you. But, he reminded himself, it was not his place to console her. He should not even claim that he could see what she was thinking. He had no excuse for his increasingly frequent propensity to make presumptions about her: he hardly knew her.

She lifted her head and started shuffling some papers on the desk.

'Anyway,' her voice was brisk. 'I want to tidy everything up before the Easter holiday.'

'Yes.'

He laid his hand on her shoulder again, and she rewarded him with a flash of her teeth, an attempt at a smile. Her words, and the expression on her face as she had looked out of the window, stayed with him through the rest of the afternoon. They did not talk again, but whenever he went into the reception, he found himself looking for her, to make sure that she was still there, as if he expected that the sight of the overfed child would have driven her from her post. Each time he did so, he found her at the desk or by the cabinets, conscientiously tucking something back or ticking something off.

Leaving the store that evening, having said goodbye to Rani, who had by then recovered some of her usual sparkle, he lingered on the street. He decided to stay on in the city a little longer. He had more than an hour before the last bus back to Cherai and no reason to rush home. His train the next day was after noon, so he could even pack in the morning.

He bought a copy of *India Today* from the news-stand and looked around. What he really felt like was a beer, but the only place he could get one would be in one of the fancier hotels on the water. He retraced his steps to Marine Drive, now even gayer, with strings of lights adding to a festive air. He passed the bench where he had sat next to the woman, now long gone, with her son, probably back to her hotel, possibly the very hotel he was walking towards. Perhaps . . . ? But he shook himself crossly: was he, now, in his late middle-age, destined to be smitten by women with beautiful legs and a charming face, of which, he was certain, there were many in this city? Had he returned not only to the place of his birth but to his younger self, complete with anxieties and fantasies and yearnings? He turned quickly into the hotel entrance, found a stool at the bar and ordered his beer. It was as chilly in the air conditioning and as soulless as he had expected. The laws revolving around alcohol seemed to allow its sale only in places which least resembled the vibrant city outside.

He had thought he was the only customer for nearly a quarter of an hour when he spotted, reflected in the large mirror over the bar, behind him and to his right, other guests: a middle-aged couple. They were positioned across the room, seated at one of the tables, eating a meal. He had not noticed them before because they made no sound. The woman was wearing a stiff, heavy sari with a wide band of gold embroidery at the edges; the man was in a brown suit, a red tie. They looked out of place in the modern trappings of the bar, handling their cutlery stiffly. Even the hotel staff seemed to be giving them a wide berth. Perhaps it was a wedding anniversary treat and they had made a special visit to the city. Occasionally, the man would look up from his food and watch the woman, who chewed carefully as if she were afraid her teeth would dislodge, fall into her plate.

They didn't speak, and their silence began to fascinate Thomas, so that he found that his eyes kept returning to them, willing them to show him a sign that all was well between them, which he finally received. The woman reached across the table with her fork, her soft plump arms crossing into the man's domain. She speared something from the man's plate, brought the fork to her lips. Her husband grunted, not looking up. Then, he pushed his plate closer to hers and with his fork and knife scooped more of his own meal on to his wife's plate, as if he were cementing a promise he had made: to take care of her, to ensure her well-being.

5

AFTER an evening spent in a chilly hotel bar, he was glad to return to the warmth of the fishing village, unchanged for decades, if not centuries. The beach resort would probably remain the only interloper from the modern world. In the morning, instead of turning right outside his house, he crossed over on to the beach. He walked near the water where the sand was wet and firm, holding his sandals in his hands. The fishermen had pulled their boats further up, near to their shacks under the trees, and were working on their nets; they did not notice him. There were at least two generations visible, maybe more. Some of the men were old, with grizzled white hair on their chests; the younger men could be their sons or even grandsons. Their skills were passed down, from father to son. Their women did the same with their own tasks: mothers and daughters would prepare the fish for market.

When he could see the tops of small kiosks peeking over the sandbank, he jogged up the bank and wiped off his feet with a handkerchief as best he could. Then he slid them into his sandals: by the time he reached the store, they would not be sandy. He appeared at the road leading to Junction from the water's side rather than from the track leading to his house, receiving some looks of surprise from the small group of autorickshaw drivers, gathered as always for their morning discussions. But then they murmured their greetings, before resuming their conversations, leaving him to chuckle to himself as he jogged further up the road to catch the bus from Junction into the city. He knew he was acquiring a reputation of sorts. For one, few men of his age went into the water unless they were fishermen; certainly he had seen none who were not guests from the beach resort, visiting from Mumbai or Delhi. For another, most in his circumstances would have bought a car by now, rather than rely on their feet and public transport. Misterthomasfromlondon and his eccentricities.

Rani was on the phone when he arrived at the store, and on seeing him she covered the mouthpiece to tell him that his first client was already waiting. It was only after the client left that he put his head around the door to greet Rani properly. He saw her standing in front of her desk, staring at her mobile phone, her brow furrowed.

'Anything wrong?' he asked.

She started at his voice and then turned to him, her face red. 'Mr Thomas,' she faltered. 'I forgot . . .'

He took a step nearer.

'Our suppliers . . .' she said. 'They want me to pick something up this afternoon. They can't bring it over themselves.'

He waited for her to continue; there was a tenseness to her voice. When she didn't, he said, 'Do you want me to go?'

'Oh no, Mr Thomas,' she said. 'You have a booking. I can go. But it's on the road to Kothamangalam. I will be at least an hour.'

She looked worried, and he realised that she was not sure whether Jos had ever wished to entrust the store to his friend without her supervision. It would be his first time on his own, and she was unwilling to voice her concern for fear of insulting him. He saw that she was looking at him with such uncertainty that he couldn't help laughing.

'I'll manage on my own, Rani. We don't have many more bookings, do we?'

She shook her head slowly.

'Well then go,' he said. He watched as she gave a small smile and picked up her bag, smoothing down her trousers.

As she reached the door, he spoke again, 'Rani, wait,' and she stopped, her hand going to her throat.

'Why don't I phone a taxi for you?' he said. 'It's so hot outside.'

Her shoulders relaxed, and she smiled again. 'You are so kind, Mr Thomas. But I'll take the bus, it's not a problem.'

When she left, the store felt empty. He wandered up and down, opened the fridge and took out a bottle, poured himself a drink, which he drank while watching the street outside. He stood in front of the desk and looked at the small piles of papers, each clearly stacked and ready for filing. He absently ran his fingers through some of the piles, wondering what he was looking for, and then admitted to himself that he was disappointed to find no trace of the bureau.

When the only booked client arrived some time later, he showed him into the testing room. When they re-emerged, the reception was still empty.

'Shall I show you the frames we have?' Thomas asked. 'I'm sorry, but Rani normally does this, I'm not sure exactly . . .'

'No matter,' the man said. 'I'll come next week. I'm running a bit late anyway. Need to pick my son up.'

As he showed the man out, Thomas glanced at the clock. She had been gone more than an hour and a half now. He wandered to the desk and opened her ledger: there were no bookings for the rest of the day. He was wondering whether to turn the sign over and go for his customary lunchtime walk when the phone rang.

'Chacko's Optical Store,' he said.

There was a sudden din in his ear, the sounds of people shouting and horns hooting, and amidst the cacophony he could just make out Rani's voice, faint, barely audible.

'Hello?'

Again the hubbub, and then a bleat: '. . . traffic block . . . delayed . . .'

'Don't worry!' He had raised his voice. 'I'm here. I can take care of things, Rani. Don't hurry.'

But her reply was a discordant chord, the concern unmistakeable.

'I can't hear you, Rani! Are you OK?'

'. . . coming soon . . . NRI . . .'

'What?' He strained to hear what she was saying.

'. . . clients . . . bureau . . .'

As the realisation of what she was trying to say dawned on him, his blood ran cold.

'. . . Vijay . . . meeting . . .'

'Rani!' The terror he felt surged out through his bellow. 'Get yourself back here this instant!'

Her voice was suddenly clear, flooding in to his ear.

'Mr Thomas! Please make sure they feel . . .'

There was a beeping sound as her signal died and he was left holding the handset. He stared at the clock.

She had arranged a meeting. She had arranged a meeting for two of her clients here. For when? He threw the phone down and ran to the door, turned the sign over to *Closed*, locked the door and peered up and down the street, as if he were under siege. There was no sign of her. And of course there wouldn't be: she was on the other side of town nearly, stuck in one of the much-celebrated traffic jams. He should have thought, he should have told her to postpone the collection from the suppliers. It was the start of the Easter weekend. There would be thousands of people in transit, cars on the road, taxis taking families to the train station: all on top of the normal traffic load. It could be an hour or more now before she returned. He shut his eyes, groaning to himself with frustration.

The knock on the door startled him; he jumped away. There was a man outside who was gesticulating encouragingly, pointing at the door: the sign had not dissuaded him. He was on the top step, his face nearly pressed to the glass, smiling widely. Reluctantly, Thomas reached forward and opened the door.

'Ah,' the man said, and stepped into the room. He was portly, but had moved so nimbly that before he could say anything Thomas saw the man had positioned himself in the centre of the reception, far away from the exit.

'Where is Rani?' he asked, pulling out a handkerchief and wiping his face, the back of his neck. He was nicely dressed, in a smart navy shirt and brown trousers, and smelled pleasantly of aftershave.

'She's . . .' Thomas hesitated. 'She's delayed. I'm terribly sorry but . . .'

'Oh, I see.' This news did not seem to worry the man unduly, but he glanced around and then looked at his watch. Then he smiled again and walked over, holding out his hand. 'Hanif.'

'Thomas.'

'Are you—?'

'No.' Thomas shook his head, not waiting to hear the question. 'No, I'm not.'

'So, you're just—?'

'Yes, that's right.'

He glanced outside at the street: still no sign. He made some quick calculations. It would be difficult to get rid of the man. And awkward to wait with him and make small talk. The less he knew about the workings of Rani's marriage bureau the better: the more innocent could be his role when all was revealed to Jos. His mind whirred. Perhaps the best solution would be to vacate the premises. He could make his excuses, leave the man to greet his date on his own.

'Please forgive me . . .' he began, moving backwards as he spoke. He stumbled against the desk, and at that exact moment the door behind him opened and a woman walked in, bringing with her the scent of her flowery perfume.

She was dressed in a smart green trouser suit that was tailored close to her statuesque frame; her hair was arranged in a bun at the back of her head. She was of Thomas's age, he guessed, some years younger than the man standing opposite, who, on her arrival, had squared his shoulders, held himself more erect. She looked from one man to the other, as they both turned to look at her, before, to his dismay, she settled on Thomas, her face lighting up with appreciation.

'I'm Sherry Varghese.'

She had a deep, warm voice: a confident tone. The man acted quickly, leaping forwards, his hand outstretched. 'Madam,' he said. 'May I call you Sherry? I'm Hanif.'

78

There was a momentary disappointment in her eyes as they flickered back to Thomas as if for confirmation. He stared on at her, aghast, unable to speak, his stagnation sufficing to inform her of her error. With a gracious turn of her head, she gave the portly man her full attention.

'Hanif,' she purred. 'So nice to meet you. But where,' she looked around, 'is Rani?'

'She's delayed apparently,' Hanif said, then, without missing a beat, 'I've been looking forward to this very much, and my expectations have been greatly exceeded.'

The woman gave a laugh, waved his words away with a flick of her wrist, but she was clearly pleased.

So far their conversation had been conducted in English: perhaps this was what Rani had been trying to let him know. It was her coup: she had managed to match two NRIs who could share anecdotes of the trials of adjusting to different climates and psyches. But then the woman turned to Thomas and spoke in Malayalam: 'I'm sorry. You are . . . ?'

'Thomas.' He moved forward and shook her hand.

'Are you Rani's assistant?' She smiled wryly.

'I'm a friend of Jos Chacko.' He added, 'I'm the optician-in-charge.'

She hesitated, a shadow passing over her face.

'I'm sorry.' She glanced at Hanif. 'You must be wondering . . .'

'Please don't worry,' Thomas said. He tried to look relaxed and made a vague gesture with his hands. 'Actually, I was just leaving.'

'Oh, I see,' she said, and her expression became more serious. And then addressing both men: 'I was led to believe that Rani would make formal introductions. I'm not sure how this will work now—'

79

'Never mind, Sherry!' Hanif piped up. 'I've done this before.'

The woman pursed her lips, and there was a silence.

Thomas began to inch towards the door, but she turned immediately and said to him directly, 'Please don't leave' and then turned to Hanif. 'You've done this before. May I ask how often?' Her voice was icy, but this did not seem to perturb the man, who chuckled.

'How remiss of me,' he said. 'I can see that my words can be misconstrued.'

Then he stopped smiling and paused, before continuing gravely, 'I have asked Rani to arrange a match twice now. You are the third.' He refrained from adding what was in everyone's mind: *third time lucky*. 'That is, over the space of six months or so, when I moved back from the States—'

'I see,' she repeated, and pulled her bag so that it shielded her bosom, as well as, Thomas thought with sympathy, her dented feelings.

'Now, Sherry,' the man sounded eminently reasonable. 'Rani mentioned that you own your own business?' He waited for her to give a small nod. 'Well then. You will know that delegating an important decision to a third party does not always produce the result you want.'

His words sunk in; his audience pondered them. Thomas found himself remembering his own question to Rani: what makes you think you are the best person? He glanced at the woman in front of him. She was regarding Hanif a little less coldly and was watching as he continued his little speech, his arms now spread wide as if laying himself open to her. 'I myself don't think I described myself very well to Rani. But it's just a platform from which to spring off, isn't it?'

He was smiling now, and the woman inclined her head in response.

'But,' he continued, 'I would hate to put you in an uncomfortable position. Shall we perhaps take a rain check?' This, delivered in English, the hint of an American accent now evident.

'No,' the woman said hurriedly, and there was now an undeniable flutter to her eyelashes when she looked at him. 'Forgive me if I offended you.'

She slung her bag off her shoulder and then walked into the reception area, sat down on one of the armchairs. 'You lived in the States?'

'Chicago,' he replied, sitting down on a chair opposite her. 'I'm a dentist. I had my own surgery. But I'm retired now. I have two sons still living there.'

'We lived in Dubai for ten years,' she said. 'But my son-in-law lives in Chicago and my daughter will be joining him soon. She's waiting for her papers.'

'Newly married?'

'Some months now. But you know how long the formalities can take . . .'

'Indeed . . .'

'I think it's a nice city?'

'Oh, a great city! But your daughter will have to acclimatise. The winters! I never got used to them.'

Thomas watched as they smiled at each other. They all fell silent, a late-middle-aged trio. A threesome, he suddenly thought, and had to stifle the laughter that arrived in his belly. Then, as if she was just remembering his presence, the woman turned back to him. 'I came for my eye test some time ago,' she said. 'I didn't see you then.'

He cleared his throat. 'I've only been here a few weeks or so.'

'Rani didn't mention that Jos is away when I called her yesterday.'

'I think she expected to be here,' he said. Then added, 'She's on her way.'

So, he thought. This was what it was all about. The two sitting in front of him might be one of Rani's more obvious pairings: both were likely to have mentioned the Chicago connection in their letters. After her initial abrasiveness, there was now a softness to the woman's air. The man, for his part, might have appeared bumptious at the start but had regained control of the situation and had defused the awkwardness with aplomb; Thomas could only admire him.

'. . . and retired last year, decided to come back,' he was saying. 'My ex-wife is still in Chicago. Her two sisters are both there, and she has an active social life. She didn't really notice me leaving.'

He paused and then grinned. 'It works better for us this way.'

'Distance always helps!' She laughed.

'When did . . . ?'

'I actually divorced ten years ago,' she said, patting her bun and weighing her words. 'The only one in the family – you can imagine the commotion!' She waited for a sympathetic nod, and then continued: 'Now both my kids are married. I need to think of myself.'

'I couldn't agree more.'

They smiled again, holding each other's eyes for a brief moment. Then the woman turned to Thomas again and asked, 'Are you married?'

Thomas cleared his throat. 'Not any more.'

The man and woman both made the same sympathetic noise in response, as if to say, look at the state of affairs nowadays! Then the woman smiled and shook her head. 'Well, at least Rani is just on your doorstep!'

She giggled and glanced at the man, who gave another chuckle, then turned back to Thomas, who decided to respond to her comment with his best guffaw.

Then Hanif stood up. 'We could stay on here and take up this gentleman's time, Sherry,' he said, motioning to Thomas, 'or I can take things in hand myself and speak to Vijay, the manager of the café. He knows me, and I'm sure we will get the special treatment.'

'Special treatment?' She was already standing, smiling broadly, her bag swung well back on her shoulder, her bosom no longer needing protection.

'A special menu, their best table . . .'

'How lovely!'

He turned to Thomas and shook hands again.

'Nice meeting you.'

This time, when the woman smiled her goodbyes, she didn't offer her hand, but lowered her eyes as if in apology for her earlier misunderstanding. 'Nice meeting you.'

'Yes, well . . .' He just stopped short of wishing them luck. He opened the door for them and watched as they crossed the road, then turned away.

He exhaled. The silence was a balm; the event had exhausted him. It had been like watching a film made for his pleasure alone, but from the inside, rather than in the comfort of one's seat in the cinema along with a hundred other members of the audience. He went and stood by the fridge in the corner of the room: he would be out of eyeshot but he could still see the scene in Green Gardens. Vijay was bowing, an obsequious smile plastered over his face as he led them to a table by the window. A nice touch: there was no pretension of hiding the two putative lovers. They were mature adults who could sit opposite each other at the table in full view of society: this was modern India after all. He watched as the man pulled out the woman's chair. As she turned back, she said something which made him laugh, throw his head back, then briefly lay a hand on her shoulder. Thomas found himself smiling, as if he had heard the woman's punchline himself. The man was saying something in return, and it was the woman's turn to laugh, and then they both looked down at the menus in a synchronous movement which made him turn away: their future was in their hands now.

He opened the fridge, poured himself a glass of water and drank it thirstily. It was the lunch hour now, and so he could leave the store with legitimacy. If Rani returned, she need only look across the street to see her handiwork. The sign was already turned over; he just needed to lock the door. The success had not been his. But he had enjoyed, even as an onlooker, seeing the spark between the man and the woman, both at an age when most would expect them to sit back and wait for life to drift by.

He gave the couple a last glance before walking down the street. When the woman had arrived, so obviously a Syrian Christian, he had felt a slight jolt on seeing her, then on hearing of her divorce. It was not just a jolt of surprise. He had felt an emotion that had arrived so easily as to be second nature, an emotion he had not thought he could unearth: disapproval. Disapproval of that woman sitting across the road, holding the menu with one hand and perching a pair of glasses on her nose with the other. In her carefully chosen attire, carefully coordinated bag and shoes. If he could feel that disapproval, however momentary, for a person he had no investment in, when he had little religious inclination anyway, then what would have been the towering wall of judgement she must have had to face from those around her? Her misdemeanour: she had refused to stay in an unsatisfactory marriage for the sake of appearances, and now she was brave enough to search for her own happiness. More than the man, it was the woman who needed to be applauded for her initiative. And Rani had played her part in offering the woman a new lease of life.

He had a warm glow inside him. The Easter weekend lay ahead, a break from his routine of travelling in to the city. The thought that he would be seeing his jolly, rotund older sister further buoyed his spirits. Just before the main road – on the other side of which lay the promenade – he turned on an impulse into a small department store. On the ground floor, he bought a selection of small gifts for Mariamma and her children: a bag, some accessories, a wallet for her son. He would present these to her in gratitude for her help since his return and in the preceding years. He held a basket and picked things up quickly, avoiding the eyes of the lone sales clerk lurking at the far end of the store. The ladies' clothing section was up a short flight of stairs. He chose a selection of ready-made outfits that he judged would be a little large for Mariamma's daughters: better if they grew into them. Then, after a moment's hesitation, he called over the young woman who was in charge of the floor. She was about Rani's size, and he asked her advice on which outfit would fit her. Fifteen minutes later, after discussions over complexion and build – clearly the most exciting thing that had happened in the sales clerk's day – he had an apple-green kurta in the basket: an Easter gift for Rani.

When he stepped back on to the street, he found his feet taking him back to Marine Drive, back to the bench where he had met the woman, her son standing ahead looking at the water. Today, the haze had diminished; it was one of those surprisingly sparkling days, when the humidity seemed to suspend itself higher above ground level so that there was some respite below. He could smell the jasmine from the nearby bushes, hear the crows cawing from the trees that dotted the promenade. She was not there, but the bench was empty and so he sat down. He felt a tug of disappointment: perhaps he had expected that she too would be thinking of him and position herself at their meeting point. He leaned back and stretched his feet in front of him. There were several people walking up and down, and groups of young men in sunglasses and jeans had placed themselves in positions along the low sea wall.

How would he have fared in a meeting with someone like Sherry? Very badly, was his conclusion. But then he remembered her eyes resting on him, the flash of approval. And he remembered how Vishukumari had laughed, touched his arm, her eyes gleaming. It was not, he realised, something he was *not* used to. In all those years in London, there had been many a stranger's eye he had caught, a backward glance, a smile thrown over a shoulder. He found himself perusing the crowds, trying to pick out the women, imagine them walking into the optical store, their hands outstretched in greeting. Among the people enjoying the promenade before him, it was clear very soon that most women were accompanied by their husband

and, if they were younger, with children in tow. There were the inevitable gangs of college-age girls, some in jeans and T-shirts, who strolled purposefully in front of the groups of young men, their hips swinging. Older women, unaccompanied, were a rare sight. But there was one, he noticed suddenly, standing out from the crowd because she had cut her hair, and it curled, streaked with grey, around her face. In her hand she carried a cloth bag, the logo of the bookshop where he had ordered his book clearly visible. It was a sign, he thought. An opportunity for a chat-up line of some sophistication: I see you like reading. He laughed at himself, but then despite himself let his eyes survey her.

She was small, curvy, with a striking profile, a strong nose which lent her a regal air. She was dressed in a chic long top, colourful scarf. She was standing alone, staring at the water, and then she turned, her eyes meeting his for a fraction of a second before they passed over him with disinterest. Then she walked away, a solitary figure with a cloth bag bursting with books, and he watched her as she retreated, until she was a small dot. The encounter, if he could call it that, had lasted seconds, and while she did not have many of the attributes he had by now listed in his mind in his hypothetical application to Rani's bureau, she had impressed him as someone with whom he could be friends. She, however, had been completely self-contained, unaware of him. The moral of the story – not everyone was searching.

He spent the next minutes casting his eyes over the passers-by, becoming, as he did so, increasingly restless with himself, so that before long he got to his feet and retraced his steps to the street. As he passed the window of Green Gardens, he could see from the corner of his eye that the couple were still there, and to his left, he saw a flash of white: Rani was back at her desk. She rose to her feet as soon as he opened the door, her eyes bright with concern.

'Mr Thomas, I'm so sorry . . .'

He held up his hand. 'Don't worry,' he said.

'It won't happen again.' She was standing with her hands clasped in front of her like a contrite schoolgirl.

'Yes,' he said, closing the door behind him. 'Yes, please. Don't let that happen again.' Then he smiled, and he saw her return his smile uncertainly.

'Did you,' she hesitated, 'did you manage?'

He gestured towards the café. 'Have you talked to them?'

She shook her head. 'I didn't want to interrupt.'

'Well,' he said. 'I didn't have to do much. The dentist handled everything.'

'That's good. He's been before.' She smiled nervously.

'Yes. He did say.'

She sat back down, her hands still linked, and he moved to the testing room, where he stowed the packages he had bought for Mariamma in his bag, leaving Rani's present on the desk. He went back out into the reception area. She had picked up a pile of slips and was sorting them into her trays; the mechanics of the paperwork remained a mystery to him. Then, from across the street, there was a movement which caused them both to look out. The man and the woman emerged from the café and stepped out on to the street. Thomas moved closer to stand near to Rani, who left the slips in her hand unattended as they both watched the scene outside. A taxi drew up, and the man opened the door, smiling, then they shook hands, and the woman climbed into the car. The man stood watching as it pulled away, his hand raised in a wave, before pushing his hands into his pockets and strolling in the opposite direction. From their positions in the optical store, Thomas and Rani could see that he was whistling.

Rani turned around and caught Thomas's eye, then looked back down at the stack of papers near her.

'Rani,' he said. She looked up, her brow creased with worry, and so he laughed and said, 'It was nice. For them, I mean.'

She did not respond, and so he said, 'I think you made a good match.'

'Really, Mr Thomas?' Her face beamed with pleasure.

'Well . . .' he gestured to the street. 'You saw yourself. It looks like they got on very well.'

'Yes, it's true, isn't it?' She sighed happily.

'Was it,' he paused, but could not resist continuing, 'was it easy? I mean, to put the two together? Was it easy to make the decision from their letters to you?'

'Not really,' she said slowly after a few moments. 'Because I was worried about Mr Hanif. He had not enjoyed the first times. This is his third time.' She looked up tentatively.

Thomas nodded.

'And Mrs Varghese just gave me a very short letter.'

She stopped speaking. Perhaps she was thinking of her ethical responsibility to guard their privacy; perhaps her reasons for the pairing were too elusive to put into words.

'Well,' he said. 'It seems to have worked.'

'Let's hope so.'

He moved back into the testing room, sat at his desk and doodled. He had a half hour before the next appointment, half an hour to dream about his first date with . . . as hard as he tried not to, the image of Vishukumari kept floating into his thoughts. He looked at what he had drawn: an abstract image of concentric circles. He put his pen down, leaned his chair back on its hind legs and stared at the ceiling.

He and Nimmy had, of course, many a time gone out for a meal, sat across from each other at a table. But they would have been married already, promised to each other; there was not that suspense of whether he would see the woman opposite him again, or whether he would make excuses and gently disengage himself. Had he ever invited a woman out for a meal? He thought suddenly to the lunch at Green Gardens a few weeks ago, Rani scouring the menu, but moved on: that did not count. There had been, once, in London, one of the assistants at the optical store. He would not pretend to himself that he could not remember her name: Victoria, like the station, she had said, smiling. She had, in her younger days, backpacked through India, had a nose ring to show off and was generous with her flirtatious glances. *She* had invited *him* to lunch at a pasta restaurant a few streets away, away from the prying eyes of their colleagues. He had, he knew, been tempted: tempted to follow through on what she offered him. She had an easy sensuality, clearly found him attractive and had a disarming disregard for his marital status. But, in truth, she had scared him somewhat with the frankness of her needs. He had handled her clumsily and had been relieved when she transferred to another branch. A faithful husband with unfaithful thoughts. Was there a name for someone like him?

The tap on the door caused him to bump his chair back on its four legs.

'Your appointment, Mr Thomas,' Rani said, ushering in a nervous-looking young woman.

'Yes, of course. Thank you, Rani.'

Attending to the young woman and her myopia distracted him sufficiently for the next half hour, and the afternoon passed at a busy pace. When he walked back into the reception area, it was close to five o'clock. Rani was dusting her desk.

'You should leave soon, Mr Thomas. The Easter traffic will be terrible; you must get your bus.'

'And you, Rani. Hope you won't get stuck again.'

She did not reply, only carried on dusting vigorously.

He hesitated. The thought of Rani returning that night to a hostel, which he had no knowledge of but which he could imagine offered few of the comforts of home was dispiriting. 'Have you any plans?' he asked tentatively. To his relief she looked up, smiling.

'I'm going to Palakkad,' she said. 'To see my father.'

'That will be nice.'

She nodded. 'And you, Mr Thomas? Any plans?'

'I'm going to see my sister. She's in a convent in Calicut.'

'Yes, I think you said.'

He suddenly remembered. 'I've got something for you.' He walked back into the testing room and found the parcel, wrapped in brown paper. She was standing by the desk when he returned, a quizzical expression on her face.

'For you, Rani,' he said. 'Happy Easter.'

She opened her mouth in surprise, and she said nothing when he handed her the package.

'Open it.' He smiled.

She did so wordlessly, pulling out the apple-green kurta with an exclamation.

'Mr Thomas!' Her eyes were shining. She held it against her. 'It's so beautiful!'

He laughed. 'It suits you,' he said. 'Is the size all right? I had to ask the girl in the shop.'

'It's perfect,' she said. She stopped, 'You made such an effort, Mr Thomas.'

'It was nothing.'

'And after I put you in a difficult position.'

'Really, Rani. In the end I have to say I rather enjoyed it.'

He felt his second glow of the day as they finished tidying away and closing up the store. She was enormously pleased with her gift, he could tell, and he was touched by this. He went back into the testing room and slung his bag across his chest, made sure he had turned off everything, switched off the lights and shut the door. The store would remain closed for the next four days.

Rani was waiting for him, her bag over her shoulder, by the door. Perhaps it was her pose that triggered a chain of thoughts. When he had seen her that morning, standing where she was now, staring at her phone, she had not looked annoyed with herself for forgetting her appointment, he suddenly realised; rather, she looked confused, indecisive. And when he had offered to stay behind, she might have been worried about her impending appointment with her clients, but she had seemed more perturbed than necessary: she could not have known she would be delayed. The idea that she did not trust him with managing the store now seemed unlikely. Why had the suppliers sent her a message on her mobile when they could have phoned the number of the store as usual? And where, he glanced around, where were the signs that she had brought back a delivery?

He looked at her, but now she was calm, content, the troubles of the day forgotten.

'Mr Thomas?' she said. 'Ready?'

He would say nothing: enough had happened today. His head was full of so many things it was easy to complicate simple situations. He nodded, opened the door and let her pass by him. On the step, she lingered a little longer. 'See you on Tuesday.'

He watched as she walked away, taking brisk, purposeful steps. Then she turned back, as if she knew he was watching, gave him a little wave and disappeared around the corner.

6

HE woke up the next day to the sound of the phone ringing. It was not his mobile, which lay near him on the bedside table, but the landline he had had installed, inconveniently, downstairs in the living room, months ago. His clock read seven o'clock: it was the latest he had slept since he had left London. He had been dreaming that he was in Tooting, taking his car for a service. In the dream, he kept missing the right turning, finding himself on a one-way street, having to reverse and make increasingly complicated U-turns on narrow streets. He was anxious, aware of the time ticking by. In the dream, the garage would charge him for a delayed drop-off.

He stumbled down the stairs. The phone lay on a tiny table which he knocked over in his haste to reach before the caller hung up.

'Thomasmon?'

His mouth dropped open: it was his mother, who had died nearly forty years ago, but who had heard that he had returned, was phoning him to berate him for not visiting her.

'Amma?' he asked incredulously, only to hear his sister laugh.

'*Eda?* Are you asleep?'

He looked around and saw the house in Cherai, tried to recalibrate his brain. He was embarrassed. His sister hooted with laughter: he could imagine her plump frame jiggling with hilarity. After some moments, she turned apologetic. A fellow nun had been hospitalised overnight over a serious asthma attack. His sister was phoning to tell Thomas that she would be spending the next few days in the hospital; his visit to the convent would have to be postponed.

'What can I do?' she asked. 'Anyway, how are you? Eating well?'

They spent a few minutes exchanging news, Thomas reassuring her that the train fare had not been exorbitant and that he would not renege: he would visit her in a few weeks.

When he hung up, he felt for the first time a vague sense of purposelessness. And some disappointment: he had been looking forward to the long train ride, and particularly to the excellent curries he knew he could expect from the nuns' kitchens. He now had four days ahead to himself. He turned away to go back upstairs and saw a ball of crumpled paper: his columns from those nights back. He picked it up and opened it out: *What I would change about Nimmy*. His words had not changed. He crumpled it up again and tossed it into the kitchen bin before going back upstairs.

By the time he reached the sea that morning, the fishermen had already gone. He felt slightly deflated: he had begun to look on their presence as a talisman for a good day ahead. Shaking off what he could see was the beginnings of a moroseness he could not afford, he plunged into the water. He had to expect moments like this. In the space of a year, his life had changed immeasurably; he needed to give himself some time to adjust. As he swam, he let himself think of the woman, Vishukumari. Why had he not asked where she was staying? Because what was the use? he answered himself. He was not going to try to seduce a married woman; he suspected, anyway, that he would have little success. But the thought of inviting her to Cherai, serving her a meal at the small table on his balcony was enticing. Her son? Perhaps he would be happy to play a game on his phone, in the gazebo. He let out a chortle, at himself and his musings, tried to rid himself of his imaginings.

The days on his own would do him good. It was time for the honeymoon to be over; there would be many such days ahead over the years. Days when he would not be working and would have only himself for company. The thought that he would miss working in Jos's optical store had never occurred to him. As he walked up the sandbank back to the house, he realised he may have to mention this to his old friend the next time they spoke. Later, after breakfast, he rang his brother-in-law, who invited him to join Nimmy's family for the weekend. But he resisted. It was tempting, but only momentarily: the joys of being plied with food and drink would also hold the burden of endless Masses for the Easter weekend, endless talk, neither of which he was ready for.

He decided that he would finish the work he had started on the gazebo, after which he could walk to Junction and get some supplies. The next day he would treat himself to a buffet lunch at the beach resort: a favourite for honeymooning couples, it was true, but over the Easter weekend it would be a popular choice for family parties. He could disappear among the throng. For the evenings, he still had a selection of books, some of which he had not made a start on.

By noon, he returned from Cherai Junction with his purchases made. In the small kitchen, he slapped at the few remaining ants that crawled along the windowsill. The heat outside flooded in through the open back door, as if a long-lost friend. He could hear Mariamma next door shouting at one of her children. He scrambled some eggs with some chillies and a tomato, then munched his snack in the gazebo, swatting away flies, but enjoying being shirtless, in a mundu, his legs stretched before him. Mariamma called over the wall: 'Too hot to be outside, Thomaschayan!'

'Not for me, Mariamma.'

'Ah, you didn't change after all that time in London!'

Her words pleased him, and he grinned. Then, remembering, asked her to wait while he went back into the house and got the purchases he had brought back with him the previous night.

'Just to say Happy Easter, Mariamma,' he said. 'And to thank you for your help.'

She exclaimed with pleasure: the children would love the gifts, it was thoughtful of him.

'Come and have lunch with us,' she said.

'No, really. You have enough people to take care of.'

She tried to convince him to change his mind, and then relented, went back inside.

He glanced at his watch and calculated that it would be ten o'clock on a holiday in Paris. He decided to try to phone his daughter again: surely Nina would be at home. He had calculated correctly: Nina answered the phone within two rings, her voice rushed, perhaps she was expecting a call.

'It's me, *mol*,' he said.

There was a short silence, and then he heard her voice again, the familiar tones.

'Pa?'

He laughed, his heart melting and aching at the same time.

'How are you?'

'Oh fine.'

'Are you still in bed?'

'Not really.' She gave a short laugh. 'Well, I am, but I've been awake a while. I'm treating myself to breakfast in bed.'

'That's good,' he said. 'Any plans for the long weekend?'

'We're actually going away later for the night,' she said. 'To see a friend in the country. But that's pretty much it.'

In the background he could hear a man's voice, and he tried to stave off the image of Nina sitting in bed, Michel lying beside her, broad-chested, unshaven.

'Good, good,' he said.

There was a pause, and then he said, 'I've tried calling you a few times . . .'

'Yes . . . I know.'

Then, a silence. With those words they had resumed their positions of old, as if their initial warmth had simply been an unguarded moment, an interval.

'Everything OK?'

'Where are you?' she asked suddenly.

'Where am I?' he repeated. 'In Cherai. In the house.'

'Yeah, but where? Are you on the balcony? Downstairs?'

'On the balcony.' He laughed. 'The sea is ahead of me. I can see only one person walking on the road below me.' He paused. 'You must come and visit, *mol*.'

She did not respond. He heard some rustling, as if she were climbing out of bed, and then footsteps. She was taking the phone somewhere.

When she spoke again, he could hear the faint sounds of traffic.

'Where are you now, *mol*?'

'On *my* balcony. Looking across at another apartment block. There's a square on my left, y'know, benches and stuff.'

'You must come,' he repeated. 'I'd like to see you.'

She did not seem to hear him. 'Are you settling in?'

'Very well, I think.'

And he told her about his morning swims, Jos's shop and Rani.

'So,' her voice was dry, 'you're doing the same job that you gave up in London . . .'

He laughed. 'Some differences. I'm more in charge in a way. And it somehow feels less like work.' He paused. 'I think living in Cherai makes the difference.'

'Right.'

She did not elaborate, and so he continued: 'I was supposed to visit Chechiamma this weekend, but she called to cancel this morning. I'll have to try to go another time. She asked after you.'

'That's nice.'

They fell silent again.

'So, everything OK?' he asked again.

'Why shouldn't it be?' Her voice seemed far away, as if she had turned her head away from the receiver, directed her words at something or someone else.

He tried to make light: 'Thought you were avoiding me when you didn't return my calls!'

'Well,' she began and then stopped. When her voice came back on her line, it was stronger, as if she had made a decision. 'Actually, I wasn't ready to talk to you, I suppose.'

He hated confrontation; he had usually left any awkward conversations with Nina to her mother. Nimmy had often

99

berated him on his silence, which she interpreted as lack of support.

He laid a hand on the railing of the balcony, shifted from one foot to the other. He could see a group of children up ahead, appearing on the sand like a lost shoal of fish, black-haired and brown-limbed, running towards the water.

'What's wrong?'

'There's nothing wrong.'

'Well . . .'

She suddenly spoke again.

'I feel a bit abandoned is what it is,' she said. 'Mum dies. Then you slope off to India.'

He stared ahead of him, over the balcony to the sea, but saw nothing.

'I have no family around me, no one within a radius of thousands of miles,' she was saying. 'I just feel . . .' and then she faltered, 'abandoned. It's the only way I can put it.'

He shifted his feet again.

'I see . . .'

'I know I have Michel,' she said. 'But I'm talking about family. Flesh and blood and all those clichés.'

'Yes.'

Then she waited. He could hear her breathing, and the sensation of holding a phone to his ear, the person on the other side expectant, was so evocative of the optical store he almost expected her to say: is Rani there?

He shook himself, tried to concentrate.

'You have your own life, *mol*, I—'

'I can have my own life, Pa,' she interrupted. 'But I can still need you. I can still need a *parent*.'

There was a long silence again, when all he could hear was a hum in his ears. His skin felt cold.

'I mean,' she suddenly started again, 'I'm just astounded. You don't seem to have any idea how I feel. How I felt seeing the house all bare and empty. The house I grew up in . . .'

'Nina, the house is yours—'

'I'm not talking about ownership. I'm talking about memories.' She paused. 'This may not be how you feel, but it was like you just wanted to erase all those years and start again. Just rub everything out.'

He was stung. Something stirred in him. 'The house you grew up in, yes, but when was the last time you ever spent any time in it? With us?'

'For what?'

'For what? To see your parents for example?'

'Whenever I came to see you, I felt like I was a visitor. Or some kind of prodigal daughter.'

He could not say anything. She muttered something he could not hear. Was Michel there?

'I suppose the truth is,' he began, picking his way around words as if they were stepping stones, some more sturdy and reliable than others, 'I feel a bit uncomfortable about the way you are living your life. You don't talk much about it—'

'What do you mean, the way I'm living my life? You mean living with the man I love? With the man who loves me?'

Immediately, he had a vision of his daughter laughing, the man in question behind her, his arm around her waist. He had only met Michel at Nimmy's funeral; he had never met any of Nina's other boyfriends, of which, he didn't know, there may have been many.

'What would you prefer?' she asked. 'That I'm sad and lonely? Like when I was growing up?'

It was like a slap in the face. He spluttered, but she was still talking.

'Everything so hidden and muffled, nobody talking about anything that really mattered? To come and just sit in your silence? I mean, did you and Mum ever think about how *I* felt?'

He heard his voice coming on to the line: 'How can you say you were sad and lonely? I won't speak for myself, but your mother was always ready to talk to you, advise you.'

She snorted. 'Yeah right. Advice? We never really talked to each other.'

They fell silent again, then he said, 'What do you mean? We always advised you, Nina, but perhaps—'

'Pa, you can't just remember what you want to remember. When I wanted to change schools? When I was having a hard time with that bunch of girls? Did you even *know* about that? Most parents would have gone to see the head at least, tried to find out what was going on—'

'Nina—'

'And when I went to New York? *New York!* Neither of you seemed to blink. Like I was going to the shops down the road. I didn't expect a farewell party or anything, but I did expect a bit of a reaction – but, no, nothing. Just the two of you staring at me, because you've never wanted to do what I am doing, or maybe it's that you've never wanted *me* to be doing what I'm doing—'

'What are you talking about, Nina?' he cried out. 'I don't understand what you're saying!'

The sound of his voice startled them both.

He was breathing heavily, his heart pounding in his chest. Her words, ringing in his ear, were at complete odds with the vista before him. He turned away from the balcony, went into his bedroom, sat on the edge of his bed. He must cut a ridiculous figure, he thought suddenly. On his own, in this house, half-dressed, in a mundu. Perhaps others were also thinking: he is here, but where is his daughter?

Now she was crying. He could hear muffled sounds, as if she had a hand over her mouth to catch the grief pouring out of her, stuff it back in. He could picture the tears rolling down her cheeks, splashing on to the receiver. Was there that voice in the background again? Of course, Michel would be comforting his daughter later over this conversation that he, her father, was holding with her. Rani had also cried, like a child who had had a toy taken from her. Now Nina. A confusing image flashed before him: of Rani and Nina sitting side by side, swiping through his phone, laughing over the photos he kept, while he sat on the other side of the table, watching them with an indulgent expression on his face.

They waited some time, his heartbeat slowed down to a dull ache, her sobs subsided. He could hear her blowing her nose.

'*Mol* . . .' he began.

'There's no point.'

'I can't explain,' he continued regardless. 'I felt like I wanted to run away, it's true. Can you forgive me for that? But in the end I haven't escaped. It's been a reminder coming here.'

Her reluctance to engage was palpable, her silence thick with frustration. But then she said, 'A reminder of what?'

He clutched for the right expression.

'The fullness of life.'

They had dropped out of his mouth, but they hit the wrong note: flowery words, empty words. What she wanted to hear was something more prosaic: that he loved her, he was proud of her, that maybe he didn't always understand her but that he accepted her. That as his only child she was more precious to him than anything else in his life. But he had missed that opportunity. He could not backpedal, so instead he sat on his bed, his hand over his eyes now.

She was silent again. When she spoke, she sounded tired, as tired as he felt.

'There's life everywhere, Pa. What do you mean?'

'I don't know,' he said.

He sat holding the receiver, miserable, staring blankly. After some time, she said, 'I'm going back in, I'm getting cold.'

'Yes sure . . .'

'And I'm going to hang up soon . . .'

'OK . . .'

'I understand, Pa,' she said, her voice was now calm. 'I understand you must feel lost without Mum. You guys were together forever. And I know that I've been away a lot. I know all of that.'

Her voice was now nearly a whisper. 'But Mum dying like that? It's just made me question a whole load of things. About me, as well as about us.'

'I miss you, *mol*,' he said, but he was not sure she heard, she was speaking again, her voice returned to her usual, slightly detached manner. They were moving into another flat, she and Michel, the next month, she was saying. It was slightly bigger but was further from the centre; they would take longer to get to work, but they both agreed that they would enjoy more space. He could tell that this was her way of coming out of it, the sadness, by returning to the civil, polite conversations they normally had about nothing very important. He hung up after they had both recovered a less strained tone, as if all that had been said could be forgotten. Yes, she would visit later that year. She would mention the trip to Michel, perhaps he would join her, at least for a week. Yes, take care, speak soon.

From having her voice in his ear, he was suddenly alone, sitting on his bed, exposed. This bed, in the middle of his bedroom, in this house, which stood alone on a track opposite the sea. Far away from his previous life as a husband. But he was still a father. He had been selfish the last year, clutching Nimmy's death to himself. He should have opened his arms to let his daughter shrug herself into his thoughts, but he hadn't. She was not a child, but his daughter was young to have lost her mother; if she had children of her own, they would not know their grandmother. The impulse that had taken him, the moment when he had made his decision to leave, as if that decision was his and his alone, he could not recall. Perhaps the idea had been less spontaneous than he imagined.

There had been that day, when Nimmy had been in the hospice for more than a week: she had said her last words to him. Her condition had deteriorated sufficiently and at such a rapid pace that Nina had been summoned back from Paris, was at that very moment in the canteen of the hospice, getting a drink. Nimmy had opened her eyes briefly and, after surveying the room with an expression close to disdain, had scratched her fingernails against his wrist. Her voice was surprisingly clear: '*Oru karyam . . .*' she had begun, then exhaled, died, her breath a punctuation mark. Something to tell you. He would have to wait now, not knowing what had weighed on her mind, if there had been anything. Perhaps the synapses in her brain had played a cruel trick, so that he would spend the next few months in an agony, searching through their paperwork at home, through her mobile phone, scraping around for a clue of what she had wanted to say. He had found none, only had reason to sift through the life they had led, the bills they paid and the people Nimmy kept in touch with. At the end of the search, while he had not found what his wife may have been thinking of, he came to his decision: his daughter was full-grown and living her own life, the ties that had held him to where he was had become irrelevant. He would leave and return home, where he would live out the rest of his years. But, he thought, not so easy.

The conversation with his daughter left him feeling listless. He went into the bathroom, where he poured a bucket of cold water over himself and then lay on the bed, the breeze rippling through the room, the sound of the waves outside. He woke up, disoriented, an hour later. He looked at the clock beside his bed: four o'clock. The sun was now beginning its descent. It would not melt into the sea for another couple of hours, but the breeze was picking up and it would be pleasant to walk outside. As he approached the main section of the promenade, he could see that Cherai had been transformed for the holiday. It was crowded with daytrippers, a row of coaches lined up near the usual cluster of autorickshaws. In the sea were dozens of people: women lifting the ends of their saris and salwar kameez, baring their calves; groups of younger men, diving in and out of the water. He walked up and down many times, the sun slipping down, lower and lower.

What had they planned to do here, Nimmy and he? He tried to remember. Nina had said in her call: you guys were together forever. What had she meant? Perhaps, on her own, without siblings, her parents had stood before her, an intimidating duo. Perhaps she was simply commenting on the longevity of their marriage, something neither of them ever considered as a feat. Even their betrothal had transpired without much effort. It was his height and bearing that had stood him in good stead when his father had approached Nimmy's father in answer to the announcement that his daughter was looking for a husband. Having secured a job in the UK, being fair-skinned and pretty enough, Nimmy had had a fair number of suitors. Thomas remembered going to see her father with his: the journey had not taken long, both families living in the hills leading to the Western Ghats. Thomas had not spoken much and had suspected that Nimmy's father had taken a dim view of the fact that at the time – and despite having finished his studies at college – Thomas had no job and was spending his days working with his father in the rubber plantation. Only towards the end of their meeting, held on the verandah of Nimmy's family home, had he got a glimpse of her: she was wearing a vivid, orange sari, and she had twisted some flowers into her hair. He had spent the journey back home with his father staring out the window, feeling that events had somehow got out of his control. He no longer felt, despite agreeing to the meeting, ready to be a husband. What on earth did one do with a wife? He was, like any young man, keen to share a bed with a woman, who would be a soft, warm presence by his side night after night. But the questions Nimmy's father had asked had pointed to a more mundane existence: what were his plans for the future, and how would he provide for his family?

Nimmy later told him that her father had advised her to accept Thomas's proposal: he is handsome, he looks strong.

Within weeks, the two had been married and, not long after, they were flying to London to begin a new life. At the airport, Nimmy had cried copiously, had clung to her mother, who even then was toothless, a crone with heavy gold rings hanging from her earlobes down to her shoulders. Thomas had been overwhelmed with the sense of responsibility: he would have to take care of his wife in a country neither had visited. In fact, Nimmy had been the main breadwinner for the first year and a half, while Thomas had taken odd jobs before training as an optician. And while Nimmy had yearned for home and her family, Thomas found he had a talent for relocating. After growing up in Vazhakulam, surrounded by the red soil and slim green coconut trees, he had adjusted, unscathed, to life in London. It became his home, the place where he conducted his married life and forays into fatherhood. And his journey in reverse had been executed with little difficulty. Was it a talent, he thought, to be so self-sufficient, or was it a curse? He could never understand the need for a circle of friends, for keeping in touch with reminders of the past. You grew older; you moved on. Nimmy had depended on him for memories of home; he must have been lacking in that way, as a companion. Yet, they had cleaved together, assuming their roles in their marriage without any practice. He tried to imagine how he would feel if Nina announced she was to marry a man she had met a few days earlier. The whole exploit seemed not only arcane but fraught with danger. When Nina had gone to university, Nimmy had broached the subject: if their daughter were engaged, then there would be less worry that she would plunge into an inadvisable love affair of her own accord. He had found himself nonplussed by Nimmy's obtuseness. By then, Nina had made clear her aspirations of living a life at odds with any edicts from her parents. And when Nimmy had insisted on having that conversation with Nina, their daughter had not spoken to them for weeks.

His thoughts were so much on the past that when he saw the young woman, dressed in a pink and blue salwar kameez, her hair adorned with jasmine flowers, he did not recognise her as Rani. She looked familiar, but he presumed that she was some-one he had known from long ago. She was facing the sun, knee-deep in the water, her hands holding up the pants of her costume. When the waves approached, she shrieked and ran back, then ran forward, laughing. She repeated her serve and volley at least five times, until a particularly large wave crashed down, splashing her nearly to her chest. Her clothes clung to her as she swivelled and ran up the sand, her mouth opened in delight. She was unaware of Thomas, standing slightly above on the promenade, who watched as she collapsed on the sand, next to a man, a red basket at his side proclaiming the picnic they must have brought.

Thomas stared. He could not see the man properly, only his back, his checked blue shirt tucked into khaki trousers. But he could see Rani's face, still wide open with excitement. He saw her lips move as she squeezed the water from her hair, pulled out a small towel from the bag and dabbed at her chest. Thomas took a step back, as if to hide, as if she would raise her eyes and see him standing on the promenade staring at her, at her compan-ion. But her eyes never left the man beside her; she turned and sat, her arms around her knees, and he stared and stared as he watched the man shuffle closer, so that eventually his head lay on Rani's lap. Now he could see more: a moustache, streaks of grey in the hair, a square-shaped face. So, her fictitious journey to the suppliers: in all likelihood she had been organising this day out or even meeting with the man beside her. Thomas turned away, glanced down the promenade, scanned the beach, but no one was paying the couple on the sand any notice.

Why had they chosen Cherai? Had she wanted to bump into Thomas? But then he dismissed the thought: look around him, hundreds of people were visiting from Ernakulam. In fact, hadn't he told her he would be in Calicut, visiting his sister for Easter? She had no reason to think he was spending his time otherwise. The sun was a red orb, teasingly suspended above the water, now turning grey. There would be half an hour of light before the dark engulfed them. The daytrippers were gathering their things, the coaches were hooting, calling for their cargo. If he stayed where he was much longer, then he would be visible: a lone figure on the promenade. As he was thinking this, they made a move, standing up and brushing off the sand from their clothes. Rani lifted her salwar to wrap around her bun, the wind whipping strands out around her face. The man – he could see him better now – took her elbow and guided her up to the promenade. She talked animatedly as they walked, throwing her head back once to laugh. Soon they were absorbed into the shadowy shapes, the silhouettes of people climbing into the coaches, the autorickshaws. Thomas stayed there until he felt sure they had gone, and then walked back along the promenade, past the cluster of huts and eateries near the road leading to Junction, then further on until the buildings disappeared, the road became a track and he arrived at his home.

7

H E was glad to return to the store when the Easter weekend was over. After the phone call with Nina and then seeing Rani on the beach, he had passed the next few days feeling troubled. He had done some more work on the gazebo the morning after but had made little progress, only succeeded in cutting his hand. His plans to have a buffet lunch at the beach resort also felt pathetic: he didn't feel that hungry in the heat, and what would he look like on his own sitting amidst cooing couples? He slept for a few hours in the afternoon on Easter Sunday and woke up bleary-eyed, his brain fuzzy, when it was already dark. He had avoided going to church that morning but then regretted it: at least Mariamma would not have thought too badly of him. While he knew she excused any behaviour she regarded as eccentric or inappropriate on the grounds of Nimmy's demise, Easter Sunday was important. The churches would be full to bursting. The phone call with Nina weighed heavily on his mind. And that, coupled with what he had seen – Rani and the man on the beach – meant that when he thought of the two young women, their images overlapped so that he saw Nina playing in the waves, then collapsing into a man's arms. It was not Michel who lay back, regarding his daughter with an easy, lustful languor, but the man he had seen, Rani's admirer. He imagined how these two would gather their things, walk away across the sand, walk away from him, her father, as he gazed at the couple's retreating forms.

That night he stared at the pages of his book, the words a blur in front of him, then pushed it aside and pulled out his laptop. As if he knew what he would do, he let his fingers tap in the words. *The Kerala Second Marriage Matrimonial Agency.* Registering took a few minutes and he used his dead elder brother's name, feeling only a brief twinge of guilt. When he was allowed on to the site, he scrolled through the endless faces, perusing the names. He recognised no one and could find none alluring. Most were near his own daughter's age but looked older, as if the first, failed, marriage had swallowed their youth. He was astonished by the sheer numbers: after browsing for only a few minutes he must have seen at least a hundred faces, a hundred failed marriages. And were spouses on the same site, so exes could track their former lovers' success in the market? He was forced to admit that he agreed with Rani's argument. Her sympathy, her discretion, and the fact that she was a living human being, all seemed wholly more desirable than posting a photograph on the site, penning a few words: *Priya, 35 years, trained in Ayurvedic massage. Status: Divorcee.* Rani's services seemed a much more palatable alternative.

A small bubble appeared at the bottom of the screen: *Hallo. Can I help you with your search?*

He stared at the words and then typed: *No thanks.*

What are you looking for?

When he did not respond, the bubble appeared again: *We offer full service. Full discretion, privacy guaranteed. Other sites available for exotic tastes.*

He closed the bubble, then the website, pushed the laptop away from him. All around him, outside, was dark, and he was alone in the room. The exchange had left an unpleasant taste in his mouth; the blink of the cursor had appeared more like a salacious wink.

It was suddenly obvious, so obvious that he wanted to laugh out loud at his naïvety. The numbers of women did not match the men; in fact, he had only seen a handful of male faces. Even in a modern India it was inconceivable that so many parents had misplaced their progeny in failed marriages. This was no marriage bureau: the website was a front, a front for a service of another kind. Only Rani would be innocent enough to take its name at face value. He would not avail her of the truth; it was her belief in romance that had prompted her to create her enterprise. She would be dismayed if she knew the sordid reality behind the promises of a second, better marriage.

He remembered how she laughed with the man on the beach, her eyes bright with delight. She had not mentioned any plans to visit Cherai; she was supposed to be visiting her father in Palakkad. Was her assignation clandestine? He wondered why he had held back from waving, calling out to Rani. It was too unrealistic, he concluded, that she would have smiled back and introduced him to her beau. She was shy enough of having a suitor to have not mentioned it.

It was a relief when he boarded the bus back into the city, the long weekend over. He savoured his approach to the shop on the Tuesday morning, pausing to look up and down the street, into the window of Green Gardens. So, he was becoming tired of his own company; he would have to remember to thank his brother-in-law for his propitious suggestion. Chacko's Optical

Store was proving an essential in his life. He saw a familiar figure move in the window and on entering felt a surge of affection that made him say warmly, 'Rani, nice to see you again.'

'And you, Mr Thomas,' she replied, the pleasure in her voice unmissable. They smiled at each other for a few moments.

'And how was your sister?'

He hesitated. 'I didn't go in the end.' Seeing a shadow cross her eyes, he lied. 'I went to stay with Nimmy's brother instead.'

There was some relief in her voice when she said, 'Oh good. Better than spending Easter alone, Mr Thomas.'

He asked as casually as he could, 'Did you have a good trip to Palakkad?'

She lowered her eyes and moved some papers. 'Yes, it went well.'

He muttered, 'Good, good,' unwilling to make her lie again. It was clear he was not able to pat her jovially on the arm and ask, so who's the lucky man, Rani?

They settled into their positions with a comfortable familiarity, and the morning passed with its usual rhythms. At half past eleven, he sent Rani across to Green Gardens to bring them back a cup of coffee each, which they slurped in companionable silence. She was organising the ledger, he could see. He turned away and leaned against the door jamb, watched the street outside with some affection. It was in full sun, with only small slivers of shade hugging the shop fronts. The man who owned the clothing shop diagonally opposite had invested in a new flashing light for his sign, which in the sun was rendered ineffective. The owner of the kiosk further down was swatting at his goods with a cloth. Thomas drained the last dregs of his coffee, turned to Rani and asked, 'Finished?'

She nodded, and he reached for her cup. 'I'll take these back.'

He crossed the street and pushed open the door to Green Gardens. The manager was behind the counter, berating a hapless young cashier. He stopped in mid-flow and smiled ingratiatingly. 'Mr Thomas!'

Thomas put the cups on the counter. 'Just returning these.'

'Oh no need, no need!'

As Thomas reached for his wallet, the manager shouted again, 'No need! My pleasure, Mr Thomas!'

Yes, indeed, he thought, pushing his wallet back into his pocket, glancing around for any likely-looking couples. But the café was empty.

When he stepped back out on to the street, he saw her further up on the other side, near the intersection with the main road, delving into her bag, wearing the same straw hat as the other day. Before he knew it, he had called out: 'Vishukumari!'

Her head snapped up and she glanced around, then saw him waving. He motioned to her not to step off the pavement but crossed the road himself to the other side. As he was walking up towards her, he noticed a hesitation, she had a slight nervous smile on her lips: she did not remember him.

'Thomas,' he said as soon as he reached her, held out his hand.

She smiled widely, took off her hat and pushed her sunglasses up her forehead. 'Of course,' she said, 'I didn't recognise you,' motioning to his chest. He looked down and realised that he was still wearing the white coat he wore for the eye tests.

'Sorry,' he smiled. 'I'm working.'

'You're a . . . ?'

'An optometrist.' He was ridiculously pleased he realised. He laughed. 'It's nice to see you again!'

She was smiling too.

'I was looking for an optician's actually.' She rummaged in her bag and produced a card, Jos's name at the head. 'They had this at the hotel.'

He laughed again. 'That's my friend, Jos! It's his shop I'm looking after while he is away.'

'Oh, what a nice coincidence.' She slipped the card back into her bag. 'I thought I'd get another pair of glasses for myself, and I have prescriptions for some friends as well. They're so expensive in the States.'

'Your son?' he asked, looking around him.

She shook her head. 'He's gone with my cousin's kids, to the water park. I thought it would be nice for him to go on his own. Truth is as well, I couldn't face it myself.'

He was grinning, then felt the need to try to compose himself. 'This is such a pleasant surprise. I so enjoyed our conversation the other day.'

She smiled widely. 'Yes, so did I. In fact, I regretted not asking you to join us on the ferry. But I suppose you were working . . .'

'I was on my lunch break.'

'I see.'

'I went back later.' Was he prattling? 'I wondered if you were staying at one of those hotels.'

She burst out laughing. 'Pinned me for the American tourist, right?'

He started to protest, but she was smiling, shaking her head. 'No, we're staying just further up from here actually.'

Then she paused. 'Why did you go back?'

His solitary drink in the chilly, soulless environment now seemed pitiful.

'I get a bus to Cherai from near there,' he said easily. 'It's on my way home.'

He turned away, gestured further down the street. 'Shall I show you the way?'

As she passed, he caught a slight fragrance, not perfume. It was the smell of her hair perhaps, which looked freshly washed, becomingly arranged with clasp and clips. She walked ahead of him, and he felt his eyes take note of the light-blue dress she was wearing that day, of the shape of her bottom, visible enough through its thin material. She turned to glance back at him, and he averted his eyes guiltily. At the shop, he saw a movement in the window as he pushed the door open for her and she moved inside.

'So nice and cool in here . . .' she sighed, then stopped.

Rani was standing in front of her desk, her lips stretched to their limit in a wide smile.

'Rani,' Thomas said in English. 'This is . . .'

'Vishukumari Nair,' she said, holding her hand out to Rani.

'Rani is Jos's assistant,' Thomas said. 'She's been showing me the ropes.'

He glanced at Rani, who was still grinning inanely, as if Thomas had brought a bride rather than a client off the street.

'So . . .' Vishukumari began.

'Yes, of course!' Thomas moved around her and stood by the desk. 'Rani, Mrs Nair would like to order some glasses. Can you take a look at the prescriptions?'

'Actually,' Vishukumari smiled ruefully, 'I didn't get a chance to have an eye test before I left.'

'If you have your old pair of glasses with you,' Thomas said, 'we should be able to get the numbers from—'

'Much better to have an eye test, Mr Thomas,' Rani interrupted. 'It will be much more accurate.'

He kept quiet: only two days ago they had done exactly that for another client.

Rani leaped behind her desk and scanned the diary. 'Your next scheduled appointment is in half an hour, Mr Thomas. You could fit madam in now?'

'Please,' she said, holding her hand up, 'call me Vishukumari. Or Vee.'

Rani gave a small laugh, her cheeks flushed. 'Oh, madam.'

Then turning to Thomas, she said in rapid-fire Malayalam, 'Tell her that if she has an eye test I can get a discount with the suppliers, if she orders from the catalogue. Delivery in two days.'

Vishukumari had walked over to the centre of the reception area, taking in the small sofas, the table covered in magazines and the glass cabinets filled with frames.

'Nice place you got here,' she said.

'Well, I can't take any credit. My friend Jos set it all up. He's in Houston for a few months, visiting his daughter.'

'Is that right? I know some people there.' She turned to both of them. 'Well, I'm all yours!'

'Yes, yes.'

He opened the door to the testing room, avoiding Rani's gaze, then busied himself at the desk as Vishukumari sat down in the chair. He adjusted the chair, bringing the seat forward, raising the height a few inches.

'We don't have all the digital equipment, I'm afraid,' he said. 'To take photos of the retina, etcetera. It's a basic sight test.'

'That'll be fine. I had the full works last year some time.'

She leaned back, watched him while he wrote her name on his pad, collected the lenses from his tray.

'There's something so comforting about seeing an eye chart,' she said. 'I had to wear glasses from age ten, so I've had a lot of experience.'

She smiled at him. 'It's so unlike the dentist's, isn't it? I just loved being congratulated on reading a few letters correctly.'

He adjusted the visor over her face, and they were silent for a few moments.

'Please read the top line.'

'E, V . . .'

He glanced down at her lap and saw how she had folded her hands together demurely, like a child in a rehearsal. She had long fingers, and her nails were painted a delicate colour. The folds of her dress had slipped between her legs and clung to her thighs. His eyes moved down to her knees, where the hem of her skirt ended, to her shapely calves. She reached the end of the chart, and he cleared his throat, moved on to the next step: 'Which is better: like this, or like this?'

'The first one I think,' she said.

Then: 'So this is what you did all those years in London?'

He made a few notes, grateful for the opportunity to collect himself.

'I worked at a large optician's,' he answered. 'It's a bit different here from the UK, or probably the States. Opticians are usually family-run businesses, passed down from generation to generation. Jos bought this store off one of the oldest, Panikkar's. Did you know them?'

She shook her head. 'My parents probably did.'

'Did you visit India much when you were growing up?'

'We came about three times?' She shifted slightly in the chair, laid her arms on the side-rests.

He tried to keep his eyes on her face, away from the slender gold chain that nestled in the hollow at the base of her throat, and then beyond. What was wrong with him? How many tests had he conducted in his lifetime? Of course he had always noticed if a female client was particularly attractive, but never before had he had such trouble in remaining unmoved, focusing on his tasks. He was acutely aware of how he was alone with her, how close she was to him in the small room, the door closed.

'I remember bits, not much,' she was saying. 'The last time I was fourteen, around Hari's age. Maybe that's why I decided to come this year.'

She looked at him, her eyes crinkling. 'Where I grew up? Queens? There was a huge Malayalee community. We did all the things, y'know: Onam, Diwali. I even learned Bharatanatyam as a girl.'

She suddenly extended her arms, one brushing against him, her index fingers touching her thumbs, her neck slender and erect.

Looking on her, he felt a desire that took him unawares. He could lock the door, lift her dress from over her, reveal those legs. Slide his hands under her and lift her on to him, with his mouth search for her breasts. The alacrity with which he arrived at these images shocked him. He had to turn away, pretend to look for something on his desk.

She dropped her hands. 'I guess my parents felt we were getting enough exposure to our heritage.'

He sat at the desk and filled in the form. He could see that she was watching him. He added a few more extra scribbles, carefully crossed his *t*s another time, dawdled over the date, absorbing her presence, like a slim blue moth in the dimness of the testing room.

'What's the verdict, doctor?'

He smiled. 'Not too bad. Your right eye is much weaker than your left.'

'Always has been.'

He stood up and replaced the visor in its holder. She swung her legs over to the side of the chair, then stopped short and looked at him.

'Thomas . . .' She hesitated, and he noticed a flush rising to her cheeks. 'I wonder. Could I ask you a favour?'

Without waiting for a response, she continued, the words a little rushed: 'I'm hoping to get some outfits ordered today as well. I just haven't plucked up the courage to go into a tailor's. Would you come with me?'

He felt a curious mixture of emotions. Her invitation had arrived as serendipitously as their encounter on the street; he should not read anything further into it. And her invitation, despite her obvious discomfort, had been made far too easily for him to discern any other intentions on her part. She could make her request because he posed no threat to her emotions. Whereas he had already broken into a sweat at the thought of spending the rest of the afternoon in her company, she looked discouragingly unaffected.

He gave her a small bow. 'Of course.'

'That's so kind of you!' Her lips turned downwards. 'I'm afraid my Malayalam isn't up to much.'

'I'm sure most will speak enough English.'

'Even so . . .'

'I'm no expert in fashion . . .'

'Oh, you won't have to be. I just need some sari blouses and a salwar kameez.'

She stood up, smoothing her dress over her hips, and he looked away, tried to focus on his notes.

'Have you a tailor in mind?'

'There's some guy near the hotel. That would be convenient for picking up . . .'

They discussed details: Thomas could be finished in another hour; Vishukumari would come back to meet him.

When she left the store, with a breezy adieu to Rani, there was a brief silence as they remained facing the door from which she had just left. Even Rani seemed to have succumbed to the aura she had created in their midst.

'A nice lady,' she said.

'Mm.' He turned to her and said sternly, 'Happily married as far as I can tell.'

She burst out laughing. 'I had such high hopes for you, Mr Thomas!'

She was grinning, and he found himself grinning back.

'Rani,' he said. 'I don't want you—'

'You're still young, Mr Thomas,' she interrupted. 'You know, you were very different when she was here.'

'Was I?' He was surprised, could not help asking, 'How? In what way?'

'More . . .' she shrugged her shoulders. 'More sophisticated. A real London man.'

She started laughing, clapping her hands to either side of her face.

'She's very beautiful!'

'Is she?' He was laughing.

'She liked you for sure . . .'

'Now, Rani . . .'

'And your English is so good! Not like mine!'

'Well . . .'

'So many words I couldn't understand!'

She was laughing like he had seen her laughing on the beach, her face glowing with delight. He watched her, thinking, this is when I should ask her. But he didn't, not sure whether he wanted to break the enjoyment of the moment. Perhaps if he regaled her with the story of the visit to the tailor's back in the office tomorrow, he could segue into encouraging her to share her story.

The next hour and a half moved sluggishly. Even Rani seemed subdued: he barely heard her in the next room. The normal buzz of the store seemed to be suspended until the upcoming events, the next instalment. Vishukumari was in the reception waiting for him when he emerged from the testing room. Rani was sitting at her desk, sitting on the edge of her seat, and had turned her chair so that she was facing Vishukumari. '. . . and then two years at Sacred Heart College, where I finished my SLC,' Rani was saying. 'I did well in my exams.'

There was a timbre of excitement in her voice, Thomas noted: she was enjoying the encounter.

'I'm sure you did.' Vishukumari was smiling.

Thomas moved to the desk, Rani standing up as he approached so they performed their exchange of seats with practised precision. He settled into the seat and tapped at the computer, feeling like he was intruding on their female collusion, a feeling that was not unfamiliar: when Nina was growing up, he had been similarly outnumbered in his home.

'Rani has been telling me about how she moved to the city from up north,' Vishukumari said. 'I've been telling her how impressed I am by her.'

'Mr Jos was very good to give me a chance.'

'Oh, I think we make our own chances, Rani. That's what I believe.'

She was rummaging in her bag.

'Let me give you my card, Rani,' she said. 'I'd like you to get in touch if you are ever in the States.'

Out of the corner of his eye, Thomas noticed a slight stiffening to Rani's posture; her expression had dimmed.

Rani was not so unaware, not so ignorant of what was available to her and what was not. Vishukumari had underestimated her. The offer may have been made with genuine intentions but the likelihood of Rani appearing on the shores of the United States was patently distant. I have probably underestimated her as well, he thought. He remembered how she had stared at Nina's photo, taken in London: oh I would love to go. Then her tact, so that he would not feel guilty about his good fortune. He tapped at the computer, but he could see that Vishukumari had extended her hand and was waiting expectantly. Rani reached forward, accepting the small card silently. Perhaps she was thinking: let me give you *my* card, Mrs Nair. Just in case your husband leaves you.

He coughed, cleared his throat.

'Thank you, madam,' Rani said, and her voice was steady. She had collected herself.

'Not at all.' Vishukumari smiled widely, turning from Rani to Thomas and then back.

He finished typing up the order and got to his feet.

'Finished,' he said to Vishukumari, who stood up herself, and to Rani, 'You'll lock up?'

'Of course.'

'Well, Rani,' Vishukumari said, and then stepped forward to kiss the young woman on both cheeks. Thomas saw Rani's hands grip the older woman's shoulder briefly. 'Thank you for keeping me company. I'll pop in later this week to pick up my orders.'

Then she turned to Thomas. 'I'm in your hands!'

'You are in good hands for sure, Mrs Nair.' Rani spoke suddenly, her tone was gushing. 'Mr Thomas has very good taste. I can tell you that the kurta he bought me the other day is beautiful.'

There was a moment's awkward silence, when Thomas saw the older woman move her head towards her in surprise.

Rani giggled. 'It was for Easter. It fits me perfectly, doesn't it, Mr Thomas?'

She was simpering in a way that Thomas had never seen before. He stared at her.

Vishukumari smiled uncertainly, and he reached forward, touched her elbow briefly.

'See you tomorrow, Rani,' he said, his voice curt.

As Thomas opened the door and Vishukumari passed through, he could not avoid looking back to see Rani, still flushed but looking crestfallen. They nodded their goodbyes, and he shut the door.

They stepped out on to the street, where the heat enveloped them, silencing them both. Vishukumari put her sunglasses on.

'Nice girl,' she said, but her voice ended on an upward note.

'Yes,' he said firmly.

They were silent for a few moments.

'Vishukumari,' he said eventually. 'I hope you didn't think—'

'Please, Thomas,' she interrupted, holding up her hand, then sighed. 'I'm not sure what happened back there, but I think I may have offended her in some way.'

'I'm sure you didn't . . .'

'Perhaps I was over-familiar? A common trait in Americans!'

She was upset but putting on a brave face. Her features were taut. He considered her anew: she was not invulnerable, and this discovery made her even more appealing.

He said nothing, but reached forward and squeezed her elbow briefly. She flashed a smile at him.

'So,' she started, and then ducked her head and rummaged again in her bag. 'I should have told you that I need to buy a couple of saris first.' Her voice was still tight, and he could discern that she was still troubled.

'No problem,' he said.

'Most men would hate to spend time in a sari shop . . .' She tilted her head to one side.

He shrugged. 'I've had quite a lot of experience.' He smiled.

'Did you use to accompany your wife?' she asked, and then, 'Do you mind me asking?'

He shook his head. 'Actually, Nimmy usually took her sisters along. I would sit in the background.'

'Nimmy . . .' she said thoughtfully, then, 'I'm sorry again. Y'know, for your loss.' Then she bit her lip. 'That sounded very insincere. I can't seem to say the right thing today.'

He took her elbow again, but this time he did not let go. She lifted her head to look at him, and they stood like this for some moments without speaking. He let himself gaze at her, careful not to let his eyes leave hers, meeting his from behind her sunglasses. He saw the tension melt from her face, the lines become softer, her eyes becoming brighter. His hand dropped from her elbow, and they started walking.

'At the moment,' he said, 'I'm most concerned about my daughter. I spoke to her the other day, and I'm afraid she's not very happy about my moving back here.'

'How old is she?'

'Thirty at the end of the year.' He turned to her. 'That probably sounds a lot older than your sons, but I'm only beginning to realise that she still needs me around.'

She was quiet and then smiled. 'At thirty, all I could think about was how to *avoid* my parents. But then, I didn't have to deal with the grief of losing one.'

They walked in silence for a few moments, then she said, 'We can't always please our children, Thomas, just as we can't always please our parents. We're people too – that's not easy for our kids to accept.'

Her forearm was brushing his and she did not seem to mind; he would have liked to have reached down and taken her hand, but the shop loomed just ahead, a flight of stairs with a security guard standing idle at the top. On seeing them, he opened the door invitingly, and they walked up, passing the window displays with ivory-skinned mannequins, brightly lipsticked, a pottu between their eyes, glittering saris. They passed through the door into the hubbub, the carnival of the sari shop: trays of glass cups filled with coffee being carried to and fro, the saris being unfurled at the merest gesture, the counters covered in silks. She was meek, quiet at his side. He adopted the requisite authoritative tone on her behalf, as he had never done for Nimmy, who had been competent on her own. Nearly an hour later, they emerged with her parcels.

The tailor across the road had the frown and disgruntled manner of someone who was secretly thrilled to be presented with an elegant foreign lady with whom to do business. He assumed Thomas was the husband, the chaperone, and neither told him otherwise. He took his measurements while Vishukumari posed before him, her arms outstretched. It was an opportunity for Thomas to gaze at her at leisure. When the tailor muttered a question at her – *'Ividey ivideyo?'* – motioning to two places on her chest with the measuring tape to show the décolletage, she had replied in a quiet voice, *'Adhyathey.'* The tailor's fingers brushed her waist, her shoulders, hovered just a hair's breadth from her breasts, as did Thomas's eyes. The tiny airless stall took on a different dimension. She was a courtesan, being dressed for his pleasure, to be clothed only so that in a darkened room later, alone, he could slide off the soft material, his fingers brushing from silk to the warmth of her flesh. As he was thinking these thoughts, she turned to look at him, as if she knew. Immediately he thought, she would let me look on her naked. With the knowledge she has of her beauty, she would stand before me and let me explore her body. He could almost feel his mouth moving against her bare skin. He stood up, moved away in the pretence of looking at some outfits hanging up, his face burning from the direction his thoughts had taken.

The tailor took the address of the hotel and promised delivery the next day.

'I can't thank you enough,' she said as they left the tailor's rooms and stepped out on to the street. The light had faded, and the evening chorus of buses, taxis, autos had risen. There was a bustle; people moved as shadows, the odd light flashing on their faces.

'Hari's not back until later,' she continued. 'I was going to have dinner at the hotel. Can I invite you to join me, as a thank you?'

All the nervousness and trepidation she had revealed in the sari shop and with the tailor had disappeared. She had made the invitation effortlessly. It was easy, it seemed, to invite a widower to dinner if you were a married woman with your affections intact. He was impatient with himself all of a sudden, and the way he had comported himself all afternoon: like some elderly count, enjoying the rarity of a lady's company.

'It's kind of you, but there really is no need to thank me,' he said. 'And I'm afraid of missing the last bus out to Cherai.'

'Oh, right . . .' She glanced away, a hand coming to her throat. Then she turned back. 'So I suppose, I should say . . .' Her voice petered away. He was surprised to see the disappointment in her eyes: so she was not used to being turned down. He made a decision.

'Actually,' he said, 'I would be happy to have a snack.' He pointed ahead to a fast-food restaurant: the cooks, all male, standing in front of hot plates, bowls of batter at the ready.

'That would be fun,' she said, smiling. 'I'd never go on my own.'

He refused the notes she tried to push into his hand, paid for a dosa for himself and an appam for her. All the tables were taken, so they stood at a high table, tearing pieces of the breads with their fingers, dipping them into the chutneys. They ate without speaking, the other diners chattering loudly around them, the two of them remaining a small island of quiet amidst the noise.

'That was delicious,' she said. She looked up and smiled. 'So that's two favours you've done for me today.'

He noticed a flash of colour in her hair, a fragment of material.

'You have something . . .' he said, gesturing to the side of her head.

She raised her hand to her hair, her fingers combing the strands unsuccessfully, until he reached forward himself. She remained still, as if aware that if she turned her face, her lips would brush against his fingers, as if she knew that he wanted to do more. He extracted the small square of silk, placed it on the table. Then she laughed, a touch nervously. 'How did that get there . . . ?' There was a silence as they both looked at the small red square between them. When he glanced up at her, she looked to him like she was holding her breath, taken unawares by how he had shown her that if he wished, he could touch her, and she would let him. He looked around him to distract himself from his assumptions; more customers were entering, eyeing their table with intent. But neither of them made a move to leave.

'I don't know what you do,' he said eventually.

'I trained as an architect,' she said. 'And I worked for a big firm for a few years after I graduated. But I run my own practice now. Just small-scale stuff.'

'I see.'

'My husband is a surgeon,' she continued. 'So with his hours, when we had the kids . . .' Her voice tailed off.

She leaned her elbows on the metal surface of the table, pushed her tray away and observed the others in the restaurant. He watched her: with her eyes now turned away, he could peruse her again at ease. It was unlikely that he would move in her social circles either in the States or in London; the irony was that it was here, back in India, that they found a commonality. Her clothes, the cut of her hair, the bracelet on her wrist: all confirmed that she was a woman unlike many of his acquaintance. Certainly unlike Nimmy, who even after thirty years in London had – with her long single plait, her choice of comfortable, affordable outfits – never shaken off the essence of the small town she had grown up in. She still exuded the simple charms of home. Thinking dispassionately about the two women, it was obvious that Nimmy had not had the beauty that Vishukumari wore carelessly. But she had had that light, the impish smile that made her look years younger. Vishukumari was a different animal. Was this why he was so attracted to her: because she was nothing like his wife, tempting him with glimpses into a love affair that he believed would be – what? – more passionate, more sensuous? Did beauty always mean passion? For all he knew, Vishukumari could be cold, reserved, an unwilling mate.

A cloud had descended, whether it had been the mention of her husband or the trail of his thoughts, but they did not speak. She may have been waiting for him to say something; perhaps he was showing himself an unsatisfactory dinner date.

'I must leave,' he said finally.

She turned back to look at him, nodded. She looked tired.

'Thanks again.'

'Really, there's no need . . .'

'I'll pop in later to pick up the glasses.'

'Yes.'

They shook hands on the street. The lights stroked her features, lingered over her lips, her throat. Once she had returned to her house, her home, her job, her life, the few weeks she had spent here would fade. She might then recall him as an interesting companion. He remembered how she had looked at the tailor's, her arms outstretched, how she had turned back to catch his eye. What had he said to Nina? The fullness of life. Did he even know what he had meant? He tried to direct his thoughts to Nimmy, to conjure up her face, but found that he could not. Can I be so fickle, he thought guiltily, and then in the same beat, crossly, and why not? Nimmy is dead, Vishukumari is still living, breathing.

When he finally reached his house, after a particularly crowded, sweaty bus ride, the darkness was his only welcome. The sea was a gentle hum to his right as he walked around to his back door. The only light shone from Mariamma's house: her back door was open and allowed a pool of light to fall near his door. It's not enough for me, all this, he thought. I've brought myself back home, but I've forgotten why I chose to do so. The thought troubled him, and he was restless in the dark, lying on his bed, the sound of the sea now louder as if comforting him: you are not alone, I am here outside your window.

8

For the first time, the next morning, he felt a reluctance to get up, get out of the house and rush for the bus into the city. Instead, he turned on his side and picked up from the floor the book he had been reading the previous night. The words swam in front of him; he could not focus. His mind was full of memories of the evening he had shared with Vishukumari. He wondered what she had made of his behaviour. Just days earlier, he had been trying to remember if he had ever taken a woman who was not his wife out for a meal; last night he had had the opportunity and had transformed what might have been a romantic dinner date into a casual refuelling. He groaned, tossing the book to one side. What was he thinking about? She was married; she was not a client of Rani's bureau seeking romance. Better that their meal yesterday had been friendly, a no-strings low-key affair. He had no doubt that when she had made her invitation she had not envisaged adulterous love-making in her hotel bedroom before her son returned; he should not assume any ulterior motives on her part. He sighed, rolled on to his back and pressed his palms to his eyes. He could picture her standing before him as she had said goodbye, the light falling across her in bands, so that at one moment her eyes were in shadow, her mouth illuminated, her throat eclipsed, her breasts aglow. And then the reverse, as if teasing him: you can kiss me here and then here. You can touch me here and then here.

Eventually, the responsibility he had to his friend, and a reminder to himself that no one had forced him to accept the position of optician-in-charge, nagged him out of his bed and on to the balcony. He could see the fishermen pulling in their nets, hear their shouts and calls interspersing the peace of the early morning. In front of the blue-grey water, the beach: bleached of colour in the early-morning light. It was the perfect backdrop to the bright colours of the fishermen's turbans and mundus, their blackened bodies, their slender boats lying like dark gashes on the sand. He could just make out their words, nearly indecipherable, punctuating the sound of the waves. He could have remained on the balcony for hours, he would never tire of his view, but he gathered himself and went downstairs to make his breakfast.

The traffic into the city was light: perhaps many had added a few more days of holiday to the Easter weekend. He got off at his stop near the High Courts and walked briskly along the promenade, the water a glittering grey at his side. It was not just the thought of working that had slowed him down in the morning, he realised: he was reluctant to face Rani after that awkward exchange he had witnessed between her and Vishukumari. He did not want her to feel she owed him an explanation and neither did he want to furnish her with the details she might request of the expedition to the tailor.

But Rani's head remained lowered when he opened the door, and he, in compensation, gave her a particularly breezy, 'Good morning, Rani!' to which she responded with a tiny quiver at her lips. He smiled widely and asked, 'Many appointments today?'

While she gave him a list of commitments, in a subdued voice, her eyes fixed on her ledger, he nodded, making a small sound of agreement after each name, until finally, with a 'Right!', he darted into the testing room. Avoiding confrontation was, after all, his forté.

The day passed as if the sound was turned down, muted noises emanating from the reception. There were no jolly gatherings, which he might today have enjoyed overhearing. Rani was perhaps, true to her word, not expanding her business. At lunch-time, she gave him a wan smile while she was opening her tiffin as he passed by for his walk and was engrossed in a magazine when he returned. He had spent his lunch hour watching the arrivals and departures of the ferry, this time unwilling to venture as far as Marine Drive for fear of bumping into Vishukumari. He had, by then, reached the conclusion that the previous evening had been an inglorious chapter of his life, and hers.

His first appointment after the lunch hour was a man of his age, with a neat grey moustache and beard, and – unusual, but not unknown – light-green eyes which stood out against his brown skin. As Thomas asked him some questions and filled in his details, he noticed that the man was smiling at him.

'You don't remember me,' he said finally.

Thomas glanced at his name on the sheet in front of him, *Pillai*, and then back at the man. His face was familiar, there was a vague recollection, and then he remembered: they had been at the same college, in the same year, the same batch. He had shared a dorm with him in their first year.

He held out his hand, and the man laughed and shook it.

'Of course,' Thomas said. 'I didn't recognise you at first. How are you?'

'Fine, fine.'

They both leaned back, the eye test forgotten for some time, and reminisced. Pillai, Thomas now remembered, had been an intellectual. Intense and driven, he had stood out among his shallower, more venal contemporaries. Rather than fritter away his time ogling their female classmates, he had organised meetings and marches. If he missed a class, it was more likely because he was taking part in a protest than because he was sitting in the cinema like most of his peers. He was no longer so politically active, he told Thomas. He and his wife now lived in semi-retirement in Thekaddy, but his son was in government, to his great pride. The Party, however, was not what it was. And Kerala now was no different from the rest of India, stricken by that well-known disease: consumerism.

'You'll have seen the difference,' he said. 'Things aren't like they used to be. Nowadays, most young people want their phones and clothes. They aren't as passionate about making a change as we used to be.'

'I'm afraid even when I was young I was never like that . . .'

'Actually, yes, I remember now,' Pillai said, laughing. 'Always reading. The girls at least were impressed by your seriousness.'

It was not a reprimand, although at an earlier stage of their acquaintance it would have been. It was more of an observation. Perhaps, Thomas thought, after a certain age you are more easily forgiven for your unremarkable contributions to society. They spoke on while Thomas carried out the test, and agreed that next time Pillai was in Ernakulam he would phone ahead and they could meet for longer. They shook hands again, warmly, at the door, before Thomas had to welcome the next client, already waiting their turn in the reception area.

After the last appointment of the day, he leaned against the desk and perused the room, still reluctant to leave the safety of the charts and implements to go back into the reception. It had been a pleasant surprise to see Pillai again after all those years. They had not been close, but he would look forward to spending an evening with him, hearing about his exploits over the intervening years. He had relied so much on newspapers for news of events in Kerala, it would be refreshing to hear of things from a more personal perspective. Of course, in a few months, Jos would also return, and they could also resume their friendship. He could picture himself picking up with old friends, gathering a group of drinking buddies; perhaps he would evolve into a more social being than he had been until now. He need not indulge in solitary drinks in an expensive, soulless hotel bar. There was one difference, however: Pillai and Jos had their wives to go home to.

He moved away from the desk and lay down in the testing chair, stretched out his legs, laid his arms on the armrests. She had posed like this yesterday, the length of her legs on full display. She had turned her head like this to look at him at his desk, making his scribbles. What had she seen?

There was a knock and then the door opened. Rani peered inside.

'Mr Thomas?' She regarded him without surprise, as if she had expected that he would be reclining on the testing chair in a quiet moment. Perhaps Jos had taken his nap in here.

'Rani. I was just . . .'

She stepped inside, moved closer and stood beside him, so that he was looking up at her for a change, she was looking down. From this vantage point, her eyes looked huge, oversized in her small face. She did not say anything but stood still, watching him, her expression solemn. He suddenly felt ridiculous, as if, despite the disparity in their size, it was he who was a small boy waiting for his mother to kiss him goodnight. He pushed himself up on to his elbows.

'Why don't you go home, Mr Thomas?' she said. 'There are no further appointments, and you had such a busy day. It's nearly closing time anyway.'

Her eyes were soft, there were dark smudges at the corners. She looked tired.

'Will you leave a bit early as well then, Rani?' he asked. 'I think you could do with a rest.'

She smiled, her first genuine smile of the day. 'I will stay just a little longer, Mr Thomas. I have a few errands to finish. And then go, if that's OK.'

He swung his legs over the side and she stepped back. He stood up and they resumed their usual positions: he looked down at her and she raised her face to his.

'Absolutely. I think that's an excellent idea.'

'OK, Mr Thomas. All the deliveries arrived this afternoon. I'll sort them out tomorrow.'

'Yes, that sounds good.'

He picked up his bag, and they moved into the reception area together. She walked with him to the door as if he were a client and she was escorting him to his exit. He glanced sideways at her; she had opened her mouth as if to say something, but she did not speak. Perhaps she had considered a reference to the previous day and then decided against any mention that would spoil their rapprochement.

'Are you reading anything interesting at the moment?' he asked.

She shook her head. 'Just a magazine.'

'Maybe one lunchtime you'll come with me to the bookshop near Marine Drive,' he said. 'I'd like to get some more books myself.'

She smiled. 'That would be nice, Mr Thomas.'

He smiled back at her. 'See you tomorrow.'

As he was closing the door behind him, he turned once again to look back at her, just as he had done the previous afternoon. She looked forlorn, somehow, standing on her own, the reception area a background. But she gave him another small smile and raised her hand as if in benediction as he smiled his goodbye in return and shut the door. It was a relief to leave, but they had ended the afternoon on a better note. He was sure that by the next morning she would have bounced back to her normal self. Most importantly she would have realised by then that he had no intention of quizzing her on her behaviour with Vishukumari, and she would have enough tact and consideration not to press him for an account of their afternoon.

The bus back to Cherai was noticeably faster, and at one point hurtled with dangerous enthusiasm through streets which were as yet unhampered by the rush-hour traffic. By the time he got back to the house, the sun had started its decline but was still strong: it would be another two hours before it melted into the sea. Mariamma's son was standing in front of the house, kicking at a stone dolefully.

On seeing Thomas, he queried hopefully, '*Urumbu?*'

He had been Thomas's second when they had tackled the ants in the house those months ago, and Thomas could remember his amusement at the boy's fastidious adherence to his instructions. He shook his head and saw the boy's face fall in disappointment.

'But,' Thomas said, 'I need some help outside. Do you want to come?'

The boy galloped into the backyard, started arranging the leftover bamboo sticks into piles according to length as asked, while Thomas went upstairs and threw his bag down, took off his shirt and changed out of his trousers into a mundu. When he went outside, the boy was already red-faced with his exertions, and Thomas dragged the sticks over towards the house where the small porch threw some shade. What more needed doing to the gazebo was best done when he was alone, without having to worry about a small boy and potential injuries. So he gave the boy a rag to wipe the sticks down while he eyed the pile and cut some strips of the tough cloth he had bought as part of his supplies. The boy worked conscientiously, only occasionally looking up to throw a glance at Thomas. He had a wiry, small frame; his skinny legs with their knobbly knees protruding from his shorts reminded Thomas of himself at that age. He watched the boy as he managed to draw out the simple task he had been given into a project of momentous proportions. He would have to find another way to occupy him: there were only so many times the boy could clean the sticks, already gleaming in the sun.

He got down on his haunches and scanned his materials, making some calculations in his head. He could fashion a small tepee for the boy and his siblings; it would not take much time, and he had yet to meet a small child who did not cherish their own hiding place. They could make a start today, and then he would discuss with Mariamma where it could be positioned.

As they worked, the boy began to speak.

'Why do you swim?'

'I love the water. Can you swim?'

The boy shook his head.

'Shall I teach you one day, when you're a bit older?'

'I'm scared.' His voice was melodious: *enikku pedi*.

'We can start in the paddy field. We won't go into the sea until you're a bit older. You'll be stronger by then.'

Then a silence while he scrubbed the sticks, before, 'Why do you know Amma?'

'Your mother has been a neighbour for some years.'

'Why do you not have a wife?'

'I did have a wife.'

'Where is she?'

'She died some time ago.'

Then, for some reason, he felt beholden to ask, 'Do you not remember her?' Of course the child didn't, he thought as soon as he had spoken. He would have been even younger when Nimmy had last been here. But the boy nodded. Firm quick movements, as if he knew from how Thomas had framed his question that this was what he should do: to make a pact, seal a pledge between them. Such was the wisdom of the very young.

After some time, when it was clear that he needed to take the big knife out, which he did not want to do near the boy, he told him to wash at the tap while he poured him some milk. He lifted the large bunch of bananas he had bought at the weekend down from its hook in the larder and asked him to choose the ones he wanted. As the boy was making his careful, serious selection, he heard Mariamma's voice, shouting.

'He's here, Mariamma,' he called out. 'With me.'

He saw her face appear over the wall. 'I told him not to disturb you! He's been in a bad mood all day.'

'He's not disturbing me at all.'

She was standing on a bucket, he could see, and another child was pulling at the end of her sari.

'I'm making a small shelter.' He pointed to the sticks behind him. 'When it's finished, I can put it up in your garden. The children might enjoy it, and I can take it down whenever you want.'

'That's so kind of you.'

'It's a pleasure.'

They both turned and watched the boy as he collected three small bananas and pushed them into his pockets. Then he ran around the house and appeared a few moments later at his mother's side. The light was fading fast now. They said their goodbyes, and he walked back to the house.

He had said to Vishukumari, that first day: it's no easier raising a girl. But maybe he would have been better with a son: at least when they were small, boys were very uncritical. Certainly he had been at that age, with his uncomplicated love for his parents. He had never ever doubted that they loved him, but neither did they ever try to remind him that they did. It just was: just as the day followed the night, just as the trees grew around them, the dry season was broken by the rains. From a young age, he had worked alongside his father in the rubber plantations, just as Mariamma's son had helped him, collecting the sap from the trees, pouring it into trays, hanging the sheets out to dry. Later, he had been charged with taking the pineapples to the market. Even in the house, his mother had enlisted his help. Both he and his older brother, unlike the other boys he knew, had their share of chores in the kitchen, helping her pound the rice, cutting vegetables. These were gentle, intimate moments, when she would tell him stories of her childhood, of her village in the mountains, of her life before she married his father, aged seventeen.

But despite the love he had for his parents, when he had left to go to college, the first person in his family to do so, he had gone with barely a backward glance – with no doubt that they would be waiting for him, whenever he visited – the promises of the city beckoning. He had not enjoyed his college days as much as he had hoped. He had found his classes irksome; he enjoyed the trips to the cinema and afternoons in bookshops far more. He remembered his return to the village, having finished his studies, with an average result from an average college. He had sat disconsolate at the table in the kitchen with his father who did not berate him for his lacklustre performance. For him, a college diploma, no matter how ordinary, was a cause for celebration. The house was quiet now, bereft, his mother having died two years earlier. With Chechiamma also gone, in seclusion in a convent somewhere far up north, the household had dwindled to the three males: his father, his brother and him.

With the certainty of youth, aged twenty-two, Thomas had sat there knowing that he had reached the end: this was it. He was back at the house with his small suitcase. He would work now for the rest of his days with his father, toiling on their small piece of land, the breeze whispering at them through the leaves of the trees that overshadowed them. As his father had got up to leave him at the table, his older brother had walked in, filling the room with his ebullience, his handsome face, his muscled frame: bright with life. At the sight of his baby brother, newly graduated but glum, in his buttoned shirt and trousers, he had whooped with laughter, slapped his hands against Thomas's cheeks, pulled at his ears. His father had muttered in irritation, swatting his noise away, then placed a hand on Thomas's head before walking outside to pick up his tools again.

Thomas had remained at the table, his shoulders slumped, until his brother had quietened, laid an arm around his shoulder, patting Thomas's cheek comfortingly with his other hand. 'Don't worry, Thomasmon,' he had whispered, his voice soft with tenderness. Then, his arm becoming a vice, Thomas now struggling to escape his grip, he had pounded at the table suggestively: 'Forget the girl, *eda*! She's already with her rich old man!' As Thomas had pushed at his sibling – who was now helpless with laughter – he had felt, despite his humiliation, that, as always, it was his older brother who could see into his heart. He had had his chance: he had gone to the city and had now returned to the village without making a mark. Not with his teachers, nor with the procession of female students he had fallen in love with from afar. His life was over.

He had been standing at the back door, lost in his reveries, the sound of his older brother's raucous laughter echoing in his ears, when the small boy scuttled back around the corner, carrying a plate, a banana leaf its cover.

'Amma said to give you this,' he said.

Thomas lifted the leaf: a plate full of ethakka appam. The aroma of the crisply fried plantain made his stomach rumble.

'Tell her thank you,' he said.

'We will work again?' the boy asked.

'Yes, of course.'

The boy scampered away, satisfied. He had a father, Mariamma's husband, who appeared occasionally in the back garden in a red checked mundu, scratching his chest and yawning. He had a father, but he still enjoyed Thomas's company. As it was easier sometimes with other people's children, so it was easier sometimes with other people's parents.

He had a sudden thought, went back into the house and collected his phone from the bedside table, ran downstairs and then took a photo of the gazebo. He was pleased with his effort. The sun, setting behind the house, lent a rosy hue; to one side the coconut trees stood sentry. He would send the photo to Nina with a caption: *You might be surprised to know that I made this. You can sit here when you visit.* He went into the house, fiddling with the controls, but then he stopped, stood still. He had never sent his daughter a photo, a jaunty note; he had hardly messaged her. Would she appreciate the sudden gesture, or would it be so uncharacteristic of her father as to appear a vain attempt at reconciliation, a sop for her bruised feelings? As if he assumed that he could erase years of misunderstandings with a swipe of his phone? He turned on the lights and carried his phone upstairs with him on to the balcony. With the sea before him now, a black carpet, he could feel more sure of himself. He would call her at her flat first and ask her if she wanted him to send some photos of the house, the improvements. He dialled Nina's number and waited as he heard the phone ring.

'*Allô?*'

It was Michel. For a moment, Thomas thought to hang up, then he steadied himself, said, 'Michel? It's Thomas,' then added, 'Nina's father.'

There was a gratifying warmth to Michel's voice when he replied in English. Nina was not back yet; he, Michel, would be leaving later to meet her. He did not like her to take the metro on her own so late. And how, he asked, was Thomas?

They spoke for some minutes, about the heat, the clouds that gathered every day, a precursor for the rains, still some months away. Yes, Nina had mentioned visiting in the summer. Would the monsoon make a holiday too difficult? Then about Michel's work, and his parents: both retired now and at present on a cruise through the Baltic States. They had arranged for Michel and Nina to meet them in Riga in a few weeks, along with Michel's sister and husband, to spend the weekend. Finally, the promise to pass on a message to Nina, tell her that he had phoned.

When he hung up, Thomas leaned on the balcony rails, listened to the waves. He looked down at the phone in his hands, smeared with dirt and dust after working with his tools. He felt unsettled and comforted at the same time. Just that short conversation had conveyed a more detailed picture of Nina and Michel's lives together than he had previously had. That Michel's parents had their own relationship with his daughter, whom they regarded as, who knew, a future daughter-in-law? He, Thomas, did not even know their names; did they know about him, about how he had packed up and come back?

And it seemed that Michel made sure that Nina was escorted home safely. Thomas had done the same with Nimmy those first years in London, before they had bought the house near the hospital. And when Nina was little, it was Thomas who collected her from nursery and then school and brought her home: Nimmy's shifts, at least when their daughter was young, were not conducive to managing the school run. He and Nina had kept each other company in the evenings. Just as Mariamma's son had studiously worked next to him earlier, his daughter had sat with him in the kitchen while he cooked, at the table with her colouring pencils, bent over her pictures with furious concentration. He flicked at his phone, pulled up the picture of Nina with Nimmy, the same photo he had shown Rani when they had had their lunch together. She had told him that she loved Michel, and that Michel loved her; she seemed to be more secure of Michel's love than she did of Thomas's. He had never required a sign from his parents that they cherished him; now he could not think of a sign that he could send to his only child to assure her of his love. A stack of bamboo sticks, trussed together, criss-crossed into a pyramid. A note: that he would build her a hiding place wherever she wished. And that he would take it down when she tired of it, when she wanted to reveal herself.

9

Hᴇ spent the journey into the city the next morning mentally constructing the tepee of bamboo sticks and then taking it apart. He had hoped his daughter would call when she returned home the previous night, but she hadn't. The photo of his gazebo remained on his phone, unsent. When he arrived on the street, the manager from Green Gardens came running out: he had clearly been waiting for Thomas.

'She's not here,' he said, pointing across the road. The door to the optician's was shut, and the sign read '*Closed*', with the opening hours listed below. 'Rani is not here.'

'I'm sure she'll be here soon,' Thomas said, surprised at the fervour in the manager's voice.

'She's never late.'

There was clearly an arrangement made between them for today: a potential client for the bureau, possible custom at the café. Thomas looked at the man. He had never, actually, paid him much attention: he was youngish, late thirties.

'She could be on her way. Her bus could have been delayed,' he said.

The manager made an exasperated noise, started to speak and then decided against it.

'Shall I let her know you were looking for her?' Thomas asked.

The manager shook his head, made his goodbyes: whatever he had expected to gain from accosting Thomas was not in the offing.

He unlocked the door to the shop, turned the sign over and walked to her desk, where lay the cream ledger that he had seen Rani use as an appointments diary. He scanned the contents. Immediately, the door opened behind him. Ten a.m.: Mr Kuriacose. He was a businessman who was flying to Delhi in the afternon and could not waste any time. Thomas ushered him into the testing room, leaving the door ajar. As he was reaching the end of the first stage of the test, he heard the shop door open and someone come in: a woman and her daughter.

'Please take a seat,' he called out. 'Rani is not here, but I'll see you in a minute.'

The morning passed in a hectic series of routine appoint-ments, all delayed as he had to show the clients the frames from the cabinets himself. By the time he reached the last scheduled appointment, he was running more than an hour late, and the elderly man who had been waiting since half past eleven was irate.

'No system. Is this how to run a business?' he asked queru-lously. Thomas muttered soothingly. As soon as he had got rid of the man, he turned the sign over: *Closed*. He could not deal with any speculative enquiries. He sat at Rani's desk and glanced through the ledger. There were three more appointments for the afternoon, the last at half past four. The next day, there was a quieter morning, the first appointment only at eleven, but the afternoon was full. Surely Rani would have made an appearance by then? Even any minute now the door could open and she would rush in, flustered, full of explanations.

At lunchtime, he went across to Green Gardens.

'She's still not here,' he said when the manager approached him. This time the man assumed an air of nonchalance.

'Some good explanation there will be.'

'She hasn't called in to say what's happened.'

'Yes. You should tell her to do so next time.'

So he had lost out on a potential deal and now he had lost interest. His words were jovial, but his manner was forced.

Thomas held him back.

'Where does she live?' he asked.

'She stays in a hostel,' the manager said, turning away.

'Yes, I know that.' Thomas could not keep the irritation from his voice. 'But what is it called? It's in Konthuruthy, isn't it? Do you have a number?'

'I will check, sir,' the manager said, so insincerely that Thomas had to bite down a retort.

The day passed unsatisfactorily: it was messy, handling both the reception and the testing room, and by the time he returned home he was frazzled. But even after an exhausting day, he felt restless, strangely awake. He was tempted to go for a night swim but just managed to dissuade himself: far too risky with the strength of the undertow and no one on the beach to monitor him. Instead, he drank a bottle of beer from the fridge, leaning against the door jamb on the balcony. He tried his daughter's phone number but got her answer machine, felt a pang as he heard her voice calmly referring to Nina and Michel.

'Just checking in with you, *mol*,' he said. 'Love to you both.' Easily said, the words tripped off his tongue as if rolling down a slope, aided by the bottle of beer.

He slept badly, falling into a deep slumber just as the sun began to rise, and woke to his alarm, disgruntled by the argument he was having with someone who remained at the periphery of his dream-vision.

Somehow he knew that Rani would not be there even before he arrived at the shop and saw the *Closed* sign. When he entered, everything was as it had been when he left the previous evening: no sign that Rani had arrived later that evening, tidied up in preparation for the new day. He glanced at his watch: one hour before the first appointment. He went to her desk and sat on her chair. The ledger was before him. To his right a jar of pens, all labelled *Jos Chacko Optician*. The telephone was in front of him, and the card machine; to his left a glass jar of peppermint sweets he knew she offered to the children who visited.

He slid the top drawer open: the inventory pads, the previous ledger, some envelopes labelled with their suppliers' names. Jos ran his shop on a minimal basis, he had told Thomas: easier to account for, less to be accountable for. There was nothing to indicate Rani's name, her address, her employee number. Nothing. The bottom drawer, when Thomas tried to slide it open, was locked. He glanced around: the key must be on the bunch he had seen Rani use. He stared at it. There, of course, could be personal details, of herself, Jos and her clients. He looked at the lock: it could easily be picked, he surmised. He was looking for a suitable implement when his first appointment arrived. Another morning of juggling, of apologies, of becoming as irate as the clients at the inefficiency of it all. When he turned the sign over for the lunch period, he sat back at the desk, determined. After ten minutes of fiddling, he heard a click and the drawer slid open with a satisfying whirr.

This drawer was more organised, with labelled folders. He worked through them systematically. No information about Rani or where she lived: it was as if she did not exist. Did Jos even have her on his books, he wondered. He had been told that Jos would ensure Rani's salary would be paid; he would not have to worry about that and indeed he had never asked her if her finances were taken care of. Towards the back of the filing cabinet he arrived at what he had expected. He took out the yellow file and opened it. On the first page, she had typed out, as if to remind herself what she held in the pages: *Rani Vamadevan, Marriage Bureau Counsellor*. It was an evocative title. He shut the folder and, without thinking further, slid it into his bag, zipped it up.

He didn't go for lunch but spent the time reorganising the frames that were now spilling out of their plastic boxes, the cabinets nearly empty, with piles of boxes on the counter. Then he scanned the diary: one more day before the weekend, and it was going to be a busy day. There were appointments morning and afternoon. After the weekend, the appointments were more intermittent: this meant people would start phoning in to book a slot. He sat at the desk, tapping his fingers, not hungry and not unduly displeased to be presented with a dilemma. He could phone Jos, but without giving Rani a chance to explain herself he was unwilling to call her employer and put her in a bad light. The immediate need was for someone to help him: to answer the phone and to deal with the front-of-house. He could, for example, block out a few appointment spaces so that whomever he enlisted would not be overrun with clients; not everyone could be expected to be as efficient as Rani. That would keep Jos's business ticking over without too much of a loss until Rani returned.

He was mulling over his next move – dismissing crossing the road and talking to the manager at Green Gardens – when he noticed someone standing in front of him, separated by the glass, waving.

He leaped to his feet and rushed to the door.

'Vishukumari!'

She gestured at the sign. 'It's very cheeky of me, I know it's your lunch hour but . . .'

'Come in, come in.' He ushered her in. 'Your son?'

'Actually, he'll be here in a moment. He just wanted to stop off somewhere, he's right behind.'

'Good, good.'

She took off her hat and dabbed at her forehead.

'I must look a state,' she said. 'It's boiling out there.'

'No,' he said, taking in the glow of her cheeks, the perspiration on the bridge of her nose, on the hollow of her neck. 'No, you look . . . fine.'

She smiled again, and his heart swooped into his stomach.

'I came to pick up my orders,' she said, looking around. 'And where is the delightful Rani?'

There was a rap on the door, and the youth gave a wave through the glass. Thomas opened the door, and he passed through with a vague smile and a duck of the head.

'Come in, Hari, come in.' Then turning to his mother, 'Well, I'm not sure where Rani is to be honest. She hasn't come to work for two days now.'

Vishukumari's eyes widened, and there was some gratification in the way she took the news with seriousness.

'Really? How very strange. She didn't call or anything?'

'No calls. It's very unlike her.'

'So how have you been managing?' This with a glance around the shop.

'I'm not really, to be honest,' Thomas said. 'I'm sure your orders are in that delivery over there.' He pointed to a box in the corner. 'As will be several other customers'. But I haven't even opened them yet.'

'Oh my,' she said. 'Hari, take a look at the box, will you, hon?'

Thomas watched as the youth slouched over and then bent over the box, looked around and grabbed a pair of scissors off the desk to slide through the packing tape. He lifted out the plastic sealed envelopes and put them in a pile, then extracted three. 'Nair,' he said. 'These are yours, Mom.'

Vishukumari turned to Thomas.

'Do you need some help?' she asked.

He looked down at her. Her expression was calm but concerned.

He spread his arms out, let them drop back and slap against his legs.

'I am floundering.'

She smiled suddenly and briefly placed her hand on his chest.

'There's something so beautiful about the way you speak,' she said. 'I could listen to you all day.'

He felt his face burn; his heartbeat quickened where her hand had been. He tried to answer flippantly: 'I would like nothing more,' hoping that the tone of his voice did not betray the very real honesty of his words. Into his vision arrived the boy to stand behind his mother.

She turned slightly. 'Hari, do you want to go ahead back to the hotel for a swim or something? And I can stay here and help Thomas out for a couple of hours?'

As her son shrugged and mumbled, Thomas made a half-hearted attempt to protest. 'I really can't let you . . . you're on holiday . . .'

'Nonsense,' she said briskly, walking over to Rani's desk and scanning the room. The boy muttered his goodbyes and was gone. Thomas watched her as she went back to the delivery box and started cross-checking the names on the delivery envelopes with some markings in the ledger.

'My only worry,' Vishukumari said, 'is if anyone doesn't speak English. You know my Malayalam is not up to much.'

He made soothing sounds; he could easily leave the testing room if the need arose.

'Mm,' she said, then delved into her bag and pulled out a pair of spectacles, then laughed. 'I should be wearing the ones I bought here. Better advertising!' Hers were tortoiseshell, with a discreet label etched into the arms. On her nose, they complemented the shape of her cheekbones.

'Shall I flip the sign over?' he said to her.

'Good to go,' she mumbled, her head bent over a selection of envelopes. As he walked to the front door, she said, 'I hope Rani gets in touch soon, Thomas. You see we're leaving the day after tomorrow.'

She was writing in the ledger as she was speaking, but she lifted her eyes for an instant to catch his before looking away quickly. So she knew, he thought. My schoolboyish infatuation has not escaped her notice. In fact, how could it not? The only wonder is that, given that she is capable of reading my mind, she has not slapped my face for my lecherous designs. He had a few seconds to compose himself before saying, 'That's a shame. At least for me. I haven't managed to invite you and Hari to my house.'

She sat back and looked up. 'Oh, that was a kind thought, Thomas.'

'Maybe next time.'

She looked at him for some moments, smiling, but there was a shadow in her eyes. 'Yes, let's say that. Next time.'

'And perhaps you will come as a family, with your husband . . .'

He need not have said it, but the words had jumped out and stood, feet wide apart, gurning at her like a troupe of warriors. He noticed her throat move as if she were swallowing her words, then she smiled and nodded. Behind him the door opened.

'Mr Thomas!' It was one of the regulars who had not ordered a pair of spectacles nor booked an eye test for two months: a client of the bureau, arriving to seek Rani.

'No Rani today?'

'No,' Thomas said, guiding him to the desk. 'Allow me to introduce you to Mrs Nair. She will be able to help you book a test or choose some frames if you already have a prescription.'

He took some cruel pleasure in directing the man to Vishukumari, who was smiling and holding out her hand. Let him reveal his pathetic longings, or make some inane excuse, leave with his tail between his legs. He dove into the test room.

She would be leaving soon, and he may never see her again. With a thumping heart he cleaned the instruments, checked the test boards. He arranged the papers on the desk, dusted and wiped the chair. Then he sat down on his stool, staring at the test board. The letters swam before him and his eyes seemed to focus on the V, the K, the M. He had only met her three times, including this afternoon. It was ridiculous to have such a crush on a married woman at his age. He blamed Rani and her talk of second chances: second-rate, second-hand.

He moved to the door and listened: he could hear Vishukumari's voice rising and falling. There were a few grunts from the other man. How small my life has become, he thought. Thankfully I have my house on the beach, he reminded himself. He closed his eyes and allowed the sea to flood his thoughts, the waves curling then dissipating on the sand, leaving a trail of shells, the sand golden and saturated. The open sky, the full horizon that he could see before him. When he opened his eyes, he felt ashamed that he had left her when she could not know the man's reasons for visiting the shop. He opened the door and went back into the reception area. The man was still there but had moved to sit on the side of the desk so that he was closer to Vishukumari. From that position, Thomas realised, he would have a clear view down her neckline at the pale swell of her breasts. She was looking up at the man, unaware, her glasses in her hand, laughing.

'Then I said to the fellow, you may be a phone-wallah but wait until the—' The man broke off when he saw Thomas. 'Oh, Mr Thomas! I'm just telling Vishukumari here about how these phone companies are destroying the fabric of our nation.'

Vishukumari.

'Have you booked for anything?' Thomas asked, surprising himself with the brusqueness of his voice.

Vishukumari stopped smiling, placed her glasses on the desk.

'No, no,' the man said, patting his pockets as if looking for something. 'I'll be going. Perhaps you could let Rani know I passed by, and give her my regards.'

He turned to Vishukumari, and she held out her hand, which he took, then turned over and raised to his lips.

'It's been a delight.' His tone was mellifluous. Who could have imagined such an assured performance from this overweight, balding, unprepossessing fellow!

Thomas went to the front door, opened it and managed a stiff smile. His cheeks felt as if they were cracking from the effort.

'*Pinne kaanam,*' he said, with a finality that contradicted his words.

'*Sheri, sheri.*' The man turned to Vishukumari. 'Safe journey.'

'Thank you.'

So he knew that she was just visiting, just helping out. He probably knew about the sons, the Italian husband. There was probably nothing, in fact, that she had reserved only for Thomas's knowledge. She was free with her information, friendly to everyone, indifferent to the effect she had on him or any other man. He closed the door behind the client, watched him cross over the road and enter Green Gardens to – who knew? – collude with the manager.

'Thomas, are you all right?' Her voice was gentle.

I'm jealous! he thought simply. She is not even mine and I'm jealous! There was a silence, and he did not have the courage to look round. They stood in this pose: he at the door, his back to her, she at the desk, like a poster for a film of an unhappy marriage. Then the door opened: his next appointment.

After the long afternoon, three clients in a row, he emerged from the testing room and found her at the desk. She stood up on seeing him and let him sit down, just as Rani would do if she were there. As he was tapping into the computer, she spoke.

'I've tidied up and sorted out the deliveries into those piles,' she pointed to the counter, 'and I've phoned if there was a phone number to say to collect next week. I thought I'd give you some breathing space in case Rani is still off. There was only one client who was leaving the country early next week, but he sent someone down a few minutes ago to pick them up, so he's taken care of.'

'Thank you so much.'

'I also took the liberty,' she continued, 'of moving your bookings for tomorrow to later next week. I explained the situation, and everyone seemed amenable.'

'Vishukumari, you've done more than you needed to.'

'I've been happy to help.'

When he finished at the computer, he stood up.

'My cousin is having us round to say goodbye tomorrow,' she said. 'I won't be able to help out again, like I said. I'll need to pack and stuff . . .'

'Really, you've done more than I could possibly have asked.'

'So,' she looked around, 'Rani may come tomorrow and everything will be OK. But if she doesn't, you have until next Thursday before you really need to worry again.'

'That's wonderful. Thank you so much.'

Then they stopped. He looked on her miserably, his heart heavy.

'Thomas,' she said softly. 'There are no more appointments for this afternoon. Would you like to come with me for a walk? I was thinking of going to Marine Drive. It will probably be my last chance.'

They stood still, facing each other, and in those few seconds several images flashed through his head. On his balcony in Cherai, the moonlight on her face, his hands in her silky hair. Lying in bed, turned to each other, her face inches from his. This was the moment, he thought, looking down at her, before him, her face lifted to his. He could almost imagine it was what she expected him to do. He could lean down and kiss her on the lips, slip his arms around her and run his hands down the delicious length of her spine and then below, something he was yearning to do.

'Thomas?'

He blinked. 'Yes. Of course. Let's go.'

They busied themselves gathering their things, as if the film from earlier was showing a flashback of happier times, of the couple leaving their home, stepping out on to the street. The heat enveloped them as always, as if to remind them that the world outside continued regardless. The sounds from MG Road, buses and cars hooting, the autorickshaws buzzing like insects, darting in and out. Across the road, Thomas saw a couple sitting in the window of Green Gardens: too young to be clients of Rani's bureau.

'Do you want to get an auto?' he asked Vishukumari.

'Do you mind if we walk?' she said.

They turned on to the main road: it was busy and the pavement was erratic, at intermittent paces disintegrating into a sandy strip or a large murky puddle. Within minutes his shirt was sticking to him; he wiped the perspiration from his face as he saw she did. It was too hot, too crowded and uncomfortable to talk. She picked her way over the pavement by his side, this time not brushing against him. Even when they reached Marine Drive they did not speak, walking along the promenade until they reached the bench, the same one where they had met, as if they were consciously replaying their fleeting relationship. Their farewell would be made near where they had met. They sat side by side and watched the sun begin its descent.

'Are you worried about Rani?' she asked.

He shook his head, smiled. 'To be honest, I haven't thought of her much this afternoon. I have a feeling she'll be back tomorrow with a good explanation.'

He cleared his throat. 'So, where does your cousin live?'

'Out near Alwaye,' she said. 'Our fathers are brothers. One went to the States, the other stayed here.' She gave a short laugh. 'It sounds like a nursery rhyme!'

He smiled, turned to look at the sea.

'And,' he started again, 'have you decided yet whether it has worked?'

When she raised her eyebrows quizzically, he said, 'Has this holiday given you that connection you were looking for?'

She did not respond immediately, then she turned and looked at him.

'Meeting you certainly has. This has definitely been the best part.'

Her eyes held his for some moments before she continued. 'I wasn't telling the whole truth. It's partly true, I suppose. But really I came here because we just needed a bit of space from each other. My husband and I. We're going through a . . . patch. I just wanted to come back and see what I would find out about myself.'

'I see.'

'Do you?' Her voice was not tense; rather, her question sounded genuine. 'Is that why you came back? To find out about yourself?'

'I'm not sure,' he said. 'The plan had always been that Nimmy and I would come back together.'

'Yes, of course. You did say, I remember.' Now her voice sounded as miserable as he felt.

'I'm not making much sense, am I?' She laughed. 'Anyway, I wish I'd bumped into you earlier. Hari and I have been here three weeks, but I've enjoyed the last few days the most.'

She had offered something with her words, made a tentative overture of sorts, but he found that he was unsure how to proceed. Either her words and their air of ambiguity, or the paralysis he felt on hearing them, meant that he did not reply. When the silence extended and he had not repaid the compliment, she gave a short embarrassed laugh. He could feel the energy seeping away from both of them and the encounter began to feel slightly anticlimactic. He could not even remember, later, what they had talked about for the next half hour before he caught his bus back. There was a vague memory of a discussion of the flights she and her son would have to catch: they would be stopping over in the Gulf for a day, though she was no longer sure that was a good idea. She had a meeting pencilled in for the day after they returned home: again, she doubted the wisdom of such, given that she may be suffering from jet lag.

They were neither of them going to reveal more of themselves. If she expected a declaration of love to rebuff, she received none. If he had expected to hear more of the tale about a lonely unhappy marriage, followed by a searching, sensual kiss – or more – he left empty-handed. Although not completely empty-handed: a card. *Vishukumari Nair, Cimini Architecture.* The name of her practice, she had told him, was taken from the mountains from where her husband's family originated. She had kept her name, but she had cemented herself through her business with her husband's birthplace.

On the street, he had hailed an auto to take her back to the hotel, thrust the fare into the driver's hands despite her protests.

They had parted with promises to keep in touch. She had then moved in towards him, raised her face as if for a peck; he had collided with her cheek, patted her on the shoulder. He had spent days imagining her in his arms, but when the opportunity arrived he had managed only a brief clumsy hug under the scrutiny of the auto driver, who was revving his motor as if providing a soundtrack. He had helped her into the auto but did not get a last glimpse of her face. Waving goodbye to the back of the auto, he thought, I am unpractised in the art of love. I was given a woman to love, and I loved her. How does one orchestrate such a huge feat on one's own? Left to your own devices you start believing that a woman, married, to all intents and purposes content enough with her life, could be the one you fall in love with, and could be falling in love with you.

On the bus back to Cherai that night, he had to stand for most of the journey. It was full to capacity, so that at one stage he was pressed against a smallish man, a civil servant-type with large glasses. He had grunted pointedly until Thomas realised that his bag was pushed against the small of the man's back. The yellow folder inside with its hard edges was pressed against his fellow traveller; he had forgotten that he had secreted the file.

That evening, after a meal of scrambled eggs – fast becoming his dinner of choice – Thomas took the folder upstairs. The night was dark outside, the swells of the sea a constant, sonorous. It was still warm despite the breeze. He took off his shirt so that he sat in his mundu, a lone figure on the balcony. If he turned the overhead light on, he would be swamped by insects, so he held a small torch. The folder lay on the chair beside him; he was still not sure if he had the licence to look through it. It might give him some clue about where Rani was, but the people who had written to her had not intended for another similarly lonely soul to be reading their words. He flipped open the cover and scanned the first page, with Rani's title. He was opening more than a folder, he knew. Along with the letters from the clients, he was also delving into Rani's dreams of romance.

He caught his breath: why had he not thought about it before? Was her absence due to the man he had seen her with last week? He spent some minutes revisiting the scene: the man had looked older than her, not terribly old, but old to be a bachelor in Kerala. They had only had a small red basket to hand: that suggested they had arrived in a car. Further, Rani had been unperturbed by her soaking kameez, which indicated that she may have brought a change of clothes. Who was he? A client of the bureau? That was the most likely explanation. He was a client who had turned his gaze on the young woman dealing with his affairs.

Sitting out on the balcony with only a torch seemed to give a slightly unsavoury aspect to his endeavours; he decided to go back into his bedroom. It was late already, and he intended only a brief look at the contents, to see if there was any indication of her whereabouts. There was a strong possibility that she would return the next day, in which case he wondered if he should try to get in early to replace the file. She would notice if it were not in its usual place.

He moved into his bedroom and lay on the bed, the folder next to him. It was, despite his first impression, scanty in its contents. The first pages held a table titled *Essential Details*, the contents of each section written in by hand. Perhaps that was how she maintained her clients' privacy, by storing nothing on the work computer. He quickly picked out Hanif and Sherry in the list, and then let his eyes run down the names. There were more than the fifteen names she had admitted to. Next to each name she had noted the date of their first applications, and he saw that one was dated a full year ago. So she had lied about how many people she had recruited and how long she had been running the bureau. What else had she lied about?

She had written down the same details for each person: name, age, occupation, residence, filled in probably when the clients were first apprised of her services. Thomas scanned the residence column: most lived in the Ernakulam area, but at least a third were NRIs – three lived in the States, one in Dubai and one in Australia. This information had been highlighted in a different colour: clearly the prospects of a long-distance relationship developing needed to be considered. There was a preponderance of women: perhaps she inspired more confidence in them, but the imbalance would not have helped her attempts at pairing them up. There was a column marked *Children*, with the ages and gender of progeny – none was younger than fifteen – and then *Interests*, with the usual activities listed: cinema, tennis, travelling. In short, the bare bones of a person presented her with an overview, but it was not what she used. It was the narrative that she chose to focus on: the letters that they wrote were her guide to their inner feelings. The amount of trust that they invested in her astounded him. But then he realised: she did not move in their circles. She would not know any of their acquaintances, friends, relatives. He had no doubt that Hanif and Sherry would not be issuing Rani with an invitation to their wedding, if it ever came to that, or even to a celebratory meal. None of the clients saw her as an equal:

for this reason they felt they could bare their souls. What had that man said earlier that day? A wallah, she was a date-wallah, a match-wallah.

The anger that he felt on her behalf spurred him on to turn over the pages. Each client was separated with a cream-coloured card, their name printed at the top. *Meena Pillai*, he read. Her letter began: *I have worked as a doctor in some of the best hospitals incl. Sri Vadya's Hospital for the sick, Mahatma Gandhi institute in Delhi. After seventeen years of marriage my husband and I divorced, one offspring*. The curt, businesslike tone continued. Above some of the sentences, Rani had made some annotations for herself, or further queries: *Lived in the North, speaks Hindi?* Further in the letter, Meena suddenly wrote: *He also wanted more children but assumed that I would stop my career to bring them up. He was only a GP, but I am a consultant dermatologist. My parents thought a doctor would suit a doctor but they had no idea of the different levels within the medical profession, or that some men are intimidated by intelligent women*. Rani had underscored the last line and written above: *High-achiever, NRI?* With her final sentence, Meena managed to sound very different from the confident woman at the beginning: *I would love to travel somewhere romantic, I never took time off before but now I am willing to with a special someone*. Rani had written at the end: *Ravi N.*

He turned back to the front page and scanned down; near the end he found *Ravi Narayan, Owner RK Enterprises*. So, how had their date gone? Had they gone on a date? She had written nothing; her work was done. He rifled through the file until he found the cream card with the titled name: *Ravi Narayan*. He glanced through the letter, at the sentences that were underscored, the annotations. *My first wife talked too much, she was an uneducated sort . . . If I have free time I like watching the cricket, I even flew to Chennai once when India were playing Australia . . . My mother has convinced me that I am handsome – mothers know best!* He shook his head in disbelief. How could she have? She would have met each in person, that was true, but even so! He spent a few moments pondering her match, and then the dentist's words returned: a third party does not always produce the result you want. He found Hanif's letter soon enough, and, just as the man had intimated, it did not do him justice: his charm and confidence were not in evidence in the paragraph which sketched out his educational background and his naturalisation as a US citizen.

He spent the next half an hour reading the entries at random, and wherever she had given a verdict he cross-referenced to find the mate that had been chosen. Some were well-matched, he conceded, matches he would have assumed himself. Others were less than obvious: Rani had alighted on a detail he could not see.

By the time he closed the folder, washed and brushed his teeth, turned the lights out and lay on the bed, his head was swimming with the stories he had read, after an afternoon spent with a beautiful woman whom he would most likely never see again. Would he be able to tell Rani about her? He could, surprisingly, imagine that conversation. She was easy to talk with: the secret to the success of her bureau. The folder lay beside him on the bed as if it were Rani herself sharing his pillow. And just as when they had spoken of her mother, of her father lumbered with four unmarried daughters, he felt his heart go out to her, felt himself making a wish: that she would find her happiness, that the man lying near her on the beach would provide for and nurture her. Her bureau had become a stage for herself, even if she had not wanted to be the protagonist; these letters, written for her to read and digest, were as much about Rani as they were about the clients. She had elicited their musings, and then she had dispensed her wisdom generously. Wisdom that was garnered not from the limited experience of her young years but from the empathy she had accrued from her own longings, her own romance. She had mulled and drawn little maps, woven fine little threads to bind these strangers together. In the hope that a spark would ignite and that she would be able to make a heart less lonely, fill in a small crevice of loss with hope.

10

O<small>N</small> the bus to the city the next day, just as they were leaving the coast road and becoming embroiled in the chaos of morning traffic, he realised that he had left the folder back at the house. He had wanted to replace it in Rani's drawer; he was sure he would be able to explain why he had picked the lock, but taking the folder home now seemed a gross breach of privacy. He contemplated getting off the bus, but the difficulties that would have ensued swayed him. His head was woolly and he could not make the decision; before he knew it, the bus had swung on to the handsome avenue in front of the High Courts.

He had slept fitfully, getting up once to go downstairs to make himself some warm milk, something he had done for Nina when she was a little girl and for Nimmy in her last months. She had hankered after Milo, the drink from her childhood; the closest Thomas could replace it with was Ovaltine, something he never developed a taste for. The downstairs of the little house had that stuffy night-time feel. Unlike the top level, there was no breeze: all the windows were shut, netted, barred – against mosquitos and intruders alike. The kitchen felt damp and dark, his fridge was making an inordinately loud humming sound, and the light from his inverter blinked on and off ominously. The overhead light, when he turned it on, revealed his kitchen for what it was: a small square with badly-made, hurriedly-fitted worktops. A sink that was awkwardly positioned in the corner rather than under the window as Nimmy had requested: the results of orchestrating an installation remotely. He did not mind but felt, in fact, a fondness for the quirkiness of the house. He heated his milk and looked at the clock: quarter past two. He could perhaps just catch Nina before she went to bed.

His daughter answered the phone in French, then turned down the music she had playing in the background, her voice rising with concern.

'Nothing to worry about, *mol*,' he said. 'I couldn't get to sleep and thought of you. I hope I'm not disturbing you.'

'That's nice.' She hesitated a little before continuing. 'Michel told me you called the other day. I got home so late I didn't ring back . . .'

'Don't worry.'

'He said you had a nice chat.'

He laughed. 'Yes, we did.' He hesitated, then continued: 'It was good to talk to him.'

'He's quite keen on visiting India, actually . . .'

'That would be very nice. It will be a chance to meet him properly.'

'Mm.'

She was quiet, and he worried that she was suspicious of his words, his motives. He wondered if he should ask her about the photos he wanted to send, decided against it.

'Did you have a good day?' he asked.

'Kind of. It rained. I've got a cold. I'm working against a deadline.' She paused. 'What about you?'

He told her about Rani, how she had not come to work for three days now, how Vishukumari had stepped in to help.

'She sounds interesting,' Nina said.

'There's something about her that reminds me of you, I suppose,' he replied. 'She's older than you, of course, but her parents also left Kerala and moved away. She grew up in the States.' After a pause, he added, 'She's married to an Italian.'

'Michel's French, Pa.' She was smiling, he could hear.

'I know . . .'

'So, what's she doing over there?'

He paused, worried that his voice would reveal his thoughts.

'Actually, she's here on holiday. I think she's leaving today or tomorrow, I can't remember . . .'

'Oh, right.'

'Yes.'

'So will you keep in touch with her?'

'Oh, yes.' How could he tell her of their lukewarm farewell? Or even the effect Vishukumari had had on him? What if Nina were to return the favour: give him a vivid description of her relationship with Michel? He gave a little cough, a short nervous laugh.

'It's nice to hear you talk about someone,' she interrupted. 'A friend.'

The warmth of her words, and their generosity – this from his only daughter, whom he had abandoned – touched him.

A bitter regret rose into his mouth like bile: he could taste it on his tongue. He regretted putting thousands of miles, oceans between them. There was no one around him to witness this realisation. His face was reflected back at him in the window, the light from the kitchen throwing him into silhouette. He wanted to reach out, to his sweet girl, with her heart-shaped face, mouth with upturned edges, hold her in his arms.

'Pa?'

Had he been silent all that time? He apologised, said he was tired, told her he would phone again, that he loved her. She murmured, 'Goodnight, Pa,' and with those words he remembered her arms around his neck, her goodnight kiss as a child.

When she was little, she had loved measuring her hand against his, her small body snuggled in his lap. When she tired of walking, she would turn to him. He would swing her on to his shoulders, a skinny leg dangling on either side of his neck, her hands clutching at his ears. The ease with which he had kept company with Mariamma's son: he should not forget that he had had the same ease with his daughter. Then, as she grew, he had felt dazzled by her litheness, her loveliness, and he had deferred to Nimmy. It was Nimmy who sent her back up the stairs to change her outfit if she deemed it inappropriate, negotiated when Nina could go out with friends; he skulked in the kitchen listening to the two voices. Before long it seemed he was always in the background, of his choosing, but unable to push himself forward. He remembered when Nina had returned home, aged sixteen, with her hair shaved off. They had both stared and stared, unable to admonish, punish; it was beyond their comprehension. Nimmy had cried in his arms that night, her tears wetting the pillow, cried as if their daughter was no more, and he had finally managed to make her laugh: 'You're right. She *does* look like your mother.' When, a week later, he had caught his daughter looking at herself in the mirror, her fingers scraping the shorn sides of her head, the expression on her face full of regret, his heart had ached for her. He could have given her a hug, made her laugh, as he had done Nimmy, but he had shrunk away, not knowing what to say, whether his daughter would welcome his remarks. For fear of offending her, he had lost a closeness with his child. There were vast swathes of time, years, epochs, from when she went to university, choosing to travel far away from home, followed by her job in New York and then Paris. Huge stretches of her twenties when they saw her once a year, when she seemed unwilling to sit still in front of them, seemingly itching to leave. The missing years, he thought.

His heart was heavy when he went to bed, and he dreamed of them all: Nimmy and Nina, Rani and Vishukumari, as if they all knew each other, as if he knew each as well as the other, feeling guilt even as he dreamed that he had relegated his wife – his wife of more than thirty years – to a similar status as a woman he had known for a few days. He was startled awake by the alarm and found it difficult to get out of bed. The sea was deep grey, the sky covered in clouds, the room already hot. He rushed from the house to Junction, boarded the bus and then realised he had left the folder by the side of his bed.

As he approached the shop, he saw a movement inside, a flash of a body passing across the reception area. So Rani was back and she would, after an absence of three days, be sure to check her drawer. Steeling himself for her questions, he pushed the door open. There was no sign of Rani. Instead, he saw that three men, wearing the familiar khaki uniforms of the Kerala State Police, were inside, filling the reception area with their stocky bodies. The air conditioning had not been turned on, and the room was hot. Through the door to the testing room Thomas spotted another police officer, looking at the walls and the testing boards, taking notes.

'Mr Chacko?' His badge read *Murugan M.S.* He was strongly built, with a thick luxuriant moustache and a full head of coarse black hair. He was sitting on Rani's chair, swivelling from side to side. His cap was on the desk, covering the ledger.

'No.' Thomas cleared his throat. 'He's a friend and owner of the store. I'm looking after it while he is away.'

'And you are?'

'Thomas. I.S. Thomas.'

The policeman made a face, shared a glance with the other officer.

'Full name? Family name?'

'Thomas Imbalil.' The underling was writing in his pad.

'Address?'

'Coconut Retreat. Cherai Beach.'

'Ah,' he nodded, smiling. He gestured for Thomas to sit down.

'How did you get in?' he asked, his question provoking a laugh from the policeman.

'Open!' was the response. 'The door was unlocked!'

Thomas said nothing. He was certain he had locked up: he remembered Vishukumari at his side while he slipped the keys back in his pocket.

The policeman continued swivelling, tapping his hand against one meaty thigh. Then suddenly he stopped moving, threw a question: 'You are from Cherai?'

'No. Vazhakulam. In Ernakulam District.'

'Yes, I know where it is.' He smiled widely, shifted his body on the chair and folded his arms.

Thomas slung his bag off and sat down in one of the armchairs.

'Vazhakulam,' the policeman repeated. 'Humble beginnings for an educated man like yourself!' Then he leaned back in the chair, smiling encouragingly. When Thomas did not respond, he continued: 'So you grew up in Vazhakulam, then worked in your friend's shop all your life?' then laughed at the absurdity of his suggestion.

'No.' Thomas found himself speaking carefully. 'No. I lived in London.'

'London! For how long?'

'I was there for nearly thirty-three years.'

'Thirty-three years!' *Muppathuh moonnu varsham!* He rolled his tongue over the words with relish, as if handing out a prison sentence.

There followed a silence. Murugan continued to smile, while Thomas began to notice more details. The yellow and cream flecks of paste on the policeman's forehead – the remnants of some kind of pilgrimage – the tobacco stains on his fingernails. The thick gold ring, the white vest under the khaki uniform, the sweat marks under his armpits. A hard-working officer for the State Police visiting a local optician's.

'And what did you do in London?'

'I . . .' He had to clear his throat. 'I worked in an optician's. I'm an optometrist. And my wife was a nurse.'

'Ah.' He nodded as if his suppositions were confirmed. 'Children?'

'A daughter.'

'Only one?'

'Yes.'

'Where is she? London?'

'No,' with reluctance, 'Paris.'

'Paris!'

'Yes.'

'She is an optician like you?' This accompanied with a wide grin.

'No. A solicitor.'

'Ah, good. Good.' He paused. 'But now you are here.'

It was a question, and Murugan surveyed him from his position in the chair.

'My wife died last year,' Thomas said. 'So I decided to come back.'

The officer's face altered a fraction. He did not say anything but continued looking at Thomas, with an expression that was still unsmiling but not unsympathetic. He started swivelling in the chair again, and for a few moments his back was to Thomas. Then he turned to face him again, to fix him with a grave expression.

'After thirty years in London,' he said, breaking what had felt like an interminable silence, 'you are understandably out of touch with the ways of your homeland.' He smiled. 'Kerala has moved on! Kochi will be the next jewel of the Arabian Sea, the next Mumbai! We State Police even have a website, have you seen it?'

He paused, encouragingly, as Thomas shook his head, then resumed.

'Yes, just the usual information. A letter from the Minister. Promises of maintaining an honest police force, no corruption.' He gave another brief wolfish grin, then leaned forward to put his elbows on his knees and continued in the same light-hearted tone: 'Do you think you can just come here and take over a business? No licence, no insurance, no permit, no registration?' He paused. 'Would you get away with this in London?'

He smiled with the last words; his reasoning was indisputable.

Thomas felt himself redden. He could sense that the other officers were standing behind him, but he did not want to turn around.

'I . . .'

'And,' Murugan continued, 'you have been broken into, did you know? Or at least this drawer has been broken into.' He slid Rani's bottom drawer out with his foot, and Thomas stared at the files and pockets.

'The lock has been picked.'

Outside an auto buzzed by; the woman from the shop opposite was beating out her doormat against the pavement. The sun was shining directly on the road, so there was no shade, and he could see a woman, her sari pallu over her head, dragging her son by the hand.

'I have received reports,' Murugan continued, 'that this shop is a front for other activities.'

Thomas felt himself turn cold. Better to stand up, he thought, which he did.

There was a loud rap at the door, and one of the policemen reached forward and opened it.

A young man came into view, carrying a brown parcel. He was wearing a black T-shirt, and one side of his hair was dyed yellow.

'Mr Thomas?'

He nodded, his mouth slightly open.

'Bimal sent me,' the young man said. 'Sorry you had to wait so long. We thought we'd bring this over as soon as it arrived.'

He glanced at the police officers but with some nonchalance: perhaps he was more used to their company.

'Just sign here.'

'Thank you.'

Thomas took the package and held it, watched the young man leave and the policeman close the door behind him.

'A package,' Murugan said, his voice rich with amusement.

'It's a book,' Thomas said. 'I ordered it some time ago.'

'An optician's book?' and he laughed, looking at the other policemen, who chuckled loyally. 'Or something more exciting?'

Thomas held the book at his side, drew himself to his full height, which, by the look of Murugan sitting on his chair, was a good half-foot taller than the policeman.

'I am happy,' he said, 'to answer any questions you may have. But perhaps I could turn on the A.C. and perhaps I can offer you all a drink. I have some water in the fridge?'

'Thank you, Mr Thomas,' Murugan said, a smile on his lips. He let his eyes move over Thomas. 'But we should go now. I need to take a statement from you at the station.'

Within minutes, they were leaving the shop. The policemen waited as he closed the door, pointedly checked the lock before turning the key. The manager from Green Gardens was watching, Thomas saw him through the window, a stricken expression on his face. When the policemen moved towards their car, he scurried out of sight.

'Get in, get in.' Murugan's manner was now affable, less threatening. 'I just need to make some stops on the way.'

They were going on an outing, five middle-aged men squeezed into a dusty four-by-four; any sense of urgency had disappeared. They were purportedly on the way to headquarters, but Murugan called on various businesses and houses en route, while Thomas was left sitting between two perspiring police officers in the back of the stifling car. This continued for two hours or more, until they drove up to what Murugan described as his final stop, a residence, an old building converted into a guest house. Thomas could see some tourists sitting on the balcony, drinks in front of them. Murugan disappeared with his lackeys into its interior, and there were shouts of greetings. The driver got out and wandered to the edge of the plot, where he then stood under the shade of a tree and pulled out a cigarette.

He was finally left alone; he was not under arrest – they had never used those words. He glanced around, cursing his own shifty behaviour, and slid out his phone. He had no idea what time it was in Houston, had no intention of making that calculation. He rang Jos's number and got his voicemail. He spoke into the phone and glanced around: the officer was watching him but made no move to stop him or motion that he end the call. Instead of looking away, Thomas forced himself to remain looking at the officer defiantly. 'Just call me as soon as you get this,' he ended the call. The officer stared on, bored. Thomas was tempted to call someone else, so pleasurable had been the opportunity to reach out beyond the confines of the airless jeep. But whom could he call? He sat as he was, then, as the minutes dripped by, he tried the door and found that it could open: he had never been a prisoner. He got out and moved to the edge of the front yard, joined the officer who nodded at him and watched without interest as Thomas wiped his forehead with his handkerchief.

Murugan came outside laughing with another man, the owner of the guest house.

'OK! OK!' He had finished his courtesy calls for the day and was ready to go back to business. They piled back into the car and then drove perhaps only three hundred metres before turning into the drive of the station.

Inside, the ceiling fans were on full speed. Everywhere, there were piles of papers, weighed down by stacks of folders, a telephone and in one case someone's tiffin. More folders stood up against the computers and on the seats of chairs positioned at the edges of the room. But there were, underneath the brown and beige chaos, some indications of order: notices detailing changes, regulations. A whiteboard was marked with the correct date. In the corner, a television set showed the news, the volume turned down.

'Come sit, sit.' Murugan spoke as if Thomas were a visitor.

'Will this take long?' Thomas ventured to ask.

'No, no. Tea? Coffee?'

The offer was surprisingly welcome. 'Yes. Coffee, please.'

A female officer appeared. 'Sir?' and then she leaned forward and spoke in Murugan's ear.

'Ah, yes. *Ippo varam.*' But instead he lingered for a few minutes, shuffling some papers, and then, without a glance in Thomas's direction, left the room.

'*Ividey irikke.*' The woman officer smiled as if she were an air hostess, pulling out a chair. She smiled again, nodding, then turned and yelled across the room. Before long, another woman, wearing a pale-blue sari, appeared with a tray of cups and deposited one in front of Thomas. And then everyone left.

He was alone in the room. Next door, life continued: drawers banged and chairs were scraped across the floor, there was laughter and a shriek. But within the room where he sat, there was nothing, no one else. He looked around and then thought of his phone, which, as soon as he thought about it, started to ring.

'Thomaschayan?' It was Mariamma, her voice stretched with anxiety. 'They are at your house,' she said.

'Who?'

'The police.'

'At the house?'

'They asked if I have a key. They want me to show them inside.'

They had taken his address, and then he had sat like a vegetable for hours in Murugan's car, unsuspecting, or underestimating, their reach. Could they just walk into someone's house like that?

'Don't argue with them, Mariamma. Do as they ask.'

'Are you sure?'

'Yes, don't worry, Mariamma. Just do as they ask.'

She mumbled her assent and rang off. He stared at the phone. How to explain the pockets of loneliness, matching a heart to another, the search for a soulmate? They would assume the worst: sham weddings, a brothel, illicit sex. He shut his eyes with frustration.

His phone rang again.

'Jos?' he barked.

There was a brief silence and then a hesitant 'Thomas?'

He felt his hand go involuntarily to his chest. 'Vishukumari!'

He could hear her smile.

'You sounded different,' she said. 'Are you OK? Are you at the store?'

'No.' He hesitated. 'The police station actually.'

'Oh my God! Has something happened to Rani?'

He thought suddenly, with a sharp clarity, yes, something has happened to Rani. Just as the previous night he had realised the key to her absence was in the folder, the visit from the police was not unconnected. In fact, that was most likely why they were in his house.

'Not sure,' he said finally.

Vishukumari was silent, then: 'So why are you at the police station?'

He tried to laugh, but the sound was more like a yelp. 'Again, not sure. I've left a message for Jos, and I'm hoping I'll find out soon what they want to talk to me about.'

'Do you want me to come?' She sounded so close suddenly that he could not stop himself from asking, 'Where are you?'

'At my cousin's.'

'No, please don't worry,' he said. 'Enjoy your day. I'm sure I'll be out of here soon. They've not arrested me; they just want some information about the store.'

'I'll talk to my cousin,' she said. 'He'll know what to do. Or he'll know someone, a lawyer or something. I'll tell him to call the station.'

'Don't worry about it now.' He paused. 'Why are you calling?'

A police officer walked in, glanced at him curiously and then walked out again. Suddenly, the fan stopped moving: a power cut. She fell silent. He could hear her breathing – she must have had the handset close to her mouth – and he put his fingers on his, as if to touch her lips. He remembered the way her head had banged against his, their ungraceful goodbye. Perhaps she was phoning to complain about his treatment of her, the undignified exit he had offered her, ushering her into the dusty auto.

'Do you know, Thomas,' she was saying, her voice nearly a whisper, 'my parents wanted me to marry someone they'd chosen. I was what, twenty-four years old? Not long graduated. They had this ideal guy, you know? Same caste as us, a Nair, a

182

doctor. He'd studied in the States. I knew him vaguely: I'd seen him at some do. Nice-looking. Y'know, the whole package.' She paused. 'Thomas, are you there?'

'Yes.' He shifted in his seat.

'But I couldn't do it, y'know?' She was speaking again, her voice so low that he could barely hear it. 'I just hated the whole lack of romance, the inevitability of it all. It all seemed so smug, so safe.' She drew in a breath. 'Plus I knew what he expected as well, the type of girl he would want. Or at least I should say, I *thought* I knew all of that. Just these last days I've started asking myself . . . what if he had been like you?'

The whole building seemed to have been silenced. He could hear no noises from next door, as if the world was waiting for his response. The fan above him spluttered into life, then after a few revolutions slowed down and stopped again. Why was she telling him all this? There was a dull ache in his chest, something he was not accustomed to. When Nimmy was dying, it was his whole body that hung heavy, no one part hurt more than the other. It was as if his wife had occupied every part of him: his shoulders and his knees as well as his heart. If that had been love, then what was this that he was feeling?

After a long pause, he said, 'Thirty years ago, Vishukumari, I was no different to any other young man.'

'I don't believe you, Thomas.'

He said nothing, waited for her to speak again. When she did, she spoke slowly, clearly, as if she were testing her words: 'I know this is unseemly of me, with a husband who loves me, two beautiful healthy boys. I should be grateful for it all. And I am. But I guess I will miss you more than I realised.'

He could have returned the compliment but he didn't.

Eventually, he said, 'Your husband . . .'

'Oh, he's a great guy,' she said. 'I *think* I still love him. But it's hard to explain. I fell in love with my husband as a person, but also with everything he represented.'

'Every marriage has its ups and downs.'

'Did yours? Perhaps I'm prying . . .'

'No, it's not that,' he said. He gulped. 'We had our hard times. There were moments when I fear Nimmy felt about me the way you are feeling about your husband.'

'What kept you together?' she asked, and now her voice was humble. 'Was it your faith, Thomas? Because of your church?'

He was not expecting the wave of sadness that washed over him. It seemed that his marriage was now open for dissection, unlike a live marriage, and he was to be attributed with some wisdom for having his wife die on him, rather than another ignominious ending. He could never before have imagined having this conversation: discussing his wife with a woman he had lusted over. The questions, in the past tense – Nimmy was dead now – however innocent or self-serving their intentions, were like an epitaph.

He did not speak, and the silence became almost tangible, as if the distance between them was entrenching itself, solidifying.

'I think,' he said at last, 'what it was, was that I never saw another life for myself, other than being married to Nimmy.'

A pause.

'You must have loved her very much,' she said quietly.

He wanted to say: if I never considered swapping Nimmy for another woman, is that love?

She waited. He heard her breathing on the phone, and the silence continued. But what else was he able to say?

'Vishukumari,' he said finally, 'I don't know your husband. But I know he is a lucky man.'

After a long silence, she said, her voice matter-of-fact, 'I'm not so sure.' Then, 'I'll talk to my cousin, see what he can do.'

'Don't worry . . .'

'I'll be in touch.'

They rang off.

He had almost forgotten where he was. The clock on the wall showed that he had been there for nearly an hour and a half. He stood up, filled with a sudden anger: what was wrong with this country? How could an ordinary citizen be plucked away from their place of work and then be subjected to an original mode of torture: an endless, excruciating boredom? He strode towards the door and, as if he had been under surveillance, an officer appeared, blocking his path.

'I'm leaving,' he said, his voice rough and harsh. 'There's no need to keep me waiting like this.'

He pushed past.

'Please sir . . .'

But then, as if on cue, Murugan came cantering around the corner.

'Ah,' he said.

But before he could continue, Thomas spoke again: 'I'm leaving.'

'Yes, yes,' was the reply. Murugan looked harried, his forehead beaded with perspiration.

Thomas stopped. 'Can I go?'

'Yes, yes.' A pause. 'Mr Jos phoned me; we have sorted every-thing out. You are free to go.'

He glanced down at his phone and saw that he had a message: Jos may have tried to contact him while he was on the phone to Vishukumari.

'OK, so . . .'

'Yes, please. You are free to go.' It seemed that Murugan could not wait to get rid of him now.

Saying nothing more, he strode out and was momentarily dazzled by the light and the heat, before flagging down an auto.

As the driver kick-started his motor, on an impulse, Thomas asked, 'If I wanted to go to Konthuruthy, how long will it take?'

The driver fixed him with a red-rimmed, scummy, truculent stare. Despite the heat, he wore a scarf wrapped around his neck and pulled over his chin and his nose: a half-hearted attempt to protect his lungs from the pollution.

'At this time, there will be traffic block. No meter. Two hours, maybe more.'

Thomas sighed. 'High Courts bus stop.'

They pulled away, and the front wheel immediately ducked into a pothole. He was thrown forwards, banging his head against a bar. And then, because he could, he spoke harshly: '*Eda*, why did you take this road? Turn right up ahead, it's quicker!' The driver did not argue, only demurred, with a surprisingly meek 'Yes, sir', as if he knew that Thomas's anger was not solely directed at him or the pothole.

The street was full of beeping cars, buses: the thralls of rush hour. He leaned back in the small seat, looked out through the flap hanging down one side. It was over. His adventure, his first time in a police station, had not even extended to a night in the cell. His covetous thoughts of a beautiful stranger: those were also over. He could look back at himself now with more objectivity. What had Vishukumari expected from the phone call? Had she wanted to press him into admitting that he had imagined making love to her? He remembered how she had handed her card to Rani. He did not even remember the moment when she had given him the same card, but he had it. She dispensed her cards at will: that man who was looking at her breasts probably had a card. He need not read anything further into their encounter. She had phoned because she was bored, out in Alwaye, at her cousin's house. Perhaps he had piqued her interest, but nothing more. On his side, well, he was lonely, that was clear. He ached – even when he did not know it, he was aching. His whole body was imploring: what now?

The roads flashed by. The shops and stalls, the people, the vehicles: all becoming a blur of grey, as if he were being spun around and around, so that he could feel time moving back, and when the spinning stopped he was presented, unbidden, with a memory. They were in a car, he was at the wheel, Nimmy beside him. They were on holiday, just the two of them. Nina had just moved to Paris, and it was the year Nimmy turned fifty. They arrived at a square, the sun was bright, the atmosphere merry. People from the bars and the cafés spilled out. There was the hum of conversation, the notes of music. Some young people were sitting on the pavement, beers in their hands; others were gathered around cars, doors open, sitting on the bonnets. Olive skin, dark hair, limbs and mouths, laughter. The church in the square stood majestic and solemn, silently observing the gaiety below.

There was a small stage to one side, a band. An arresting singer, her long hair tied up in a scarf, long gypsy skirts swirling as she danced, her voice surprisingly throaty for her slim figure. The crowd was dancing, and he and Nimmy got out of the car, mesmerised. They watched, occasionally turning to each other to exchange a smile; the atmosphere was infectious. Then she had said, I've never danced like that. I want to dance, will you come with me? He had resisted, she had implored him, and eventually he had relented. They had stood awkwardly among the others – not all young, there were at least two other middle-aged couples, moving effortlessly in time to the music. And then Nimmy had swayed, laughed, swayed again, and they had continued, Thomas's hand on her waist. They moved jerkily, out of time, the rhythm was unfamiliar, but, he remembered, they moved in step with each other.

The motion of the auto mimicked their movements, and he was transported. He spent the rest of the journey to the High Courts and then on the bus back to Cherai celebrating his wife, his Nimmy, whom he had loved without knowing what love was. The tears in his eyes splashed on to his lap, so that the woman sitting beside him queried quietly if he was all right, to which he had replied that he was. He was well.

Later that evening, before he went to sleep, and after the lights in Mariamma's house had gone out, he went outside to his back garden, and near the gazebo he found a tin bucket. The yellow folder had been where he had left it, on his bed, among his other books. If the police had searched his house, it had not appeared ominous enough to warrant their attention. It burned quickly and easily, he found, the pages crackling as he fed them one by one into the fire. The letters written for Rani by the lonely people who had traversed her path. Their chance for another life, a date at Green Gardens, a love in their later years, when the fire finally went out were only dust and ash, which, when he had walked across the road and then the sand, he poured into the sea.

11

Jos had been apologetic when they finally managed to talk. He had telephoned the chief of the sector, a friend of the family, who in turn had rebuked Murugan for abducting an innocent citizen: all this while Thomas had been left alone in the office at the police headquarters. But some face had to be saved: a fine of some kind would need to be paid for not registering Thomas as an employee or caretaker. Along with the fine, Jos had to fax a letter confirming Thomas's status and documentation regarding the lease of the shop and its purposes.

'They were implying that I was running more than an optician's,' he had said, while Thomas made disbelieving noises.

'It's jealousy,' Jos had concluded. 'The Panikkars didn't want to sell to me in the first place. But they couldn't afford not to. Prime real estate, you know. They probably didn't want me to make a success of the business. And so they've started a rumour.'

In fact, Thomas suspected some of that was true. The other businesses on the street may have surmised that Rani had an agreement with the new café, Green Gardens. Whether anyone had known about the bureau was another matter. A disgruntled former client may have decided to mention something to someone, and eventually that may have trickled across to the police. He decided to be honest with his old friend. He told him that

Rani had now been away from work for nearly a week, and Jos agreed that it would be difficult for Thomas to run the store on his own. They would close the shop early for the week and put up a sign notifying customers that it would reopen on the following Thursday. When Thomas telephoned the hostel where Jos had said Rani stayed, they told him that she had moved out three months ago. She was still staying somewhere in Konthuruthy, she had told them, and had been collecting any letters herself rather than give a forwarding address. The only way to try to find her was to go to Konthuruthy himself and make some enquiries. Surely someone local, a stallholder perhaps, would know where she lived.

He had made this decision the previous evening, but when he woke in the morning he realised he felt unsettled, like something was bubbling below the surface, something he was unable to grasp. He was still confused over the phone call from Vishukumari: what had she expected? Why had he found himself angry with her by the end of their conversation? His thoughts of her from the previous evening now seemed harsh. She had regarded him as a friend: didn't one share difficulties with a friend? He, who had few, was unaccustomed to the workings of a warm, sympathetic human being which she had proved herself to be. What had she made of the brevity of his answers, his trite pronouncement of her husband as a 'lucky man'? Was it now unlikely that she would keep in touch with him, and if she didn't, would that make any difference to his life as it was now?

Thinking of Vishukumari helped him avoid thinking of Rani. Burning the folder had seemed unavoidable after yesterday's events, but now, in the morning, his actions seemed disproportionate. Why would the police be looking for the folder, and what could they do if they found it? Why hadn't he simply hidden it? Why had he cremated it and scattered the ashes, as if he were a grieving relative? It gnawed at him. Rani's absence, the appearance of Murugan and his officers, the man he had seen on the beach. He could not regard each in isolation.

In the morning as the sun was rising, he left his bedroom, crossed the road as he had done the previous night and plunged into the sea. He swam out with strong strokes: the waves were immense. When he staggered back on to the sand, he noticed that one fisherman, an orange mundu tied around his waist, was watching him as he mended his boat. He waved, and to his surprise the man did not just wave back but walked over to him.

'You are Misterthomasfromlondon,' he said, and Thomas nodded. He picked up the towel he had left on the sand and rubbed his face and his hair.

'The sea is strong,' the fisherman said. He was young, his teeth white in his dark face, his smile accentuating his chiselled cheekbones. 'Some have died.'

'Yes,' Thomas replied, and then because he felt that he was being given a warning, he said, 'I am a good swimmer.'

'Yes, I can see. Even though you are an old man,' the fisherman replied. 'I swim also. You live there?' He pointed to the house.

Thomas nodded.

'You want fish?'

'I do sometimes.'

'Whenever you want, just tell me and I will keep some aside for you.'

'Thank you.' Thomas paused. 'And for Mariammakutty. Do you know her?'

'Oh yes.' The man smiled again. 'I can keep for her as well.'

'Well, I will pay for both houses from now on.'

'I understand.' Then he asked, 'You are a Christian?'

It was the question that Vishukumari had asked: was it your faith? He had wanted to answer her then: *her* faith. I was never a believer. Now the fisherman had asked the same, but before waiting for his answer – and with a name like Thomas who needed to ask? – he continued: 'And yet you give offerings to Kadalamma.'

It was only later, after Thomas had smiled politely and walked away from the fisherman, had washed and was standing on the balcony, when he saw the fisherman still mending his boat, did he realise that the young man must have seen him the previous night, emptying the tin bucket into the ocean, and imagined he was making an offering to the god of the seas. He turned away. The police had come and gone and found nothing. Jos had paid his fine and had smoothed over any difficulties. There was no use being paranoid, but the unsettled feeling continued through his breakfast and his journey back into the city, to post a note on the door of the shop, and beyond to Konthuruthy.

He asked to be dropped at the large white church, well known and not far from the hostel where Rani used to stay. The auto skidded to a halt just outside the entrance. A small crowd had gathered nearby, he saw, as he paid the driver and got out. A car had knocked over a wheelbarrow of fruit on the side of the road. The vendor had emerged from a tea-stand and was berating the driver, a bespectacled youth in dark jeans and

T-shirt. He was shouting, 'Look, will you buy these now?' And as if to prove his point, he squeezed the mango in his hand until the pulp oozed out. The youth stood, befuddled. His car looked new and expensive, probably his father's.

'Pay now! You have to buy everything because no one else will! I have four children—'

'Let him buy half,' a voice came from the crowd. 'You always leave your barrow in the middle of the road—'

'He has eyes, doesn't he?' the vendor roared.

There were already fifteen or more people closing in on the pair. There were layers of chatter, reams of advice. For a moment, he enjoyed the spectacle. But then, perhaps because of his earlier melancholy, he turned his enjoyment into a rebuke. By not shouting out advice like the men around him, he did not risk derision from the crowd, who may even turn on him with malevolence: he was not a local. But by not calling out, he was, as always, an onlooker. Even with his daughter, he was an onlooker. He stirred himself: he had come here for a reason, and he moved away from the crowd.

One other man was standing slightly apart, a rolled-up newspaper in his hand, observing the scene with an amused expression.

'Do you know the Holy Mother Hostel?' Thomas asked him.

The man glanced at Thomas, then pointed. 'End of the road.'

The young woman in reception repeated what had been said on the phone. Rani used to live there but she had moved away a few months ago.

'Has she been recently to collect her post?'

The young woman disappeared through a door behind the desk. Thomas looked around: it was neat and clean, a ceiling fan wobbled sluggishly, polished floors, a large cross above the door. As he was waiting, three girls emerged from a side door and walked briskly past. One clambered on a scooter parked outside, the others squeezed behind her, giggling, before they sped off.

'No post.' The young woman had returned.

'So she has been to collect it recently? Do you remember?'

The young woman stared at him blankly.

'I'm looking after Chacko's Optical Store,' he said. 'Rani hasn't come to work for some days now.'

The young woman hesitated and then said, 'Wait here.'

This time Thomas turned and went outside, stood on the verandah. He could see ahead that the crowd had dispersed. The altercation had ended; some resolution had been reached. He wandered out of the shade of the verandah into the small dusty forecourt where the sun massaged his arms, which still ached from his morning swim. When he was a young man, few of these hostels existed. The female students at his college lived in college residences; after graduating, most moved back home to await marriage. Those three young women who had sped off on their scooter had appeared self-possessed, in charge of their lives. They had hardly glanced at him, and why should they have?

Behind him he heard someone step outside. It was a man close to his age, his hand extended.

'You are a relative?' were his first words.

'No,' Thomas said, then stopped. What was his relationship with Rani? He was not her employer per se, but neither could he describe himself as a friend. He remembered the obsequious manager of Green Gardens: we all want a daughter like her.

'We work together,' he said. 'I'm a friend of Jos Chacko, he owns the shop Rani works at.'

'Yes, I see.'

The man looked down, as if he were making a decision. 'She moved away some months ago,' he said.

'And you have no idea where she may be? Konthuruthy can't have so many hostels.'

'Well, we don't know that she moved to another hostel,' the man said reasonably.

They fell silent.

'Friends?' Thomas asked. 'Does she have any friends who would know?'

The man nodded. 'That's a possibility. I am just not sure if I should be giving out this kind of information.' He smiled. 'I've never met you before.'

Thomas nodded. 'Can I leave you my number? Perhaps you can speak to one of her friends and ask them to call me if they think they can help. Rani may have mentioned my name. I've been working with her a few months now.'

'Yes, good idea.'

As he wrote his phone number down, he felt some irritation. In the old days, people would have accepted his respectability; his demeanour would have sufficed. But, he told himself, these are not the old days. He looked up: the man was standing before him, waiting, watching him. Thomas handed him the piece of paper and turned to go.

'Wait,' the man said.

Thomas turned back to him.

'There is one thing,' the man said, then paused. Thomas could see that he was trying to make up his mind.

'She called a few days ago,' the man said finally. 'She asked if there was a space in the hostel. She wanted to move back.'

'When was this?' Thomas asked.

'Hard to say, it was a quick call. Two, three days ago?'

'Thanks for telling me.'

'Yes,' the man continued. 'But we're full up. That's what I told her. She moved out a few months ago now, and her space has been filled.'

'I see.'

Thomas held out his hand. 'Thanks,' he repeated.

He went back out on to the street. There were the usual stalls and kiosks. After a moment's thought, he went into the tea-stand. The vendor of fruit was inside, revisiting his triumph of earlier: Thomas could overhear that the young man had agreed to pay a flat fee and had driven off with a carload of fruit in various states of wholeness. 'Do you know Rani Vamadevan?' he asked the vendor as he ordered a coffee. The answer was no, but the coffee was hot and sweet. He stayed for a few minutes, listening to the men around him chatting. Then he went out on to the street and asked the same question in each of the small stalls lining the road. Rather than wait hours or even days for the chance that one of Rani's friends would phone him, he preferred to at least try on the street. In each stall he was rewarded with a jerk of the head: no one could tell him where Rani lived. He had no photo to show, could only show with his hand: she is this tall, her hair is this long. He could be describing a million girls, he knew. She did not stand out; she blended in.

He found that his feet had brought him back to where he had started, the church. He was not a spiritual man, and yet his relationship with God had been queried twice in the space of a day, by Vishukumari and then the fisherman. Was it a sign? That he should call on God's help to find Rani? He shook himself impatiently. The interior of the church looked cool, which was appealing in itself. He stepped inside. It was quiet, with the only sound coming from a woman in a red cotton sari, the pallu tucked at the waist, who was sweeping using a straw brush. The floor was stone, cool under his feet: he had left his sandals at the door. The ceiling was high, the several large doors were all open allowing a breeze to pass through. There were some people dotted around, but no sign of any Mass. He leaned against a pillar, viewed the altar.

He had not drawn away from God; rather he had felt less and less a need for belief. If his parents could die, his brother, if in the end he would also die, then what was the point? Most people sought solace in a religion, something he could only find by himself. Even with Nimmy's diagnosis, he had felt no need to talk, pour his heart out. She had, in contrast, spent hours with the parish priest; her friends had organised prayer meetings. He knew that her thoughts had been less on survival, more on Nina and himself. She prayed because she needed to believe that death would not be the end, that there would be an afterlife in which she would again be entrusted with their safe keeping. She spoke to God, and she spoke to friends. Yet Thomas had had very few moments in his life when he had found that to talk to anyone, friend or higher being, even Nimmy, was to soothe, to heal.

There was never a question, however, that Nimmy's funeral would take place anywhere other than in the bland modern church a few streets away from their home: a church she had attended piously, even when he had stopped accompanying her. It had been filled to capacity, hundreds squeezed in to pay their respects. Nina had been silent beside him, tears collecting in a pool in her eyes. At one point she had leaned in against him, and he had felt grateful. Surrounded by mourners, evidence that his wife had forged friendships and ties with others without him, he needed to feel needed. Even if just to remain upright, to hold his daughter's weight, to prevent her from falling. She had chosen to lean on him at that moment, rather than Michel, who stood on her other side, holding her hand. It had not been the most auspicious way to meet Michel, this man who Thomas could see was handsome, with his beard and intelligent eyes, but with whom he had only exchanged a few words. Later he had seen them standing outside together, slightly apart from everyone but close to each other. Michel was smoking a cigarette, and Nina was now leaning against *him*, her hip pressed against his.

The dinner held at the house after the funeral had been organised by the ladies from the community. Nimmy's friends clucked around Nina, their husbands keeping Thomas stolid company. Afterwards, Nina stayed the night with him, while Michel took the late flight back to Paris. Thomas had not seen their farewell; he had shaken Michel's hand in the kitchen. His daughter had gone straight upstairs, to cry perhaps, before coming down. Neither had wanted to eat again, and so they had gone for a walk. He had held her hand, he remembered, but they had spoken little, about practicalities. He had not mentioned Michel again, and neither had she. They had tiptoed around each other for years: the lost years, he thought of them. And would they be any less lost, the years to come, if he were here, thousands of miles away, and she was there?

It was tempting to spend the rest of day where he was, in the cool and quiet space, but he left the church and his memories, and went back out on the street. The sun was lowering. A fruitless search. He tried to rationalise: in all likelihood, Rani had returned to Palakkad. Perhaps something had happened to her father, a sister, and she had left in haste, been unable to leave a message or was too distraught to phone. What else to do? Perhaps he should stay on in Konthuruthy, wait in the streets, try to catch a glimpse of her. But it would be futile, he thought immediately. The weight of the darkness offered little respite: it was like having a blanket thrown over your eyes. Feeble street lights, chaotic flashes from passing vehicles did not help. He had wondered what he would find most difficult to adjust to. Now he knew: it was this swift descent into the darkness of the nights, the feeling that everything had to be accomplished before the sun disappeared, the dark arose. Some more people had started filtering into the church: perhaps there would be a service soon. He would not stay. His expedition looked unlikely to garner success. He decided to leave.

His friend's shop was undisturbed; the sign still read *Chacko's Optical Store*. Nothing had changed since he had been there that morning. He stood outside re-reading the sign he had pasted on the door, then turned round and crossed the road. He pushed open the door of Green Gardens and went inside. There was a young woman at the counter: the manager was in the back office, she would fetch him.

'I'm worried about Rani,' he said without preamble when the manager appeared.

The younger man did not express any surprise or dismay at these words; he may not even have heard them. Instead, he peered at Thomas anxiously.

'The police yesterday?' he said.

Thomas shrugged. 'They're carrying out spot checks in the area,' he decided to say. 'Making sure papers are in order, employees registered. That sort of thing.'

He held the manager's eyes, did not blink. The manager twitched.

'They'll be back soon, they said,' Thomas lied easily.

'Oh.'

'So,' Thomas started again. 'About Rani. Do you know where she is staying?'

'The hostel—'

'She moved out.'

Again, this news was received with neither surprise nor dismay; the manager's thoughts were on other matters. His accounts and employee's ledger, thought Thomas savagely. There was little hope of learning anything from him.

'I'll be going then,' he said. At the door, he turned back. 'How's business?'

The manager twitched again.

'Oh. Fine.'

'That's good.' He took a cruel pleasure in seeing, as he left, through the window, the manager hurrying back into his office.

He opened the door, kicked aside a pile of post and entered the office. He had no wish to carry on as normal: look into the ledger, go into the testing room. He turned the computer on, stared blankly at the screen while it whirred and booted up. Then he searched for the website and dialled the number.

When his call was answered, he said, 'Can I speak to Officer Murugan?'

'This is incident number.'

'I know. Sorry, but I was at the station yesterday.'

'This number is—'

'Yes, sorry. Could I please talk to him? He'll remember me.'

There was a short hesitation and then, 'Who is calling?'

'Tell him Thomas Imbalil.'

'Hold, please.'

There was little chance he would catch him: it was past six o'clock, and anyway, didn't the police work in shifts? It was possible that Murugan was not working today or could be out of town.

'Mr Thomas.' His voice was wary.

'I just wondered,' Thomas said, 'how to go about reporting a missing person.'

'A missing person?'

'Rani Vamadevan. She is the assistant at Jos Chacko's store.'

Murugan did not speak, and in the background Thomas could hear overlapping voices, the sounds of doors opening and closing. Not the empty silent room he had sat in for hours yesterday then.

'How do you know she is missing?' the policeman finally asked.

'She's not come to work.'

'She could be ill.'

'She would have phoned.'

Murugan sighed. 'Mr Thomas, I'm a busy man . . .'

'Is that why you came yesterday to the store?' Thomas asked. 'To find her?'

The phone clicked, and the line went dead.

He sat at the desk, opened the blinds and stared out past his reflection, on to the street. He thought back to the responses he had received from the stallholders, none of whom knew Rani. Each shake of the head, each dismissal was a confirmation that the image he had had of her early on, of being one of the multitudes, held true. *I am from an ordinary background.* More than ever he felt that he needed to find her, to assure himself that she was not unfindable, would not disappear into the depths, leaving no trace. He had burned her folder – none of that remained; he could not let her join those ashes he had thrown into the sea. He pressed his fingers against his temples. He had the sensation that he had to keep his mind clear, focused. There was something at the back of his mind which was trying to come forward, but he had allowed it to be suppressed.

There was a tap at the door. How long had he been sitting there? It was now quite dark in the office; he hadn't turned on the lights. He stumbled to the door and opened it. The manager from Green Gardens was standing outside, looking harried.

'One of the waiters says he heard her talking on the phone once. About an apartment.'

Thomas waited, looking down at him.

'One of those timeshare places. You know, you can stay there for a certain number of months per year?'

'Where?'

'I don't know. We don't know. But my uncle has one of those and it's in Konthuruthy. I don't think there can be many like them.'

'How do I find it?'

'Blue Lagoon. Any auto driver will know it.'

Thomas nodded. 'OK, thanks.'

The manager nodded, turned away. Then stopped. 'I hope she's all right.' He looked younger in the dim light of the street; his expression was concerned. Rani was not just the conveyance through which he built more custom at his café. He cared;

she made people care for her, Thomas thought. He locked up and paused briefly to look back at the sign, then up and down the street.

If he moved away from this spot he was standing on, he was making a decision: to uncover his eyes, his ears and his lips, to learn. He was not reluctant, he realised. Rather, he was filled with suspense. The sensation that he was travelling towards something, towards an understanding of sorts, was hard to shake off. The same words arrived that had repeated in his mind those weeks before leaving London: could he do it? All through the auto drive back away from the centre, back through the streets he had only just left, back to Konthuruthy, the feeling grew stronger that he was arriving somewhere.

It was easy to locate: the large tower block, fallen on slightly hard times, with the disused swimming pool at the side, the vestibule with a flickering TV screen. A second-rate hostelry, a refuge. As soon as he saw it, he knew it was the right place. So that the moment he knocked on the door, watched it open, saw her face – small, pale, exhausted – what he had been trying to excavate surfaced, and when it did, the realisation came to him without much surprise. Her story was unremarkable: the man was married, with a wife and son. This discovery had led to an argument during which it was revealed that he and his family were moving to Australia. The lease for the apartment he had moved her into was near its end, and she could find nowhere to go. Over the last days, she had been paralysed by heartbreak.

On hearing her words, seeing the tears in her eyes, her body defeated, he knew. Perhaps he had always known, known that even Vishukumari had appeared, like a siren, solely to distract him from what he might have been allowed to understand much earlier. When she had raised her hand in apology that last day, it had not been in benediction as he had thought. It had been a plea: to ask him to wait, to accept what she seemed to have knowledge of already. This was why he had come back. She needed finding, and he had returned so that he could find her.

12

WHEN he woke the next morning, he could hear Rani breathing next door. It was a strange sensation: there had not been anyone, other than himself, sleeping in the house for the last months. They had arrived late at night. Rani had been tired: the events had drained her. She had fallen asleep in the taxi he had hired, her head against his shoulder, her feet curled up on the seat, like a small animal beside him. Her small suitcase of belongings, already packed when he had arrived at the door of the apartment, lay by his feet. He could see faint lights in Mariamma's house. Normally, it would be quiet, dark at this time; it was late for her to be up – perhaps a child was unwell. The sky, covered in clouds, as it often was in these months before the monsoon, was black. He had shaken her gently to wake her, and she had appeared disoriented, staring at him for a few seconds before saying his name.

He had offered to cook something quickly, but Rani had refused: she simply wanted to sleep. Upstairs, he had shown her the bathroom and given her a towel. While she was having a wash, he had gone into the second bedroom, realised that he had forgotten to fix the shutter that he had found broken months back on his initial return. The room was dusty, sand had blown in, and it had an inhospitable air. He decided to sleep in there himself. He put a clean sheet on the bed in the main bedroom and left another folded for her to cover herself, moved his books out and a few clothes. She had not argued when he told her to sleep in the bigger room, with the bigger bed. She had swayed slightly on her feet, as if she would fall asleep standing up. In the dim light of the room, all he could see were her collarbones, her narrow shoulders, stooped with the weight of her worries. He had patted her shoulder, then briefly clasped the back of her head, before going downstairs.

He was starving: he had not eaten all day. When he opened the fridge, he saw he had only a few slices of bread, a potato, half an onion, a few sprigs of coriander and remembered that he had intended to stop at a shop on the way home. So, he reflected, he really *hadn't* expected to be returning with Rani in tow, another mouth to feed. Yet, he still remained unsurprised that he had. It was lucky that she was not hungry, he thought, as he made his paltry meal of fried bread and potato. As he ate, he heard her footsteps above. When he himself went upstairs later, the bedroom was dark, and through the door that was left ajar he could see her lying on her side on the bed, her shoulders rising and falling.

As he was taking off his clothes in readiness for a shower, his phone had rung, under the pile of his clothes. He scrambled for it. For some reason, he half-expected it would be Murugan, the police officer, phoning to check that he had indeed found Rani and brought her back with him, as if it were the officer's doing. Instead, he had a confused conversation with a distant voice that he strained to hear, until suddenly the voice became strong and loud in his ear. It was the agent he had left in charge of the house in Tooting, apologising for calling after hours. He glanced at his watch: seven o'clock in the evening in London. He found his brain readjusting to the news: the boiler had been causing problems, and the tenants wanted it repaired or replaced. The gas technician who had made the recommendation came with a trustworthy reputation. After a brief confabulation, it was decided that a new boiler would be ordered, the amount debited from Thomas's account.

When he hung up, he had stared at the dark outside for a long while, listening to the sound of the sea. The world was still out there, and it had been his world. Perhaps he had dreamed it all. He would wake up and find Nimmy sleeping beside him, her mouth slightly open as happened when she slept at her deepest. Perhaps he would reach over and touch her, feel for her head, his fingers reaching coarse skin: she was in the middle of chemo. He had dreamed it all: he had thrown himself into a future which had never happened. Nimmy was not dead, she was still fighting the cancer. They were talking about moving back to Kerala after her treatment was over, but they had not yet displaced themselves. Rani: a figment, conjured up because somewhere in his psyche he knew he had been lacking as a father. Vishukumari: a pathetic fantasy of a different sort in his late middle age. It was only when his mind alighted on Nina that he balked. He had not dreamed that: her anger, the way he had disappointed her. If only he could have dreamed the fact that his only child felt he had abandoned her. But he could not. He lay in bed later that night, Rani fast asleep next door, as Nina should have been, and he yearned for Nimmy.

He crept past Rani's door in the morning. The sea looked especially inviting; he would feel ready for anything after a swim. He crossed the road and walked across the sand. The fishermen were talking loudly and did not acknowledge him. He paused to enjoy the feel of the sand, already warm beneath his feet, deliciously soft. He breathed in the fresh air. As he raised his head to look at the sea, he saw a flash in the corner of his vision: the young fisherman had raised his hand. When he dived into the waves he felt better. Everything was as it was, and that meant it was as it should be. He swam out as far as he could, turned on to his back, rolled in and out and then let the waves help him find the shore, his feet scraping the sand. As he was drying his face, he looked up: there was a figure on his balcony, in a green housedress. He waved, and after a moment he saw Rani wave back.

He washed quickly at the tap outside in the back and then walked down the road, across the bridge to Junction. The talk in the shops was of the latest plans to increase the tariffs at the toll booths: a blow to taxi and auto drivers who would have to increase their fares accordingly, an inevitability which would displease customers. He collected some groceries and walked back, across the backwaters. The bridge was a natural mound of earth, the ground packed hard by the feet of the thousands of people who had crossed over the backwaters, the brackish water that stretched for miles further south. Before him was the strip of land and then the sea, the sky. It was a place one could come for comfort, he thought. Whether you believed in a god or not, the harmony of the elements could console. Rani would feel the same, he was sure. When he arrived at the house, he saw that Mariamma was in her front yard. He paused, she looked up and smiled briefly.

'Mariamma . . .'

'Thomaschayan . . .'

He walked towards her; her wall was low, and he could look over it with ease. She was sweeping her front area with a straw brush, and through her open door he could see one of her children at the table, writing conscientiously into a notebook. There was no sign of the small boy: perhaps he had gone somewhere with his father. When she saw him waiting, she stopped sweeping.

'I have a visitor, Mariamma,' Thomas said. 'Jos Chacko's assistant, Rani. She needs a place to stay and will be staying with me for a few days.'

A few days. In fact, nothing had been decided yet.

Mariamma tilted her head in acknowledgement, saying nothing.

'I hope the police didn't give you any trouble the other day,' he continued.

She shook her head; her eyes were not unfriendly but did not have her usual warmth.

Thomas nodded, tried to smile. As he was turning away to return to his house, she spoke: 'Thank you for the fish. The man brought some yesterday.'

'That's good, that's good.' He was glad to speak of something else, even fish. He turned to face her.

'It's my pleasure,' he added. 'I can't thank you enough for keeping an eye on the house all these years.'

'I still have yours. It's in our fridge.'

'Keep it, Mariamma. I won't be cooking it soon.'

She gave him a small tight smile, then bent down, carried on sweeping. Upstairs, he passed his bedroom doorway and glanced inside. Her suitcase was lying open on the floor. She had folded her cover sheet neatly, and on the table at the side there was a small pile of clothes. He could just make out a figure through the doorway: she was still standing on the balcony. He had a quick shower, and as he dressed he inspected the shutter in the second bedroom. It would not take long to fix, and then he would have more reason to tidy up in that room. He skipped downstairs and inspected the food he had bought, prepared a menu in his head, then called up, 'Rani?'

She appeared at the head of the stairs. 'Mr Thomas?'

'Come and eat something.'

He had spoken to her as if she were his daughter, and she behaved as such when she limped down the stairs and then sat on a chair watching him at the counter. She didn't offer to help, but sat at the table listlessly, as if she were only having breakfast to please him and was not beholden to assist. He made an omelette with tomato and chillies, fried slices of plantain with cinnamon and sugar, toasted some bread. He boiled some coffee and cut some slices of pineapple.

'I don't always have so much,' he said smiling. 'It's nice to have a guest.'

They sat at the table and ate silently, the ceiling fan turning slowly overhead. He refilled her coffee cup, gave her more toast when he saw that her plate was nearly empty. She leaned back in her chair, her hands cupped around her cup.

'Do you want to tell me more?' he asked quietly.

She shook her head, put her cup down and pulled her kurta over her knees, stared at the pattern. He stood, gathering the plates, and took them to the kitchen sink. Again, she made no move to help him. When he had finished washing up, he called to her, 'Come, let's sit outside.'

She followed him, and he led her to the backyard.

'This is nice,' she said, gesturing to the gazebo.

It was good to hear her voice, and he felt some relief.

'Thank you.' He patted one of the supporting poles and grinned. 'I made it!' Then laughed at her surprise. 'I wanted to be able to sit outside, even in the afternoon.'

'It's so nice.' She inspected it, her face full of wonder. 'I can't believe you made it.'

'I'm from the hills,' he smiled. 'A village boy.'

He motioned for her to take the only chair, a rocker made from bamboo. He watched as she sat down, her smile fading. Her hair was parted neatly to one side, her long plait lay down one shoulder. She looked clean, fresh, young; her face was brighter than yesterday evening when he had found her. But the difference between the girl before him and the busy, occupied receptionist he had known scurrying around in the optical store was stark. That was because, he reminded himself, they were not in the optical store. She was sitting in his gazebo in his backyard in Cherai.

'And you also swim so well,' she said quietly, as if stating a fact.

He lowered himself on to the floor of the gazebo, next to the chair. His calves ached, possibly from climbing the stairs yesterday to her apartment. The lift had been out of order, in keeping with the general feeling of malaise in the block, and he had found her on the fifth floor.

'My brother taught me how to swim,' he said. 'In a river near where we lived in Vazhakulam. Even my older sister swims really well. That's what I remember from growing up: the three of us in the river. It seemed like we were never out of the water. Then, in London I went swimming nearly every week. I joined a club.' He laughed, glanced at her; she was watching him, her gaze steady. 'To learn proper strokes. I taught Nina how to swim, or at least I started her off.'

'Does she swim like you?'

'Probably better than me,' he smiled.

'And your wife?'

He shook his head.

'No,' he said. 'Nimmy never learned.' I never taught her, he thought. I'm discovering all the things I didn't do.

She continued to watch him, as if she were waiting for him to continue.

He said, 'What about you, Rani?'

She shook her head, saying nothing.

'And your sisters?' he said. Then changed tack: 'Where are they? Do you keep in touch?'

She plucked at her kurta.

'One is married, living in Bangalore. One is in Palakkad, with my father. One is in Kottayam, working in a hotel.'

'Do you see them?'

'My sister in Kottayam came to stay with me last year.' She stopped, then said quietly, 'I couldn't tell them about my life.'

They fell silent. He remembered how she had come to Cherai with her erstwhile beau, the married man. They had probably wandered up and down the promenade; they could even have sat at one of the eateries.

Perhaps because of his silence, she lifted her eyes and held his. 'What do you think of me, Mr Thomas?'

They were large, dark pools. She held her face to him as if she were expecting a blow, as if to show him that any punishment he decided to mete out, she would accept.

'I don't think badly of you, Rani,' he said. 'And I'm really not in the position to judge anyone. I'm not perfect by any means. And I have been lucky all my life, much luckier than many people.'

'But,' she said, 'if you found out your daughter was in my situation, wouldn't you be angry with her?' A tear rolled down her cheek.

He reached over: even from his position at her feet he could lay a hand on the top of her head. He felt the warmth of her skull, the slight oiliness of her hair. She did not look up or make any sign of acknowledgement. She was a heart-breakingly vulnerable figure, the folds of her clothes enveloping her slight frame. She wiped her nose unselfconsciously with the end of her kurta. He dropped his hand and touched her arm briefly.

'I would probably be more upset that she hadn't talked to me,' he said finally. 'I wouldn't be angry with her. I don't think so. I'd be angrier with the man.'

She sniffed, raised her eyebrows.

'I don't know him, but I'm angry with him,' he said quietly.

'I'm so ashamed.' This delivered in a whisper.

They listened to the sounds from next door. Mariamma's voice was raised; there was a bleat from one of her children.

'Things are never black and white, Rani,' he chose to say eventually, but his words seemed generic.

Even with a long marriage in his repertoire, he was less experienced with the workings of a love affair than she. If she were waiting for his wisdom, or worse, an absolution, he felt ill-prepared. She assumed that he was horrified that she had given herself to someone her father had not chosen for her. Of course he did not feel that way, but he had implied the same when he had spoken to Nina, suggested he felt uncomfortable with the way she was living her life. What had been her response? Everything so hidden, so muffled.

'My daughter never really talked to me about anything much when she was growing up,' he decided to say. 'I'm not saying that was her fault. I don't think I made it easy for her to talk to me. At the moment, she is living with a man. They're not married. I'm sure she's had relationships that I don't know about.'

When he glanced at her, he saw her eyes were steady, large; she was listening intently. This was what she wanted to hear, he could see. Stories of love, or of the search for love, had fuelled her endeavours: they had all fed into her own story of love. He had an image of her folder, the flames crackling, the pitiful amount of ash that had resulted. He waited for her to ask, Did you open the drawer? Did you read through my folder? But she didn't speak.

They remained silent for some time, and then he elected to say, 'You'll feel better if you go back to work, start getting busy again.'

'We came here, you know,' she said suddenly. 'We spent the whole day in Cherai.' Her face was in repose, as if she was watching herself, the moments from that day playing out on the sand before them. 'We spent the afternoon on the beach, before it got dark.'

Thomas remembered how he had seen her, laughing, teasing the waves, running in and out. Barefoot, the pants of her salwar kameez soaked where the waves had taken her unawares. She had run back and thrown herself on the sand next to the man.

'Yes, I saw you,' he said, and her head snapped up in surprise. 'I didn't go to stay with Nimmy's brother over the Easter weekend,' he continued. 'I stayed here.'

She looked down, and he saw a flush rise to her cheeks.

'And you didn't go to Palakkad,' he said.

'No.'

'Do you want to go? Do you want to go home for a bit?'

She shook her head.

'Would your father . . . ?'

She shook her head again.

'Rani . . .' He moved closer to the chair, laid his hand on her shoulder. They stayed like this for some minutes, and then he ventured, 'If he is indeed an ambitious man with a wife and child, it's best if you try to put the episode behind you.'

'You're right.'

'Take your time. I'll help you find somewhere else to live when you're ready, but until then you are welcome to stay here.'

He got to his feet and moved away, busying himself with checking the generator, the water pump. When he turned around, she had left, gone back inside.

They spent the rest of the day in different rooms. He fixed the shutter in the second bedroom, swept up the sand and dusted the furniture. As he worked, he caught glimpses of her: she was often sitting on the bed, her knees pulled up. Once he saw her on the balcony, looking out. At one point he knocked on the door and went into his bedroom. She was lying on the bed, on her side, and she watched him solemnly as he took some more clothes out of the wardrobe. If she felt any consternation at occupying his bedroom, inconveniencing him, she gave no sign. The events surrounding her were larger, he could see. In the same way, she had made no effort to dissuade him from taking her away from the apartment, no move to decline his offer of bringing her back with him, as if by appearing at her door he had registered himself as caretaker and would therefore fulfil all accompanying responsibilities.

When the sun was at its hottest, he lay down on the bed in the second bedroom, heard her breathing steadily from the next room. She must have fallen asleep. He found that he was restless, so he started writing a letter to his daughter. He was not sure if he would ever send it, but he felt that he needed to try to express himself: impossible to do in a phone call or an email. *I feel*, he wrote, *coming back here, like a young man in an older man's body. Every day I seem to remember something, not always about my life here, but also about your mother, our life as a young couple. I remember what I felt like as a young father with a young daughter. Perhaps that is what growing older is about, endless memories. I'm not sure where my life will take me, so I focus on what I did. And by doing so I realise there is much I would change.*

After some time, he went back downstairs into the yard and swept the back step. He had an idea to have an area of potted plants to one side, and some months ago he had organised a delivery of earthenware pots and topsoil. He cleaned the pots, set them out and filled them with the soil, work that soon had him sweating in the heat. He could at least start by growing some chillies, then later some flowers. He spent the next hour making the tepee for the children next door, half-expecting the boy to appear from around the corner; he would have enjoyed his company. When the sun began its descent, he jogged over to the beach resort to order two meals to take away. The dining area was empty; only a few members of staff drifted around, languidly swatting at the tables with dust cloths. A few guests lingered, but most seemed to have barricaded themselves away in their chalets to escape the heat.

He returned to the house and went straight into the bathroom, where he washed and dressed in a clean mundu. If he had been on his own, he would have remained shirtless, but he put on a clean T-shirt, then called her.

'Rani.'

He was arranging a small table on the balcony, two chairs, when she appeared and stepped outside.

'I've brought some food,' he said. 'I thought we could have it here and watch the sun set.'

He set out the plates and cups of water, started opening the boxes of food.

He glanced at her, and she gave him a small smile. 'This is nice.'

He had not seen her go downstairs once and get a snack all day, and she ate ravenously.

'You can help yourself whenever you want,' he said when her plate was empty. 'From the fridge, I mean. Don't wait for me. I'm no good at keeping an eye on the time. I've got used to eating when I'm hungry.'

'I didn't know I was so hungry.'

He stacked the plates on to the tray, moved them to one side. The breeze was a balm after a hot day.

'Are you not lonely here?' she asked.

He turned to her; she was watching him.

'Not always,' he said. 'I like the peace and quiet.'

She plucked at her kurta. 'Has Mrs Nair left?'

'I presume so.' He paused. 'She came and helped me, you know. One day at the store.'

This time when she smiled she looked like her old self. There was a mischievous glint in her eyes when she said, 'She liked you for sure.'

'Well . . .' he said. 'And I liked her. I hope we'll stay in touch.'

'Did you think she was beautiful?'

He glanced at her. She had turned away and was looking at the sea, her fingers playing with the end of her kurta.

'Yes,' he said. 'I suppose I did.'

She was quiet for some minutes, and he searched for something to say, but then she spoke again: 'You wanted her to stay longer?'

'It wasn't my decision to make.' He waited and then continued: 'I would have liked to get to know her better, I suppose. As a friend. Because, as you know,' he gave a long look, 'she's a married woman.'

She laughed and so did he, relieved. The atmosphere lightened, but then seconds later a shadow flitted over her face.

'I'm sorry about that last time,' she said. 'I think I wasn't polite. I was angry with her for some reason.'

'Don't worry.'

'Or jealous maybe.' She sighed. 'I think I was jealous of *her* and also jealous of how I could see that *you* liked her,' she said.

He digested her words, could think of no response.

'What were you making this afternoon?' she asked.

So at some stage she had left the bedroom and watched him; he had had no idea.

'The pots?'

'No. With the bamboo.'

'A smaller version of the gazebo,' he smiled. 'For the children next door.'

'Who lives next door?'

'Mariamma and her children,' he said. 'And her husband. I'll introduce you tomorrow.'

She nodded, saying nothing.

'My book arrived,' he said finally, and stood up, went back into the bedroom where the parcel lay, only partially opened. She watched him brandish the brown package as if it were a prize and gave him a small smile. He remembered how she had slid her copy over for him to see, that day in the optical store, how he had had to disguise his surprise at her choice of reading material. She was looking at the cover as if she was remembering the same.

'Actually,' he continued, 'it arrived when I had some visitors to the store. The police.'

She stared at him, opened her mouth to say something, then closed it.

'For some reason the police came. They said it was because Jos hadn't registered me, but I'm not sure I believe them.'

She was still staring at him intently.

'Was it because of your . . .' he struggled for the right word, 'your friend?'

She looked down, 'Mr Thomas . . .'

'Is he a policeman, Rani?'

She shook her head slowly.

'But he has friends in the police?'

She said nothing.

'Who is he, Rani?'

When she spoke, her voice sounded older, dismissive: 'Just a man.'

He waited and then, when she did not continue, he spoke. 'And he was a client.'

He didn't ask a question this time, and her silence was enough of a confirmation. He looked down at her, at the top of her head, the neat parting, then her small hands laid on her lap. How could she have thought that delving into people's desires and loneliness could be done from afar, as if she could stand by the side and watch people plunging into a pool: did she never think she would get splashed?

'Rani,' he spoke clearly, so she would hear him. 'I destroyed your folder. When the police came, I got worried. I thought they were looking for it. I burned it. I burned it and then I threw it into the sea.'

She did not turn to look at him; her eyes were fixed ahead, beyond the balustrade of the balcony, as if she would see the folder bobbing up and down in the waves. When the silence lengthened, he reached out and laid a hand on her shoulder.

'Rani?'

She said nothing, seemed not to feel his touch.

By now it was dark; he would have to go inside and turn a light on. He turned to collect the tray and saw that she was crying. He took one of her hands and pulled her to her feet, so that she was standing against him. Just as he had held Nina, all those months ago, he held Rani, her head reaching the collar of his shirt, her tears soaking into his chest. She kept her hands at her mouth, so that his arms encircled her completely. At one point he put his lips against her head, her hair, feeling the stiffness of each strand.

Below he heard a clink: Mariamma on her way with her empty bottles to the kiosk. She looked up and saw them. He raised his hand in a wave, but she turned away quickly. He had told her he had a visitor; now she had seen the visitor in his arms. A young girl, younger than his daughter. If he could only have shouted down, I wanted another, Mariamma! You never met her! I had a dream to bring Vishukumari here, watch the sunset with her beside me, then take her to bed.

In his arms, Rani was still, as if she had fallen asleep. When he held her away from him, peered into her face, he saw that her eyes were dry and open.

'Are you all right?' he asked.

She shrugged, and with that action he felt her shoulder blades move under his fingers. He released her, let his arms drop to his sides.

'I'm sorry,' he said.

'Thank you for dinner, Mr Thomas.' Her voice was steady, quiet. 'I'm just going to lie down. I'm so tired.'

'Yes, of course.' He moved aside for her to go back into his bedroom.

He took the plates downstairs and washed them up. He could hear her moving around upstairs in the bathroom. He pulled the fridge away from the wall and swept up the dust and dead ants. He mopped the floor and then laid some more bicarbonate of soda along the skirting boards. Then he went and sat out in the gazebo with a torch and a book until the mosquitos defeated him. The house was dark and still; she must have gone to sleep. He was not tired enough to go to bed, and so on an impulse he walked along the road until he returned to the beach resort, ordered a beer and drank it at the bar among the chatter and music and lights. The dining area was crowded now, people he had never set eyes on in the village or near the kiosks. When he left, the road back to his house was pitch-black. He walked with his arms extended before him, brushing against the odd bush.

Once, an animal: a goat? When he reached the house, he didn't turn on the lights but crept around in the gloom and climbed into bed.

He woke up with a start; he had no idea how much later, perhaps there had been a noise outside. The waves were crashing against the sand, the wind blowing into the room. A storm, out in the ocean, the remnants touching the shore. He turned on his side, closed his eyes. In the house, aside from the white curtains billowing like sails, all was quiet, still. He sat up instantly, a sudden fear setting his heart pounding. He rolled off the bed, walked out on to the balcony and peered through the doorway into Rani's room. The bed was empty, the cover sheet lay crumpled at the end. He hurried back through his bedroom, into the bathroom – it was empty – then back out on to the balcony. Just below, crossing the road, he saw a slight form in green.

The sky was black, the moon hidden behind fluffy, innocent clouds. He ran, his chappals flapping against the soles of his feet. He had tried to call out, but his voice had plunged into the depths of his stomach. When he reached the sand, he could not see, but with his sense of touch heightened the sand felt incredibly soft. There was blackness all around, no sign of the detritus and piles of litter near the edges of the beach: just a sense of open space before him. Then the moon came out from behind a cloud, and he saw her standing by the water. Her hair hung loose: he was surprised to see its length, to the small of her back. Her arms were wrapped around her body, and the wind was whipping her housedress against her figure, her hair a fan behind her.

'Rani!' he called.

Did she hear him? He could not tell; the wind seemed to take his words and place them further along the beach. Whether she stepped into the water herself, neither could he tell. All he saw was the giant wave finding its zenith then crashing down, less than a foot away from her. Then the moon slid away again, and when it reappeared he saw her in the sea, like a green bird, struggling in the vastness of the grey water.

He dived into the water and it hit him like a shock, so that he felt his chest constrict in protest. The water rolled and rolled, and he rose and fell, a roaring in his ears. His mundu was torn from his waist, and he kicked it away so that his legs were free. Then the cool, clean, sharp water was all around him, welcoming him back. It was useless, he thought, he could hardly see his own hands. Then he felt her hair. He twisted his hand in it and felt a curve, a bone, a shoulder. Her hair was now in his mouth, they were rising and falling together, her nightgown was a ruff around her chin and then seemed to disappear, so when his hands finally found her body, he could feel she was naked, his hands grasping her pelvis, her breasts, her ribs. They went under together, her hair wrapping itself around his eyes; he was being pulled deeper. He thought she was dead already, then he felt her hands claw, so that they clung to his neck, her body pressed against his, pulling him into the sea as if she were in control and this had been her plan all along. They would die together, he realised, be washed up on the shore in the morning, entwined like two lovers. This would be the narrative; his daughter would never know the truth.

Suddenly, he felt another hand, an arm around his shoulders as strong as his, even stronger. And then one of Rani's arms was taken away from him, so her weight suddenly dropped away from him. He could rise, feel the wind on his face and gulp the air. Another arm, a foot kicking, and he kicked also, and they rode the wave, so that they could find the sand, suddenly scraping against his feet, against his body. The fisherman's teeth gleamed white in the dark as he pulled Rani across the sand, then returned and grasped Thomas, his hands in each armpit, his breath, redolent with paan and spices, momentarily replacing the cool night air. Then he turned again to Rani, as she lay naked, as thin as a girl, her body a sheath on the sand. The clouds had scudded away and the moon shone brightly so that Thomas could see, on his knees, his own breath coming in gasps, as if lit for a play, the fisherman's blackened body bend over Rani. He took off his mundu, which was tied between his legs, and covered her. Then he breathed into her mouth, his hand cupped around her nose. No one else arrived, no sirens wailed. Only the sea kept up its roar, the waves crashed. For what may have been minutes but which appeared to be an endless moon-touched moment, Thomas watched until she coughed and spluttered, and the fisherman, too, coughed, and wiped his mouth with his hand.

Later, he had carried Rani in his arms, effortlessly, as if she were one of his catch, to Thomas's house, strode across the backyard and deposited her on the floor in the living room, waited while Thomas fetched some towels from upstairs, before lifting his hand in a salute. Thomas had struggled up the stairs with Rani in a deep slumber – not dead but sleeping, breathing in and out heavily. He had covered her with a blanket from his wardrobe. His arms were aching, his body exhausted, as he tucked the rough cloth over her feet. When he looked at her face, he saw she was shivering now, but her eyes were open, bright. Her lips moved, and he bent near her to hear her words, not knowing whether he would hear gratitude for extracting her from the sea or admonishment for not letting it consume her.

But he only heard her say, 'Ammachi.'

And again, 'My mother.'

And lastly, before her eyes closed again and she fell asleep, 'My baby inside me.'

13

H E dreamed that he was on a ship, at a table in a dining area, heavy white material under his right arm lying on the table. His hand was palm up, balancing a glass. The whole room was being lifted and dropped in time with the swell and ebb of the sea, the liquid in his cup swilling from side to side. Nimmy was on his right dressed in a red sari he did not recognise. Her expression neither did he recognise: her eyelids were at half-mast, her jaw slack. She was speaking, but he was not aware of what she was saying. His left hand under the table, out of sight, was placed just under the hem of the skirt of the woman to his left, his hand sliding up a silken thigh. He was aroused; Nimmy beside him was slurring a remonstration. *Veshya*, she was saying, a word he had never heard her use. *Veshya*, who is she?

He woke up covered in perspiration and his heart thumping. His eyes tried to adjust to the bright light pouring into his room from outside; last night's storm had moved on. He tried to move his arms and legs, which seemed to suffer from an incredible weight. He lay on his back, his eyes open, seeing nothing. He could hear noises outside, but nothing from the room next door. He was sure, however, that Rani was still in bed: somehow he knew that she would not make the attempt, if it had been an attempt, again. There had been something so satisfied in her expression when she had laid down in the bed, when he had covered her with the sheet, the blanket. Perhaps his actions reminded her of being a child: being tucked into bed, a bedtime ritual.

He lay quietly; the bed was a sanctuary. At some point he had to get up and deal with the situation, but for the moment he preferred to stay still, with his thoughts. He turned on his side, breathing slowly. He had rarely felt so disturbed, troubled; he had always been able to face a crisis with some degree of equanimity. The last few months had seen him ruffled more often than was usual. He knew that his mildness had both soothed and agitated Nimmy's more expressive temperament. He wished she could see him as he was now: cowering in his bed, uneasy and uncertain. He could imagine her amusement. She would laugh at him, waggling a finger.

But of course, over a marriage of thirty years, he had not been perpetually unperturbed: she had seen him very much shaken once, when his brother had died. He couldn't explain to Nimmy, with her sprawling, untidy family, about the closeness he felt to his siblings: a small tight unit. The day he found out was etched in his memory; when he recalled it, it always reappeared before him in slow motion. A letter had arrived from Chechiamma, and Nimmy had opened it. When he had arrived home from work, she had said to him immediately on opening the door, there is some bad news, come, sit. He had reacted in an uncharacteristic way: tell me, he had said roughly. But her voice had been choked with tears, so he had had to push past her, scan the kitchen where the letter was lying on the table. When he had read that his older brother had died so easily, so suddenly, he had cried out, made a noise that he had never heard himself make. More than any bereavement he had suffered to that date – his father, his mother – it was losing his older, stronger brother that had devastated him. Even Nimmy had left him quietly, with time, given him a chance to prepare; there was not the brutality of having a brother one day, not the next. What had been equally painful as the loss itself was that he had had no inkling of his brother's death for weeks. He had carried on living, innocent of this momentous change in his life. The letter had arrived weeks after his brother's funeral had taken place. With both parents dead, his sister in a convent, it had fallen to a cousin to make arrangements. He had not thought to call Chechiamma, certainly not Thomas, thousands of miles away in London, as if the distance was evidence that Thomas had relinquished his ties with his family. He had not attended his brother's funeral, and it was more than a year later when he visited his grave. By then he had learned that there were no words to assuage the pain; he alone was his own healer.

He turned over on to his back, let out his breath. His brother would have known what to do about Rani, but he was no more. He had no confidant to hand, but he could talk to Chechiamma. He got out of bed and went downstairs, where his landline sat on its stool, waiting for him. His sister was called to the phone. In the background, he could hear the rustling of garments, shouts and calls: all sounds of a busy convent life.

'Thomasmon?' His sister was pleased to hear from him. She assumed he was calling to rearrange his visit. When he started talking about Rani, she remained silent until he had finished. For some time, they were quiet, the words hung between them as if Rani herself was before them, turning herself this way and that, smiling shyly, allowing them to inspect her.

'Not what you expected in your retirement,' she said finally.

He cleared his throat.

'I wondered,' he began, 'if you knew of any place near here where we could get some advice? Someone she can talk to? I'm not sure I'm any good at this sort of thing.'

His sister did not speak for some time, and he could hear a door close. She had moved to a quieter place, where any shouts or calls were more distant.

'These things go two ways, Thomasmon,' she said, and her voice was different, severe. 'You are asking me, and so I would direct her to one of the licensed homes we run for unmarried mothers.'

He waited for her to continue. When she didn't, he spoke: 'And the other way?'

'You need to ask?' She sounded genuinely irate. 'Family planning centres. Termination of the pregnancy. Of course I cannot recommend any of those places to her.'

When he did not speak, she spoke again: 'If you ask me to find someone to help, you are choosing a direction for the girl that she may not wish.'

He was quiet. Was it the right moment to go upstairs, gently waken her? Rani, what are your intentions? Do you want to keep the baby?

'I'm not even sure if I heard her correctly,' he said finally.

His sister sighed. 'Then maybe you should wait and see?'

Again a silence. He was tired, he closed his eyes, covered them with one hand, made his decision as quickly as he had made the decision to return to India.

'I need help, Chechiamma,' he said. 'I have no idea what to do with her. Anyone who can talk with her will be a big help.'

His sister remained silent for some time on the other end of the phone. He held the handset away from his ear for a moment, strained to hear if there was any movement upstairs, but he heard none.

'Are you fond of the girl?'

Her question silenced him. Was he fond of Rani? He had never asked himself that before.

'Yes,' he said. 'Yes, I am. I suppose we've become friends . . .'

'But she has a father?'

'Yes.'

'Should he be the one you contact?'

'But . . .' Again he stopped. 'She may not want him to know, about the . . . situation.'

'She may not want it, but might it be the best plan? Then he can take responsibility for his daughter.'

'Maybe . . .'

When his sister spoke next, her voice was firm.

'You have to look into your heart, Thomasmon. Think about how much you want to help this girl. Because once you offer a helping hand, you cannot then withdraw it at a later date when it suits you.'

He marvelled at his sister. He had allowed himself to forget her talents, her perspicacity. She had always, from an early age, shown a strength that he did not feel he had. She had taken herself to the convent, providing some relief to his parents, he was sure, for not needing to find her a husband nor pay a dowry. She had done so, not to alleviate any burden they might have felt, but because she had a conviction that that was how she wanted to devote her life. She had thrived in her environment, winning a scholarship to study in Rome, then later the Philippines. She had travelled and studied through her vocation.

In her younger days, she had set up the psychotherapy centre, liaised with the government on both state and federal level. Despite living her life in a type of solitude, without dependants, she had involved herself with the lives of those around her more than he ever had. He need not patronise her.

He heard her sigh again. 'I know someone,' she said. 'I know someone who runs one of the homes in Ernakulam. Let me call her, and then I will call you back.'

He hung up the phone and went to stand outside in the backyard. To his right, he could hear voices from Mariamma's house. He would have to explain, if she had heard, the commotion from last night. The fisherman might have brought her his catch in the morning and already apprised her of the situation. And what was the situation? In his house, in his bed, lay a girl, sleeping. She was unmarried, pregnant from an affair with a married man. He did not need much imagination to recognise how violently Rani's plight broke the norms that were expected of her.

He was not sure how long he had stood outside, absorbing the warmth as if it could erase the shock of the water the previous night. But not much time had passed before the phone rang again: his sister had arranged that one of the nuns who worked at the centre would drop by at midday.

Thomas glanced at his watch, it was nearly nine o'clock. He climbed the steps and walked towards the room, pushing the door open quietly. She was still asleep; the blanket lay on the floor beside her, the sheet was a tangle around her body. He stopped short, one foot poised above the ground. She was still naked. In the light that filtered through the thin curtains, she shone among the neutral tones around her, like a copper sculpture. She lay away from him, the sheet around her waist. He could see the line of her spine, the delicate indentations in her back, the slim waist and gentle curve of her hip. Her hair, unharmed by the seawater of the previous night, had fallen in a sweep from her temples and lay like a puddle under her neck, covering half her face. Her shoulders rose and fell: a deep sleep. But as soon as he had that thought she stirred and he slipped back outside, paused a moment then knocked on the door.

'Rani?' he called, and he waited to hear her murmur a response, waited for her to realise her nakedness, cover herself.

'Rani, can I come in?'

'Yes.'

She was half-sitting up, the blanket around her shoulders. She looked pale, but her voice was strong and her eyes were luminous.

'Good morning,' he said.

'Good morning.'

He stepped into the room.

'How are you feeling?'

She shrugged her shoulders, tilted her head. Then said, 'How are *you* feeling Mr Thomas?'

He shrugged his shoulders in mimicry, wondering if that would make her smile, but her expression remained grave.

'All right. A bit tired.'

She nodded, drew her knees up to her chest, put her arms around them. Then she lifted her face to his, and again he stopped short.

It was like he was seeing her for the first time, as if when she had emerged from the sea she had been redrawn, so her features were more distinct in her face. The shape of her eyes, the symmetry of her nose. Her hair hung heavy down one shoulder, arranged as if for a soirée, the blanket framing her shoulders like a cloak. He wanted to say, Rani, you look beautiful: it might be just the compliment that would cheer a broken heart. Somehow he realised that she might have hoped that he would have said this to her the previous night on the balcony. But the moment had passed, he had missed it, and this was not the time to make reparations.

He stood at the end of the bed.

'Are you hungry?'

She considered the question, then nodded her head slowly.

'I'll make you something soon.'

He stood silent for a few moments, then said, 'Do you remember about last night?'

Tears welled up in her eyes, magnifying her dark irises, her lower lip trembled, but she held his gaze, nodded her head.

'Do you remember what you said to me?'

Up and down. She nodded slowly.

'Is it true?' he asked quietly.

This time she spoke. 'Yes, Mr Thomas,' her voice a whisper, a tear fell on to her cheek. She wiped it away with the back of her hand, then resumed her position, hugging her knees.

He tried to look reassuring, but he was sure his smile was hideous.

'Don't worry.' He had to stop himself from adding *mol*.

She looked down at her arms around her knees.

'Do you know,' he asked, 'how many months you are . . . ?'

She made a movement with her head, neither a nod nor a shake. Perhaps it meant: what difference does that make to you?

'Does he know?'

234

The question brought further tears to her eyes, which she wiped away again. She shook her head, let it fall on to her chest.

'I'm sorry,' he said. 'I'm sorry that you have had all this worry by yourself.'

He came and sat on the end of the bed, reached forward and put his hand on hers, felt just below it her angular knee. She raised her head to look at him but said nothing.

'Rani.' He cleared his throat. 'I've spoken to my sister. She knows someone who can talk to you. Offer some advice.'

She looked down again. A tear trickled down her cheek, splashed on to her wrist. She touched it with one of her fingers, then looked back up at him.

'Do you want me to speak to her, Mr Thomas?' she whispered.

He shifted closer to her, tightened his hold of her hand with his.

'Yes, please,' he said.

They remained like this for some time. Then he stood up, moved to the window and opened the curtains. Outside, he had a view into Mariamma's yard, to his right the road, and beyond a glimpse of the beach. All was quiet. When he turned around, he saw that she was watching him.

'Is she a nun?'

'Yes.'

'Does she know I am not Christian?'

'It won't matter.'

'What will she talk to me about?'

'Just to find out how you are feeling. What we can do.'

The 'we' had slipped out – whether she noticed or not he could not tell.

He pondered this when he went downstairs. As he toasted some bread and brewed some coffee, he heard Rani getting up and moving to the bathroom, heard the water running.

Afterwards, she called downstairs. 'Do you mind if I stay in bed, Mr Thomas? I'm feeling a bit weak.'

'I'll bring you something up on a tray.'

They sat together, and he watched her eat the toast he had made, slurp the coffee. While he had made her breakfast, she had washed her hair and plaited it loosely, still damp. Dressed in a kurta, her hair pulled back, she had transformed herself back into the Rani he had known at the optician's. When she had finished eating, he took the tray from her and laid it on the floor. Then they waited until they heard the car outside. From the window, he saw the driver manoeuvre the car until he had it parked in the sliver of shade by the road. The nun alighted from the passenger side.

He met her at the door; she was out of breath, round, with glasses and a light moustache.

'Thomasmon? I am Sister Beatrice.'

'I haven't discussed much with her this morning,' he said. 'She's very tired. Did Chechiamma tell you what happened yesterday?'

The nun nodded. 'It's best I talk to her alone. If she is still upstairs, will you wait downstairs?'

'I'll go out,' he said. 'I want to stretch my legs anyway. If I come back in one hour or so, would that be all right?'

They exchanged phone numbers: the nun would call him if she needed him to return.

He walked out into the sun, the heat. In the distance, he could see her driver, sitting under a tree, smoking a cigarette.

He turned right, walked along the road, the bank to his left eclipsing any view of the sea: he was not sure how he would feel about it after last night. As he walked past the beach resort, a couple emerged, carrying beach towels. The woman was speaking, her voice a whine: 'You said that last time . . .' He passed them, exchanging a look with the young man. A honeymooning couple enjoying a honeymoon argument.

At the end of the track, the autorickshaw drivers were gathered under a tree, along with the man from the kiosk. One driver remained in his auto, sitting sideways, his legs planted on the ground, a newspaper on his lap. He looked up briefly as Thomas passed, then looked down again.

He paused. 'Anything interesting?' he asked.

The driver glanced up, raised his eyebrows, then looked down, muttered, 'The usual.' He was chewing something, then he spat it out, away from Thomas, to his right, near his feet.

He looked up again; his expression had cleared. 'Strike is planned.'

'Right.'

'One was planned last month also.' Then he grinned suddenly, revealing a row of over-large, tobacco-stained teeth.

He walked up the bank and looked at the sea. It was glittering, calm. The storm had blown away any clouds, and the sky was a clearer blue than he had seen over the last few weeks. At this time of the year, each day was spent examining the sky, gauging the movement of the clouds, predicting the onset of the monsoon. The whole vista seemed to be pensive, as if mulling over the events of the previous night, when he had tried to tear a girl away from the arms of the sea, had himself been entangled in its embrace. He glanced to his left, but there was a curve in the bay that he had forgotten about; he had no view of the fishing boats, but he knew that at this time of the day the fishermen would not be around.

He leaned forward and picked up a handful of sand, watched as it slid through his fingers. There had been, of course, all those thousands of years ago, his namesake, the Syrian. The apostle who had landed on these shores, who might even have walked on the same beach. The sand from two thousand years earlier may have been sifted through time, reclaimed by the sea, but it could just as well be exactly the same. How could one tell? Each grain might hold a memory of the sermons which a people, parched for something, had believed. Perhaps two thousand years ago, with little knowledge of what lay beyond the water, the Syrian had brought words of comfort. Your children will die, but they will live again. You are poor, but you are blessed. Some of his remnants were buried in an ivory-coloured church on the Bay of Bengal, the rest had been shipped to Mesopotamia. Even hundreds, thousands of years ago, after leaving a homeland, the desire was to return. He dusted his hands on his trousers. If Nimmy had not been so pious, he thought, he could have brought back her ashes to scatter in the hills of her birth.

His thoughts were crowded. He realised that he was losing a sense of time. He had grown accustomed to the changes in the seasons that would allow him to punctuate the year with little milestones: he needed new milestones. He walked up and down, as he had done a few weeks ago, or was it months? What had he gathered so far? Only a crush on a married woman who had returned to her husband thousands of miles away, resentment from his only child, and a new role of caretaker to a young girl who, no matter how lovable, was, ultimately, not his responsibility. He had written in his letter to Nina, the unfinished letter he was not sure he would even post, *I would change much*. He replayed the conversation he had had with her, weeks ago, when she had been tearful, finally voicing what he had always suspected: that he had, if not failed, then not excelled as a father. The events from the previous night, along with the image of Rani on the beach with her lover, mingled in his head, and as before it was Nina who emerged as protagonist in his recollections.

He was tired, clearly, after last night, and he had not eaten much. His stomach rumbled accordingly and made him glance at his watch: an hour had nearly passed. He turned back; the sea was now on his right. What would have been talked about, decided in this short time? He had no idea how much of her disastrous love affair Rani would have revealed. He found himself chuckling. She may have felt constrained by the veil and habit, but she would have no idea how much a nun relished stories of iniquity. Their innocence of the ways of the world was not manifested in a distaste for it; rather there was a vicarious enjoyment in discovering that the world they had forsaken was indeed as unpleasant and sordid as they had imagined. Of course a young woman allowed to live on her own in the city would yield to its temptations; of course a married man would betray his wife, given such an opportunity. All was right in the world.

When he passed the crossroads, he saw that all but one of the autorickshaw drivers had gone. The one who remained was not the one he had spoken to, but another lying in the back of his vehicle, a handkerchief over his face. The kiosk owner had retreated to the interior of his stall. Thomas could see him bent over a table, eating a chapati from his tiffin. He walked back along the road; there was music playing from the beach resort: it was the time of their lunchtime buffet, which he had yet to enjoy. The nun's driver was now back in his car, in the front seat, the radio playing. He heard voices as he rounded the corner to his backyard and saw the nun talking to Mariamma over the wall.

Something in their demeanour made him pause, one foot ahead of the other. Mariamma was speaking animatedly, Sister Beatrice was nodding, arms folded. The sight of the two women, separated by the familiar, cream-coloured wall, covered with a tangle of bougainvillea, seemed to encapsulate a familiar motif in his life: Nina and Nimmy, Rani and Vishukumari. Now Sister Beatrice and Mariamma. He knew, inexplicably, that they were discussing him, and with that realisation came an urge to turn around and leave. But before he could move, they both turned round and regarded him, their expressions solemn. The nun said something to Mariamma, who nodded and turned away, moved back into her yard without a word of greeting to Thomas.

Sister Beatrice walked over to him briskly and then motioned to the gazebo. 'Shall we sit there?'

She settled into the chair, and he stood before her.

'Is she all right?' he said. 'Did she talk to you?'

The nun nodded. 'Yes, she talked.'

She paused. 'And she is well, considering. What happened last night, thank God, has not harmed her.'

He waited for her to continue, and when she remained silent, absently fingering the beads of her rosary, he said, 'Should we contact her father?'

The nun said, 'She says you are the father.'

For a moment, he thought he had misheard.

'Her father?'

'The father.' The nun cleared her throat. 'The father of the baby.'

The heat was strong, too strong to be sitting outside even in the shade of the gazebo. His shirt was sticking to his back, and Sister Beatrice pulled out a handkerchief and wiped her forehead. He could hear Mariamma's voice behind him, raised, and then a growl: her husband was at home.

'Well,' he said. 'I'm not sure why she told you that. But it's not true.'

The nun nodded but did not say anything. She was watching him; her eyes held a light interest, but her whole manner was quiet, unconvinced. They remained like this in an almost companionable silence. Thomas swatted away a fly.

Finally, he said, 'And do you believe her?'

She smiled slightly, and when she spoke she had that same, light, detached tone.

'Why do you think she would lie?'

'I have no idea.'

She nodded again.

He looked down at his hands and to his surprise he saw that they were shaking.

Sister Beatrice started to speak. 'You lost your wife recently, and you must be lonely. You must miss her.'

He raised his head to look at her in astonishment. 'You believe her . . .'

'You came back home for what? To live all alone in this house, full of memories of your wife? I talked to your neighbour. She says you have been different.'

He stared at her incredulously.

The nun nodded. 'You have been spending too much time on your own. No visitors. Even at Easter you spent the whole weekend on your own. You didn't go to Mass . . .'

Thomas looked down at the small woman in the chair across from him. Her face was impassive, her forehead beaded with perspiration.

'You have been spending time with Rani in the store, and it is natural that you should become friends. She told me you have been very kind to her.'

'Sister Beatrice—'

'You've been buying her presents. Books . . .'

'Books?'

'. . . clothes . . .'

'One kurta!'

'Mariamma says she has seen the two of you embracing,' the nun said with finality.

Thomas turned away and left the gazebo, stood in the middle of his backyard with the sun beating on his head: anywhere was better than being near to the nun.

Then he turned around. 'She was crying . . .' he began but could not continue. He was not even sure she could hear. He walked back towards her and spoke a bit louder.

'Sister Beatrice,' he said. 'None of this is true. Why would I ask Chechiamma to find someone who could help her? Why would I invite you here if I thought she would tell you this story?'

He watched as she struggled to get to her feet from the depths of the low rocker; he made no move to assist her.

'Thomas,' she said. 'The girl is going through a trauma. She needs someone to listen to her, not question whether she is telling the truth or not.'

'So you *don't* believe her?'

The nun stepped out of the gazebo to stand directly in front of him. Her veil was grey, a white band at her forehead. Her moustache glinted in the sunshine.

'Perhaps what is more important is what Rani believes. She seems to believe that you are the father.' She paused. 'And she seems to believe that you will accept the responsibilities.'

He gazed down at her, his arms at his sides.

She sighed. 'I think you will agree that in the circumstances it is inappropriate that she stays here with you. I can arrange a place for her at our centre, but any donation towards the cost of her board over the next months will be appreciated.'

She lowered her eyes as she said the last words. 'You can visit,' she paused, 'so you can make arrangements.'

'Arrangements?'

She sighed again, heavily. 'From what she says, she is not more than three months expecting. If you decide to take responsibility, no one need know, and she can escape any shame or stigma.'

'Can I see her? Can I talk to her alone?' His voice was rough, and without waiting for a response he ran to the back door – *his* back door – then through the kitchen and up the stairs.

'Rani!' he shouted from the landing, and then pushed open the door to his room.

She was tidying the bed. Her suitcase lay on the floor beside her, half-full. She did not turn to look at him.

'Rani,' he said.

She stopped and then lifted her face, turned to face him, her expression calm.

He found he did not know what to say. She waited a few moments and then turned away, bent at the waist and picked up a hairbrush from her suitcase. His eyes travelled over her person, over her slender middle, her narrow hips. There was no sign of a bump, and although her kurta was loose, it was made of thin enough cotton to show any swelling.

He watched her for some time: she undid her plait and brushed her hair, now dry, turned away from him, looking at her reflection in the inlaid mirror on his wardrobe. Even through his confusion he could feel a subtle change in the atmosphere. The way the two of them were posed, a man watching as a woman brushed her hair: a picture of intimacy. He waited for her to speak, to chatter, to say something, but it was as if the events had endowed Rani with a composure he was unaccustomed to witnessing.

'Did he give you the book?' he asked finally.

She paused, the brush poised in mid-air, then she put it down on the bed beside her, started dividing her hair into three, replaiting it.

She nodded. 'It was a birthday present,' she said. 'He brought it to Mr Jos's store. I think Vijay must have told him it was my birthday.'

She tied a band at the end of her plait, then bent again, took out a small pot of talcum powder, dusted her cheeks and neck, completely unselfconsciously, as if it was the most natural thing that Thomas should be watching her toilette.

'Why did you lie to Sister Beatrice?' he asked quietly.

She flung her plait away from her neck, kneeled down and closed the suitcase.

'Why, Rani?'

She stood up, quietly patted the folds of her kurta. Then she went still.

'Did you tell her about him?' Her voice was low.

He shook his head. 'No,' he said.

'Thank you,' she whispered.

'But why did you lie?'

They heard the nun's footsteps, heard her breathing heavily as she climbed the stairs. She appeared panting at the doorway.

'Could you leave us for a minute?' he said, his voice tetchier than he had wanted. He saw the nun's eyes flicker to Rani, saw her nod, remembered suddenly the same nod she had given to the manager of Green Gardens, months ago. So, collusion again, another conspiracy.

The nun said, 'I'll wait downstairs.' As she turned to go, she added, 'I have another appointment in an hour.'

Another girl in trouble? Thomas wanted to snarl.

They waited until they heard the nun descending the stairs, one at a time, and then Thomas sat on one end of the bed, Rani did the same on the other end.

'Tell me,' he started again. 'Tell me why you told her that I was the . . .'

She smiled slightly, without looking at him, her hands lay palm to palm on her lap. And then she spoke. 'Because I knew you wouldn't deny it,' she said. The simplicity of her statement, the trust in her voice smote him. He stared at her, at her profile, her eyes not meeting his.

'But I did,' he said quietly. 'I told her it was nonsense.'

'But you won't go any further,' she said. This time she turned her head and looked directly at him. She could have continued: You won't demand proof, you won't shame me, denounce me as a liar. How could she have been so sure? Perhaps he had revealed more of himself than he had ever imagined, when he had shared the office with her in his friend's optical store. Perhaps she was taking a gamble.

The gamble, if that was what it was, paid off. He found he could not speak, and so they sat together, in silence for many minutes, until they heard the nun call again from downstairs. Then Rani stood up and picked up her suitcase. He watched her, made no move to help: he knew it did not weigh much, her belongings were negligible. Before she left the room, she briefly laid her hand on his shoulder – whether in comfort or gratitude he did not know. He said nothing, did not even look up.

But when he heard voices outside, he moved to the window. The driver was stowing her suitcase in the boot; the nun was climbing into the front seat. Rani opened the passenger door at the back and then looked up so that their eyes met. She raised her hand as she had done that last day at the optical store, and he found that he was doing the same. Then she ducked her head and climbed into the back as, in a cloud of dust, the car pulled away.

14

THERE was someone waiting outside the store when he turned the corner on to the street. All was normal, as if the last few days had not caused any stir in the workings of ordinary life. As always, there was a woman in a sari, dragging a child with reluctant feet. A waiter was cleaning the windows of Green Gardens. An autorickshaw was scuttling further along towards the main road. In the distance, Thomas could see the familiar signs that a ferry had arrived from the islands: a cluster of people were on the other side, waiting to cross.

It was a middle-aged man, wearing a beige bush shirt, the style of which Thomas had not seen for at least a decade. He was not anyone Thomas recognised, and when he saw Thomas approach the store, with keys already drawn, he tutted in irritation.

'I've been waiting half an hour,' he said. He took out a hand-kerchief from his breast pocket, wiped his forehead.

'Do you have an appointment?' Thomas asked.

'I had one for last week.' The man could not conceal his vexation. 'That was rescheduled for today.'

Thomas glanced at his watch: it was nearly eleven.

'For today?' he murmured.

'Yes, today,' the man repeated. 'A foreign lady phoned. On your behalf, she said. And explained you would be open again on Thursday.'

So it was Thursday.

'I'll need to check the diary . . .' he began.

'Come on, man!' the man suddenly exploded. 'What way to run a business? I've waited a week for my bloody eye test!'

'Of course, of course,' Thomas murmured hurriedly. 'I'm sure I can fit you in.'

He had turned the key in the lock without realising, and the door gave way so that he stumbled into the reception area. The air was stale, lending an ukempt feel, but everything was as he had left it. He picked up the post that had been shoved in through the slot over the week, and the pile that he had kicked aside the other day, stood to one side and let the man enter.

'Where is Rani?' The man looked around impatiently.

'She is . . .' Thomas faltered, then looked at the man again surreptitiously. He was older, as far as he could remember, stockier. But that day on the promenade, he had been standing some distance away. There was a strong possibility that the man would return to the store, try to make amends for their argument. He held his breath: could it be?

'Your name, please?'

'Paniamparambil,' the man muttered, wiping his brow again. 'Muhammed. Can you turn on the damn A.C. at least?'

'Of course, of course.' The unit started with a gurgle and a clank, as if protesting at being neglected so long. When it had churned into life, Thomas opened the diary and saw Vishukumari's elaborate Ls and Ps.

'Good, good.' It seemed that he was unable to say a word without repeating it. He cleared his throat.

'So you know Rani?' He asked this while pretending to collect something from the top drawer.

The man was standing near the door to the testing room. He shrugged impatiently.

'Know her? Well, she's been dealing with me and my family for the last year. Where is she?'

Thomas moved towards him, gathering his thoughts, pretending to scan a sheaf of papers he had picked up randomly from the desk. When his eyes focused, he realised they were fliers. *Joshi's Retirement Village*, he read on the first. Then *Sapna's Beauty Salon: Lulu Mall*. Why did Rani keep them?

'Are we ready?' The man was staring at Thomas. It was not him: if he were Rani's companion, then he was remarkably focused on having his eyes tested. And after an acrimonious break-up, it would be risky to choose the optical store as the location for any reconciliation. Thomas showed the man into the testing room.

The next hour and a half was a reminder of his previous five months, only there was no Rani in reception, no sound of chatter and laughter. It seemed like years ago that he had enjoyed a quiet routine, looked forward to his lunchtime walk, enjoyed the cooling breeze from the windows on the bus back home in the evenings. Only one other client arrived: perhaps many had made alternative arrangements on hearing of the store's temporary closure. He felt a momentary pang of guilt for his friend whose business he seemed to be running into the ground, but then dismissed the thought. He had other, more complex, concerns. Jos would be able to regroup when he returned from Texas, take charge and add a new vigour to his store.

When half an hour had passed and no one else had walked in demanding an appointment, he turned over the sign on the door – *Closed for lunch break!* – and locked it from the inside. He pulled down the blinds, then picked up the post that he had left in a pile on the desk and sat down on one of the blue armchairs: he was unwilling to sit at Rani's desk. Among the usual circulars and industry catalogues there was a small cream-coloured envelope, his name written on the front. No stamp or address: it had been hand-delivered. He opened it and immediately saw the letterhead of the hotel down the road.

Thanks for letting me know that the police didn't keep you, she had written. *To be honest, I wasn't much company for my cousin. I pestered him about calling his friend but in the end, when I got your message, we didn't need to. I'm leaving in an hour for the airport, but I'm having a last walk before the taxi comes. I just wanted to write to you before I left, and I promise I'll write you when I get back home.*

He stopped reading. There were a few more sentences, no more. She had not dated the letter, and he found it hard to remember exactly when the last time he had seen her was: she had said she was flying out two days after. Anyway, by now she would be back in the States, her husband would have told her that he had missed her dreadfully, the short time apart would have done them good. Thomas closed his eyes, leaned back in his chair. A nice meal, wine, to bed afterwards. Perhaps she talked about her trip as she undressed; he would be lying in bed waiting for her. Would she claim to be tired, jet-lagged after the journey? Probably not. The lights would be turned off, they would slide into each other's arms. I don't know your husband, he had said. But I know that he is a lucky man.

He opened his eyes, read the last of the letter.

I'm sorry I got so emotional on the phone. It was very selfish of me, especially when I think of your loss. I have no excuse, only the deep fondness I feel for you. Please stay in touch, Thomas, and come and stay if ever you are out this way. Vishukumari.

He examined her name. She had written Vee, and then scrawled over her full name. He let the letter flutter to the ground, stared at it for some time. Then he leaned forward and picked it up. He folded it into a small square and pushed this into the pocket of his shirt. His phone rang.

'Pa . . .'

His daughter's voice was like nectar: that was the phrase that rushed into his mind. He clutched the small device to his ear.

'Nina. *Mol.* How nice to hear you.'

'Is this a good time?'

'Absolutely. Are you at work?' He glanced at his watch.

'No, I've got the day off. I'm just lounging around. I'm meeting up with a friend later.'

'Good. That sounds nice.'

They exchanged some news. He told her about the boiler in the house in London; she told him about a case at work that was particularly complicated. They spoke for many minutes, easily, without restraint. He walked up and down the store, opening the blinds and surveying the street as they talked, then turned away, moved to the testing room. The charts, the desk, the instruments – all lay untouched and as he had last left them. As he spoke, his hand went into his pocket and drew out the folded square, the letter Vishukumari had left. There was evidence, therefore, that she had been real, not part of a dream. More dream-like was the situation with Rani, whom he did not mention. Then there was a pause, which extended to a short silence.

His daughter spoke.

'I've been thinking about you, Pa,' she said. 'About what you said. About what I said. It didn't come out the way I wanted it to—'

'Nina—'

'I didn't say the most important thing. I just went on about being abandoned and all. I didn't say that I don't just miss Mum. I miss you too.'

He gripped the phone tightly. His daughter, his only child, had spoken. He had heard her words in a way he may never have heard them before.

'Nina,' he said, steadying his voice. 'Do you want me to come back?'

In the moments before her response, his mind travelled, across the seas, carrying the same suitcase that he had arrived with, the same clothes. He saw himself as if in a film, but in reverse, so that with jerky speeded-up movements he was moving backwards, away from his bedroom door, backwards down the stairs, out into the street, into a taxi which reversed back to the airport. He could return: the other way this time.

But even as he was watching himself he could feel the fingers clutching somewhere at his chest. And he could picture another image, of himself watching himself. The two selves both clearly him, but one real and present, the other gone now, departed. There was too much here, he realised, too much had appeared in his life; it was not as simple as pressing a rewind button. Even Vishukumari seemed more attached to his life here than she would in London. And then there was Rani. But he had said the words and could not un-say them. If his daughter responded, Yes, I do, Pa, I want you to come back, what would he do?

He stayed motionless for an age, holding his breath. It would be easy in some ways. If he were confused over what to do, how to proceed with the dilemma he found himself in, then what simpler solution than to let Nina decide for him? My daughter needs me you see, he imagined himself saying – to whom he was speaking was not clear.

'That's not what I mean,' Nina said. 'And not even what I want. We'll come and visit in the summer.' She paused before speaking again. 'I'm not sure why, but I just needed to tell you that I miss you.'

He swapped the handset from one ear to the other.

'*Mol*,' he said, 'I miss you too. Very much.'

She laughed, but she said, 'I'm crying, Pa. I just can't seem to stop crying these days.'

He put a hand on his chest, where it felt hollow and full at the same time.

'We are learning about each other,' he said finally. 'With your mother gone, we have to let ourselves learn more about each other.'

He heard her blow her nose, and then she said, 'That's a good way of putting it.'

When she hung up a few minutes later, the tightness in his chest had not subsided. He had not told her about Rani, but he had not known where to start. He sat for some time, tapping his fingers on the seat beside him. Then he stood up, turned off the computer, the air conditioning, and, locking the door behind him, left the store.

The action of leaving its cool interior and stepping out into the heat and glare of the street was comfortingly familiar. He walked with long strides towards the sea, then turned right on to the main road. The bookshop was open, and within minutes he had found the youth with the earring, stacking books from a box on to a shelf. The young man turned on his approach and gave a small smile of recognition.

'Could I ask,' Thomas said. 'Am I the only person who has ordered *Chemmeen* recently?'

The answer came much more quickly than he had expected.

'Actually, no. When I put in the order, I found out that we had ordered the book for someone else just a few months earlier. One of the others must have put it through.'

He smiled sheepishly at Thomas. 'It was only after you came in that I found out what a huge sensation it had been. It's a bit embarrassing. My parents, my uncle who owns this store . . . they've all been really happy that someone has reminded them of it. Anyway, you can see we've ordered a few now to make a display.' He pointed to two neat piles of books on a small table, a small poster showing a black and white photo of the author.

'In fact, I've sold a few copies to tourists,' the youth was saying, 'even if they can't read Malayalam, it's a different type of souvenir.'

'Oh good, good,' he said. Then, as casually as he could: 'Who ordered the other copy?'

He would receive a steady stare, he knew, an appraising gaze before the need to protect a customer's privacy would be reiterated. He had come prepared with a story: he was trying to start up a fan club, a book club, and he was procuring members. But the young man asked no questions, walked over to the monitor on the cash desk and tapped on his keyboard, then scoured the screen.

'Vishal Kumar,' he read.

And immediately Thomas knew: it was a name he recognised from the folder.

'I'm thinking of starting a book club . . .' he began, but the young man was already reading more out.

'We delivered it to his work address,' he was saying. 'He's a lecturer at the Government Law Colleges on Marine Drive.'

How easy. He left the bookshop and crossed over the main road.

The sea was flat, grey, the only ripples came from the ferries churning through the water from the islands across the bay. Today, the haze enveloped the vista. There was only the occasional splash of colour from a glimpse of a sari on the ferry, a flag on one of the larger vessels moored offshore, all barely visible from where he stood. Some miles further north, opposite his house in Cherai, the sea was different: unleashed from the confines of the city which surrounded it here. Blue-green, immense. No wonder a book would be written with a deity constructed from its waves, Kadalamma. For what better reminder could there be of the fragility of human life, with its delicate dramas: birth, love, marriage, death. All diminished by the strength of the sea. Two lovers washed up on the sand, a fisherman breathing life into Rani. Had she been with child when she had stepped into the water or had that, too, been the sea's doing?

He shook himself, turned and walked further to the start of the promenade. A few weeks ago, he had walked along here and had met Vishukumari, now far away across the oceans. Years ago, he had made the same stroll, Nimmy at his side. The promenade was, as always, gay. If he walked on for another twenty minutes, he would reach his stop, opposite the High

Courts, where he could board an earlier bus back out of the city, to Cherai. And just next to the courts, as there had been all these days, weeks, years, was the law college. He had passed the building nearly every day, Rani's paramour comfortably installed in its halls.

He might not be there – hadn't he told Rani he was leaving? Although that too might have been a ploy, a ruse, just as he must have engaged in a certain amount of deceit and deployed a certain amount of charm to engage the young woman's consent. Or maybe in Rani's case not much was needed: a few kind words, some attention, a simple gift. Her face had lit up when Thomas had presented her with the kurta. He could well imagine her pleasure at being given a book that implicitly told her what the giver hoped for. Her defences may not have stood strong for very long.

He looked across and saw that he was drawing near to the law college: a large cream building, with pillars and a red-tiled roof, set back from the road, surrounded by coconut trees.

The steps to the main door were freshly polished, and just inside he saw a woman cleaning the far end of the entrance hall, a bucket in front of her.

'Vishal Kumar?' he asked her. She shook her head, glared at his feet in their sandy sandals.

'Sorry.'

He walked down the hall, the sunshine through the archways punctuating the gloom in bursts. A group of students were huddled in one corner, peering at a sheet of paper pinned to the wall.

'Vishal Kumar?' he asked, and one answered, hardly turning round.

'International Law. First floor.'

At the top of the stairs, there was a glass-cased noticeboard with photographs of members of staff, name tags beneath each. *International Law Faculty Welcomes You* read the title card. Vishal Kumar's photograph showed an open friendly face: a square jaw, smooth skin. His specialism was international mercantile law, and his office was further down the corridor. As Thomas approached the end of the corridor, he saw a man leaning against a door jamb, talking to the person inside.

'I would say five o'clock max,' the man was saying. 'Then we make our excuses.'

There was a grunt from the interior. The man leaning against the door turned to Thomas and watched him approach.

'Yes?'

'I'm looking for Vishal Kumar.'

'Is he expecting you?'

He had the hauteur and curt manner of most people in authority. Replace him with a shorter more hirsute version and he could be the policeman Murugan. If the thirty years Thomas had spent in London still showed, the man would be even more resentful. There was them and there was us: those who stayed and ran the country, those who left. But it was not always the case that those who left were the most privileged; rather that they had a much greater hope of finding their fortunes else-where. This was a discussion which Thomas knew he would have little success in winning with the man opposite him, who was waiting for a response, his expression imperious.

'No.'

Thomas drew abreast with the man and glanced into the office. There were boxes everywhere, the walls were bare. There was another man, in a blue-checked shirt, leaning over the desk that was covered in papers, the metal bin beside him crammed with crumpled sheets. He looked up as Thomas's shadow fell into the room.

He looked older than in his photograph down the corridor, but younger than Thomas had imagined from that glimpse on the beach. He was no more than forty. He was slimmer, too, than he had appeared that day, when Thomas had discerned an incipient paunch: perhaps it had simply been the way he was lying down, perhaps he had been wearing a money pouch. He put down the books he was sorting on to the desk, saying nothing.

Thomas spoke in English.

'Kumar,' he said, 'I'm looking after my friend's shop. Chacko's Optical Store off MG Road.'

There was a silence. The man leaning on the door jamb looked from one to the other, straightened up. 'So, what is it—'

'I'll see you at the reception,' Kumar interrupted. His voice was deep, pleasant. 'See you later.'

It was a dismissal, and the man nodded, moved away. Thomas watched as he walked down the hall, saw him look back once more to eye him with curiosity, before going down the stairs. When he turned back to Kumar, he saw that the younger man had moved away from his desk and was looking out of the small dusty window. He entered the office, stepping over boxes, and joined Kumar at the window. He was a head shorter, but his body underneath the collared shirt was wiry. He had his hands in his pockets, a slight smile on his lips and had assumed a relaxed pose by his window. It was only the twitching of his jaw muscle that showed he was in any way perturbed.

Behind the law colleges was a small patch of grass, and then, beyond, the swathe of coconut trees, swaying in the eternal breeze, claiming the land as their own, so that the college buildings, even in their grandeur, were reminded that they were an upstart, an interloper, never to displace the red earth, the green, the blue sky.

'It's beautiful, isn't it?' Kumar said.

Thomas nodded.

'I've always wondered why they haven't built on this part, like they have on everywhere else. Must be a reason. Foundations or something.'

He cleared his throat. 'I'm from Kottayam originally,' he continued. 'My wife too.'

The last words were said with a nonchalance, but their significance was clear. He turned to face Thomas, held out his hand: 'You are . . .'

'Thomas.'

'Ah. I see.'

They shook hands: he had a firm grip, dry skin. His eyes met Thomas's briefly, then he looked down. He moved away and sat down on the desk, gestured at the room.

'Sorry it's a mess. I'm leaving in a few weeks—'

'To Australia,' Thomas interrupted. 'Rani told me.'

'Yes,' he nodded. 'I see.'

He said nothing more, but fingered the thick gold band on his finger.

'Kumar,' Thomas began. 'Rani has been staying with me. She had to leave the apartment.'

The younger man nodded slowly. 'I know,' he said, and again Thomas thought what a pleasant voice he had. It was easy to imagine him giving lectures, advising students.

He raised his head.

'You see, I went there a few days ago,' he said. 'They told me she had gone.'

There was a noise at the end of the hall, a group of people were laughing and talking loudly. Kumar got up and closed the door, then resumed his perch on the desk.

'Why did you go back?' Thomas asked.

'Because I felt bad. We'd had an argument. I realised that the lease was running out. I wanted to see what she wanted to do. Whether she wanted to go back to her hostel.'

Thomas watched him. The anger that he had expected to feel when he confronted the man was difficult to find. Instead, the calm answers, the absence of denials, were disconcerting.

He realised Kumar was speaking again.

'The relationship is over,' he was saying. 'I feel terrible, but I need to try to make my marriage work. I have a son . . .'

'Rani is pregnant,' Thomas said.

The words were crisp, clear, there was no ambiguity. Kumar remained still for some time, his hands motionless on his knees. Then he stood up and moved back to the window.

And then the anger arrived, like a tide, so that it rose from his belly and fell into his mouth, swirling around his tongue and his teeth. It was an anger that he had been trying to unearth for days, months, years.

'Did you hear?' he said. 'She's pregnant.'

The blue-checked shirt didn't move. Thomas looked around the room, for a weapon, an object that he could pick up and throw at the man. He was breathing heavily; his heart was thumping.

'What were you thinking, man?' He didn't recognise his own voice. 'What were you thinking when you—'

'I wasn't thinking.' Again, the deep notes, the pleasant tone. 'Clearly, I wasn't thinking.' He delivered his words as if to soothe. All was well. Admission of failure, let's move on.

'Can you at least turn around so we can talk face to face?'

Kumar obeyed, a small smile on his lips. They stood at opposite ends of the room, as if in a duel, and then the younger man moved back to sit on his desk.

'Please,' he said, and pointed to a chair that Thomas hadn't seen, behind a tower of boxes.

He moved around the tower, pulled the chair out and sat on it. The room was becoming hot now with the door closed, the window barred. He could feel his heartbeat slowing, and he relaxed back into the chair. He had not realised the tension that had built up inside him. He could have closed his eyes then and there, fallen into a slumber; the wave of tiredness that engulfed him suddenly was overwhelming. But he tried to focus his thoughts. No matter what would transpire from this moment, what else would be said between the two men, he had already learned something at least: Kumar's demeanour made it clear that whatever Thomas had expected to gain from this meeting was not to be.

The man was still perched on the desk, his feet scraping the floor. He was looking at his hands, but not in a shamefaced way; rather he was examining them as would a pianist before a concert.

'Did you send the policeman?' Thomas's voice was abrupt.

Kumar smiled again, this time rather sheepishly, and raised his head.

'I hope you weren't too inconvenienced.'

'Did you? Why?'

'I helped his son out some years ago,' he said. He held Thomas's gaze. 'I just wanted him to make sure that Rani had not left my name lying around. After our argument, I was worried about what she would do.'

'You were a client of the bureau?'

He did not reply but looked at Thomas for some moments before saying, his tone non-commital, 'Hasn't she told you all this? How we met?'

'She said you were a client.'

Kumar made a face. 'I wouldn't call myself a client of anything. She's not running a business. It's more like a hobby, although she would probably call it a vocation.' He slid his hands into the pockets of his trousers, then regarded Thomas calmly.

'I was intrigued by the business card. I suppose I was intrigued by her as well. I pretended I was divorced only so that I could see how far it would go, what would happen . . .'

He stopped talking, his hands jiggled in his pockets.

'Then you bought her *Chemmeen* . . .'

Kumar smiled, his shoulders moved as if in a shrug. 'Do you know it?' he asked without looking up.

'I read it when I was at college. Many years ago.'

'Yes.' Kumar pulled his hands out from his pockets, placed them on the desk on either side of him, the muscles twitching in his forearm. He pushed himself further back on the desk so that now his feet were suspended from the ground.

'Yes, I bought her the book, then I took her out, and things just happened.' He smiled slowly, paused. 'I've never done this kind of thing before. I've been married, happily married, for fourteen years.'

He had bought her a book, a meal, inveigled himself into her affections. That world seemed so far removed from any Thomas had known. And why had Kumar chosen Rani when he could have chosen someone more his equal: in temperament, schooling, position? He let himself think the question, and then his mind moved towards finding a response. If he had not seen Rani that morning, her back bared to him, he might never have been able to imagine an answer. But something had stirred at the sight of her slender figure. He remembered suddenly the two of them in the water, her hair in his mouth, her fingers scratching at his neck, the bones of her hips under his hands. It was her vulnerability: the absence of any robustness. Her fragility had enticed the man before him: the chance to hold something wafer-thin in his hands, something that would fracture under the slightest pressure. The delicate balance that he would control must have been intoxicating.

'She's pregnant,' Thomas repeated. 'At the moment, she is staying at a licensed home.'

'I went to the store when I couldn't find her at the apartment,' Kumar was saying, as if he had not heard. 'To give her this.'

He reached behind him, twisting his body so that his shirt opened at the bottom revealing a hard brown stomach, a cluster of hair around his navel. When he had twisted back, Thomas saw that he had an envelope in his hand.

'I wanted to pay for another month's rent at the apartment,' he said. 'So she would have time to find another place.'

'Finding somewhere to live is not her only concern now,' Thomas said.

'No. You're right.' His voice was low; he tapped the envelope against his thigh.

Suddenly, Kumar raised his hands to his eyes. The envelope was now crushed against his nose. The gesture was so at odds with his previous measured countenance that it was all the more shocking for its rawness.

'It's such a mess,' he said, his voice muffled. 'What a mess. I never want my son to find out how stupid I've been. He's ten years old. What would he think?' His voice was higher, less pleasant, imploring.

Thomas could say nothing. He watched as the man exhaled slowly, straightened up, patted at the crumpled envelope, and then folded his arms. When Kumar spoke again, his voice had returned to its normal, pleasant tone.

'I decided to end it all some time ago but could never find the right moment. When I told her I was going to Australia, she followed me, saw my son.' The rest was easy to imagine, and as if to prove this Kumar fell silent.

Thomas looked around the room: a good-sized office with a nice view. The man opposite him would be considered success-ful by most standards. And he would not be going to Australia if others, not only those close to him, did not feel that he had credentials. He enjoyed an influence and prestige that Thomas had never commanded. Just as he had felt that the way Rani had been courted was out of his sphere of experience, so was this environment intimidatingly unfamiliar. Only the very clever managed to get into this college: the entrance exam was notori-ously tough, the fees were high. If he had studied here, he might have embarked on a respected career, he might even have prac-tised in court. But when he was a young man, from an unexceptional family from the hills, with unexceptional grades, it had been clear that he would never ascend to such lofty heights. It was Nimmy who had prised them both from the inevitabilities of their future.

The tiredness had returned, and his eyes felt heavy. He might have fallen asleep and woken up hours later. For a brief moment, he could not recollect why he was sitting in this chair, in this room.

'I wonder,' Kumar's voice cut through his thoughts, 'I wonder why you are here?'

He let his words sink in as he looked coolly into Thomas's eyes.

Thomas opened his mouth, but Kumar was speaking again, choosing his words with deliberation, as if he was in one of his lectures and about to reach his final, irrefutable argument.

'Rani was fond of you. She spoke of you often. You said she was staying with you?' he said.

'She was,' Thomas answered, then stopped. A silence ensued, but then he continued as if he was himself only now discovering the reason for his visit: 'She was until yesterday. But I live on my own. My wife died . . .'

Kumar was staring at him, his expression inscrutable. 'I see,' he said finally.

What do you see? Thomas wanted to ask him. An old man? A lonely man? The encounter had reached its end, he got to his feet. Kumar did not move; his feet were swinging slowly.

'She is in the licensed home near Mattancherry,' Thomas said. 'I thought you should know that. And the . . . circumstances.'

Kumar nodded again. Then he extended his hand with the envelope from earlier.

'Can you give this to her?' he asked.

What had he hoped to achieve, Thomas thought, by coming here? The anger returned, but this time over his own foolishness. He had nothing more that he wanted to say. He took the envelope and pushed it into his pocket. Then he moved to the door and without turning back he walked out.

When he reached the stairs, he heard steps behind him. Kumar was jogging down the hall and had raised his hand as if to stop Thomas. Then, as he drew nearer, he slowed to a walk, pushed one hand into his pocket so that his attitude looked more relaxed. But his hand was clenched into a fist, evident from the bulge.

'You see,' he said, as if they were continuing the conversation, 'my wife's family own a lot of property in Kottayam. And both my parents are still alive. I am considering their feelings as well.'

Thomas nodded, turned away and started down the stairs. When he reached the end of the first flight, he looked back. Kumar was still there, watching him, standing still, silhouetted against the light behind him. They stared at each other, not speaking, until Thomas continued down the stairs, out of the building and back on to the street.

15

A WEEK passed. No one came to see him in Cherai. There were no phone calls, no nuns in habits appeared at his door, no irate policemen tapping their batons impatiently against their thighs. He did not go back into the city but resumed the routine of his first weeks: waking with the sun, plunging into the sea, working in the garden. Evenings were spent on his balcony, the breeze his companion. He finished the mini-gazebo and left it one morning in Mariamma's front yard, hoping that the small boy would knock on the door, ask him to help set it up in the back garden. But when he returned some time later from a walk, he saw that the gazebo had been moved, was probably already in position, being used as a hiding place. There was no sign of the boy.

One afternoon, he climbed on to the roof from the balcony to bolster some tiles that had loosened in the storm. As he was sprawled precariously on the roof, the sea behind him, and in front of him, at his eye level, the green fronds of the coconut trees framing his house, he looked down to his right. Mariamma was hanging some washing in her garden, was standing still, a garment clutched to her chest, staring aghast at his form. He smiled and gave a quick wave, to reassure her, and she turned away quickly. He realised that he had not considered how dangerous his actions were – a missed foothold, a panic attack. When he had finished his task and was inching backwards, then lowering his feet over the edge to find the balustrade of the balcony, his hands, slippery with sweat, gave way an inch. For one heart-stopping moment he thought he would lose his balance and crash down on to the sandy square in front of his house.

The next morning when he was leaving the water to retrieve his towel, he saw the fisherman running lightly over the sand towards him. The red cloth tied around his head, and the green mundu tied around his waist the only clothing he wore, a bright contrast against his sinewy black chest and limbs. He was a man of the sea, a merman, who could pull humans as well as fish from the waves.

'Misterthomas.' His teeth were a white flash against his dark skin.

Thomas held out his hand, and the fisherman took it.

'Thank you,' Thomas said.

'The girl is all right?'

Thomas nodded. 'What's your name?'

'Krishna.' He was still smiling. With his free hand, he pointed at Thomas's house. 'If you need to fix something, then just tell me. My brother and I can help you. If you need someone to cook for you, my sister can cook for you.'

It was not just information; it was a request. He may have thought that he was alone, but there were eyes: Mariamma from below, the fishermen from the sea. Even the coconut trees had been watching him. He would ask the fisherman's sister to come to the house and talk to her: perhaps he could ask her to cook a few times a week, even clean. He didn't need the help, nor was he particularly inclined towards the intrusion, but the message was implicit. Just as the sea needed the land in order to be the sea, he needed others in order to be who he was. Even his arrangement with the fisherman – over the fish that was brought to his house and Mariamma's – was more than a contract: it was an assertion of the larger ecosystem.

He nodded, let go of the man's hand.

'And I'll bring fish?' the fisherman asked.

Thomas nodded again. 'Thank you again.'

The encounter with the fisherman, that the young man had asked after her, was the only confirmation that Rani had stayed with him, that she existed. The days passed, and no other reminder arrived; he could live on in his solitude undisturbed. The heat intensified, the air became heavier, the sun was relentless. In the evenings he grew melancholic, ignored his books, including *Chemmeen*, which remained in its brown packaging, turning instead to the small shoebox, sealed with elastic bands, that still remained in his suitcase in the wardrobe. It was full of photographs he had brought with him from London. He lay on his bed at night under the fan, naked except for a mundu, and scattered the images over the bedspread. He did not want chronology; he played a game with himself. He would select a photograph and try to remember where and when. It had never been his task to assemble the photographs in their house. Even Nimmy had been rather haphazard. After the first years of neatly arranged albums, the photos then stayed in the envelopes, in a cupboard. Their house in Tooting had had the same displays for nearly thirty years: in the living room the wedding photo taken in Kanjirappally a few weeks before they left for London; in the hall, photos on the wall of baby Nina in her mother's arms, Nina in her First Communion dress, Nina in school uniform. Later, a graduation photograph appeared on the mantelpiece. But there were few other displays: neither Thomas nor Nimmy were very sentimental. The photographs that he had in his hands now were testament to their nonchalant attitude to their life. Perhaps Nina was right: her childhood might have been colourless. Both parents consumed by the difficulties of being displaced from their homeland, they treated the joys of life with a cavalier attitude. Neither realised that it was not enough to simply provide their child with a house: they had to make it a home.

He picked up a photograph: Nimmy and Nina in front of a lake. It could be a picnic they took to Hyde Park. Behind them were swans, groups of people in pinks and browns. Nina was wearing purple trousers tucked into brown boots, her two plaits reaching to her elbows, a woollen hat on her head. From the gaps in her teeth, Thomas guessed she would be about eight. So Nimmy would be thirty-two or thirty-three. He peered at her. She was wrapped up in a large beige woollen rollneck, blue jeans ending in trainers, her thick hair parted to the side, then disappearing behind her. Smiling widely, her arm around her daughter. He stared at the photograph for minutes, hours. The others lay around him, a mass of multicoloured squares, but he seemed unable to let go of this one. Behind the camera he stood, aged thirty-five. The angle of the shot, the way the two girls were looking up, betrayed his height. The sun shining on their faces, his back to the sun. Just perceptible in the corner was his shadow, half an arm. He stared at it, but nothing moved inside him. He knew he would feel differently if he had Nimmy standing in front of him, Nina sitting beside him, but he could not shake off the feeling of distance he felt between himself and the man behind the camera.

He stood up and pulled his laptop from under his bed, then rifled through his clothes until he found her card. He typed in the name of her website, and the internet whirred before settling on an image: a wood frame, the shine of glass. So she was based in Missouri; he had not asked for details. At the corner, her name in discreet letters, a contact link.

He clicked on it and a page opened, a notepad on which he could write a message.

Rani is well, he wrote. *I went to find her at her hostel and it seems she was having problems with the landlord. She is living in better lodgings now. My friend Jos will be back in a few weeks. I may ask him if he still wants me to help him out. I'm hoping my daughter will visit soon. She told me she wanted to come during the monsoon! Hope you are doing well.*

Thomas.

He clicked send before he could change his mind, and then spent the next half hour browsing the pictures of her previous projects, scouring the images for a glimpse of her. He found none, only several recommendations: *Vee seemed to know exactly what we wanted. I'm delighted with the extension that Vee designed for us. It's really filled our house with light.*

He woke up an hour later, the lights still on, his beer bottle empty beside him. He swept all the photos off the bed and into the box, the albums he left on the bedside table. The photo he had pored over he propped up against his lamp, and before he turned off the lights he had one last look. The next morning he left the house, walked to the end of the road and caught his bus into the city, then the ferry across the water.

It was not a journey he had made very often. When he had first arrived in Ernakulam for his college studies, a group of friends had taken the ferry from the mainland across the grey water to the peninsula. That day, the most interesting aspect for the young men had been the quartet of backpackers who had been on the ferry with them: with long blonde hair, glistening light hair on their forearms, naked shoulders showing the stripes of where their brassieres had been. Years later, he had made the same journey with Nimmy and a young Nina in his arms. Again, four backpackers had boarded with them, two men and two women whom Nimmy had helped, advising them on directions to the bus station for their journey back. One of the young women, when they had arrived at the jetty and were gathering their belongings, had pressed a small bead bracelet, which she had been wearing herself, into Nina's hand. So many years ago, he thought. And now Nimmy is gone, Nina is far away. The ferry moved up and down, the waves were strong, and he could see that they were drawing towards the jetty.

The home was on a quiet road in the hinterland between Fort Cochin with its famous church and stately elegant architecture, and the narrow alleys of Jewtown. There was a gate with a sign, a long path and a series of low white buildings far enough in the distance so that the people moving inside were only visible as shapes. The bushes and flower beds were well cared for: an old man wearing a white vest and a mundu was on his haunches tending to one near the gate. Thomas pushed the gate open, and as he closed it behind him he saw a figure hurrying towards him on the path, her face encircled by a grey veil, the creamy folds of her habit flapping around her legs.

'Yes, please?' she called.

Thomas stopped and waited for her to draw near. She was young and slim: not unlike Chechiamma on her first visit back to the family home, complete with habit and veil. This young nun, with her vow of chastity sealed, now surrounded by reminders of carnal desire.

'I'm here to see Rani, if I may,' he said.

'Rani,' she frowned, her forehead crumpling momentarily. Her hand went up to the rosary at her chest. 'Sir, can you wait here please. Your name?'

'Thomas.'

She nodded, then turned back up the path, moving in that distinctive way that could only mean a nun, he thought.

A face appeared briefly at a window far away, then drew back. A form appeared on the verandah of one of the buildings. He was at one end of the path, and on the other end was another world. Something made him look back over his shoulder. The old man was still there but standing up, a trowel of some kind in his hand, watching Thomas. He had clean white hair, light-brown eyes in an ancient face, his skin etched with lines. After some time, the old man gave him an imperceptible nod, then turned away and bent back down over his beds.

There were footsteps approaching. Sister Beatrice he recognised, and with her, a head and a half taller, another woman, in her thirties he guessed, but not wearing a habit; she was in dark-blue jeans and, most noticeably, her hair was cut into a short, swinging bob.

'Ah, Mr Thomas,' Sister Beatrice said. She spoke in English, and so Thomas replied in the same.

'Maybe I should have rung,' he volunteered.

'No, no need. But we have some regulations, you understand. To ensure the girls have some privacy.'

'Yes, of course.' He felt angry at himself for his not thinking of that. 'Sorry . . .'

'No, no,' Sister Beatrice was saying. 'Can I introduce Dr Dasgupta?'

The younger woman's gaze was frank. She had a firm grip.

'Hello.'

Sister Beatrice said, 'Dr Dasgupta has been staying with us for some weeks now.'

The younger woman broke in: 'Basically I'm trying to find out exactly who ends up in these homes.'

'She's been investigating interventionist policies,' the nun said, then dropping into Malayalam: 'Family planning, etcetera. Not something I can approve of, but I've turned a blind eye.'

She had on her face the hint of a smile. She was not without a sense of humour, Thomas realised. Then, reverting back to English, she said, 'I wanted to introduce you to her because Rani has been helping her.'

'I can't speak Malayalam.' The younger woman shifted on her feet and shaded her eyes. 'I'm from Calcutta. One of the nuns has been helping translate for me. But of course, it's not easy for the girls to be open and honest with a nun!'

She laughed, glanced at Sister Beatrice, who inclined her head in acknowledgement.

'But now Rani is interviewing the girls, sharing her experiences and getting theirs. It's been a very effective technique. I'm hoping that she'll carry on working with me for as long as possible.'

'I see.'

'She's good with people.'

'Yes,' he said, grateful for something he could say with sincerity. 'She is.'

'They open up to her.'

'Thank you, Beena,' this from Sister Beatrice. The younger woman seemed to recognise her cue, turned to Thomas and offered him her hand again.

'Nice meeting you . . .'

She walked away, and he was left with the nun, who touched his arm briefly, smiling widely. 'Shall we sit over there?' She pointed to a bench positioned under some trees near the fence. They walked along the meandering path, interspersed with flower beds.

'We grow nutmeg trees,' she said, as if she were giving him a tour. 'We can sell the fruit, and the girls help with looking after them. Also, we have a vegetable allotment.' She pointed to some beds further away, then to a small cream building set apart from the others. 'A craft workshop, set up by an NGO a few years ago.'

They arrived at the bench, in a pleasant shady spot, and sat down. The nun arranged her habit over her legs and exhaled.

'So hot,' she said.

He asked her: 'And Rani? Is she all right?'

'Yes, yes. Settled in nicely.'

'And is she . . .' he hesitated. 'Is she really expecting? I mean . . .'

The nun looked at him curiously, her gaze steady, then nodded.

'Will I be able to talk with her?'

'She's busy at the moment,' Sister Beatrice replied. 'But I'm sure you will be able to in a while.'

He nodded, glanced down and saw her feet in comfortable black chappals, dry skin at her heels. Her toenails needed cutting.

'I'm from Calicut,' she said, apropos of nothing, but it seemed to Thomas, in explanation of her toenails. 'I've lived down here for about six years now. My adopted home.'

'Is that where you met Chechiamma?'

'Oh no,' she smiled. 'Sister Grace and I studied in Rome together, at Sapienza. We were the only Keralites, and we became good friends.'

They sat quietly, until he began to feel impatient. But he did not want to break the silence, unwilling to be the first to broach the subject that was hanging over them. Then the nun folded her hands neatly, one over the other, and turned to him.

'Rani insists you are the father.'

There was nothing to say. He settled for, 'Do you believe her?'

She shrugged. 'That's what she tells me!'

Her tone of voice was light-hearted, but her eyes were grave, searching his.

He tried to gather his thoughts. He had not really expected Rani to change her story. Perhaps she hoped that in his confusion he would in turn start believing that he was the father of her child. She did not know that he had confronted Vishal Kumar, that he had met her real-life lover.

'Has she told you anything else?'

'A lot.'

He looked at her in surprise. His expression must have shown some consternation, for she reached out and patted his arm again.

'But not about you. I meant about her. Her family, her childhood. You know. And,' she lowered her head so she was regarding him slightly askance, 'she's told me about the matchmaking.'

'I had no part in that!'

'I know. She told me how you've destroyed the evidence.' Then her body started shaking against his as she laughed. 'She has initiative, that girl!'

He ventured to join her with a smile. 'Yes, she has.'

'And so many people joined! She said about twenty!'

'Mm.'

'Anyway,' she sighed, fingered her rosary absently, patted down her habit over her knees. They lapsed into a silence that felt, he tried to resist, contemplative: as if the nun beside him expected him to start praying for his future. He stretched out his legs, crossed his ankles, folded his arms, determined to appear relaxed and unperturbed by her comments. The silence continued: an impasse.

Then from somewhere, perhaps the edge of the peninsula, from where the old church stood, from where the elegant, spidery fishing nets vaulted up to the sky and then down to the water, a breeze arrived, whispered at his neck. And the nun said, in an echo of Rani's words those months ago, 'Tell me about your wife.'

He wanted to give a little laugh and make the same excuse as when Rani had asked him: maybe some other time. But she was regarding him with that same expression as when she had been sitting in his gazebo, reminding him that he must be lonely, that his house would be full of memories, and he found himself speaking slowly.

'After she died, I felt a strong urge to come back.'

She was watching him, her eyes grave, her lips pursed.

'I left Kerala when I was not yet twenty-four,' he said. 'A young man. I grew up here, but I became a father, was a husband, had a job, all these things I did far away. I'm not the kind of person who has many friends. I depended too much on Nimmy. Not,' he turned to her, 'in the way that most people think. I cook, I helped with the house. No, I just left her to do everything else. Raise our daughter, make a home for us in London, keep in touch with family back here.'

The old man had walked over to near where they were, his old body with its brown thin muscles now bent over the flower beds to their right.

'She must have been exhausted with all that responsibility,' Thomas said. 'I exhausted her.'

The words remained suspended in the air, then he imagined the old man catching them between his fingers, so that he was now at this minute interring them into a small grave among the flowers. The nun didn't respond for a long time, but she placed her hand on his arm again, and after some time she spoke. 'Grief hits us in different ways at different times.'

They sat quietly, but there began a change in the atmosphere. The breeze left; they were alone again. Behind them somewhere they could hear a bell ringing and then shrieks, shrill laughter: lunchtime at a nearby school. He had had his chance to have his say. She had listened to him quietly, and now he found he was holding his breath.

'About Rani,' Sister Beatrice began.

'Yes.'

'I'm not sure how much you know about these homes, but she will not be able to stay here for ever. A few months after the baby is born, no longer.'

'I see.'

'As for the baby . . .' She opened her palms. 'As I've already told you, the options are limited. Either the girls give the babies up for adoption, which is not an uncomplicated process. Or they try to raise them by themselves, which, as you can imagine, is tremendously difficult. They may not find a job, and they will probably never marry. Most girls I know who have taken that path have ended up working in the sex industry.'

The contrast with her habit and the benign environs made her words even more shocking.

She waited, as if she wanted her words to sink in.

'It is one of the greatest paradoxes in this country which is full of paradoxes,' she continued eventually. 'A woman who is a mother is revered. A woman who has desire, well . . .'

She smiled at his expression. 'You are shocked at my words, Thomas. But these girls,' she gestured to the buildings in the distance, 'look how I have to hide them.'

They both turned and looked at the small, low buildings. From this distance, they appeared not unlike chicken coops. Behind the netted windows, the hens were waiting to lay their eggs.

Sister Beatrice spoke: 'She doesn't want her father to know, and she seems confident that he will not try to see her in the near future. That gives her some leeway. If she were to marry in the next few weeks,' she paused as if to acknowledge the impact of her announcement, 'no one need ever know what we know about her. She could present her father with a fait accompli.'

It was not a surprise: hadn't he arrived here knowing what would be asked of him? But even so, it was many minutes before he could speak.

'I'm not sure,' he said, 'that a widower in his fifties would be what her father had imagined . . .'

The nun laughed. 'You are still . . .' she searched for the word, 'youthful, Thomas. And,' then she turned to him with the same wry look as before, 'an older man with a young wife is not something we are not used to.'

He considered her logic.

'She's younger than my own daughter,' he said finally. 'And I think of her like my daughter, not . . .'

But he could not continue. These were fripperies, he could see the nun thinking. And therein lay the problem. For all the empathy and wisdom a woman like Sister Beatrice could hold, she did not have any insight into the daily intimacies of married life. She had never, he glanced at her, shared a bathroom with a man since she had joined the convent. Beneath the veneer of an impossible request, however, there was a truth. The surprise that many might have when Thomas revealed his young bride would fade fast: he was lonely, he had a long life ahead of him, how could he remain alone? Rani, on her own in the world with her baby, the product of an ill-fated love affair, would not be afforded such sympathy.

He could not help but admire the nun. She had asked him to talk about himself so that he could see his woes placed within a grander narrative. Look around you, was her message. Open your eyes. He thought: how could I return and think I could live a life that was immune? It was as if his homeland was chewing him slowly first, deciding whether to spit him out or allow him to be swallowed, down her gullet, into her belly. I left a long time ago, he thought, and now I am being welcomed back. With a poisonous kiss: the beauties of the land caressing my right cheek, its injustices my left. He remained silent, then watched as she stood up, smoothed down her habit.

'I'll tell Rani you are here,' she said. 'God bless you,' then she turned away.

He kicked at the ground with his heel, looked up and watched her disappear down the path and then into one of the buildings. He got to his feet and looked around him. The gate was only a short distance away. He could walk away. He had spent the last week undisturbed; he could spend the next twenty years in similarly quiet isolation. He had never heard of this home, and he could let it slip from his memory. It was unlikely that this flock of nuns would pursue him; Rani certainly did not have the means to do so. Even Chechiamma, he was sure, would not refer to it again. So it was true, he thought. She was a disappearable; she was one of the unfindables, indistinguishable among the multitudes, invisible. He walked towards the gate, and then a movement to his left caught his eye. He had forgotten the old man, with the ancient face, the white hair, on his feet now, holding his trowel up as if it were a cross with which to give a blessing.

Behind him he heard footsteps, and he glanced back. He saw Rani skipping towards him in a light-pink salwar kameez, the loose tunic flapping against her body, her hair in its familiar plait hanging down one side. He turned back and saw the old man still standing there, his light-brown eyes watchful. For a few moments he was suspended between them, then Rani drew up to him. She was smiling, her face as bright as when he had first met her all those months ago in Chacko's Optical Store.

'Mr Thomas!'

'Hello, Rani.' He turned to face her fully. 'How are you? You look well.'

'Yes,' she brushed a strand of hair away from her cheek, 'keeping well. Are you?'

He smiled. 'Not bad.' Then, 'It's nice to see you.' The words came easily to him.

'Yes.' She clasped her hands together, laughed.

They remained like this for a few moments; behind them Thomas could sense the old man moving away.

'Shall we sit down?' He pointed back to the bench.

'Or shall I bring you a coffee? Oh, I should have asked the Sister!'

'Please, don't worry,' he said. 'Let's sit.'

He led her to the bench, waited until she had sat down, then sat beside her.

'How are you?' she repeated.

He looked at her, her face open and shining.

'I've been a bit worried about you,' he smiled.

She laughed. 'Oh, Mr Thomas, you are so kind. But I feel well, like I told you. And I've been helping Dr Dasgupta.'

'Yes, I heard.'

'I speak with the girls, then we try to translate into English.'

'I see.'

'She says she may need me for some time!'

'That's good.'

'Are you still swimming?'

He smiled. 'Yes.'

'And eating well, Mr Thomas? Don't forget to eat!'

He smiled but said nothing.

'And how is the small house you are making? For the children?'

'It's finished.'

'Oh, you will have made them so happy!'

'I hope so.'

'Yes, for sure. You made me happy,' she said. 'I felt happy in your house.'

He smiled again. 'That's good.'

They could carry on like this, he could see, for many minutes, even hours. He remembered her sitting on his bed in Cherai, in the morning light, her knees drawn up, her hair loose around her.

He took a deep breath and said quietly, 'Rani. You're telling everyone that I am the father.'

She looked back, a small smile on her lips. Then her smile faded, and she looked down at her hands, her face grave. He watched her: there was a new softness to her cheeks, like a slight blurring, so that the lines of her profile were less defined. She did not speak but played with the collection of bangles on her wrist.

'I went to see Vishal Kumar,' he said.

His words stilled her. She did not turn to look at him but whispered, 'Where?'

'At the law colleges.'

She nodded as if to say, yes, that's right, that's him. Then, finally, she spoke.

'I don't miss him any more,' she said, her voice low. 'I was afraid before. But I'm not now. Speaking to some of the other girls here, I think I was lucky.'

She lifted her head and looked at him. 'Some of them, I haven't talked to all of them yet, but some of them . . . it was their uncle. Or their cousin. And they didn't want to . .' She shook her head. 'It wasn't for love. But some of us, it was for love. With Vishal . . .' she paused. Then she said slowly, 'He lied to me about his wife but that is the worst thing he did.'

Thomas reached into his pocket and pulled out the brown envelope. 'He wanted me to give you this,' he said. 'To help you out over the next few months.'

She didn't take it, gave it a sidelong glance. 'I don't want it,' she whispered.

'What do you want, Rani?' he asked.

She was quiet for a long time, then placed one hand on her belly. And when she did, he could see the shape of the small mound, barely perceptible but there, nevertheless, under her fingers. When she spoke, her voice was matter of fact.

'I want my baby to have a chance in life,' she said.

Before he could respond, she had turned to him, so that her face was lifted to his, her slim figure twisted next to him.

'You know what I want, Mr Thomas. What I want you to do.'

'Your father, Rani . . .'

'He will not object,' she said. 'He will be pleased . . .'

He said, 'Is it just my decision, Rani? You're forgetting my daughter.'

She shrugged her shoulders, turned her face half away. 'She could know the truth, everything. Wouldn't she understand?'

It was like arranging your personal dramas in a line, as if for a beauty pageant, he thought. At the lower end, the disgruntled clients of Rani's bureau, now wondering why her services had disappeared and what their next port of call might be. Then Jos and his annoyance at losing his trusted assistant. Further along, perhaps he could place himself: his loneliness, his yearning to be with and taste a woman again. Then Nina: the loss of her mother, compounded by her bewilderment at her father's behaviour. How could all of these trials win against helping a new life, a child? Two children, he thought, glancing at Rani, who looked impossibly young, like a schoolgirl, fresh home, now out of uniform. As he had glanced down at Sister Beatrice's, he glanced at Rani's feet: small and narrow, her baby toes curled inwards as if seeking comfort from the rest of her body.

'Mr Thomas?'

She was speaking again, but he was no longer listening. He could only hear the faint noises from the street beyond the gate, now bright in the full sun. Busier now with carts carrying sacks of flour and rice, cars and bicycles. People going about their days: getting a meal ready, washing clothes and cleaning rooms. Waiting for a respite from the heat, waiting for the rains to arrive.

16

THE road snaked up, not much wider than a track, trees on either side, the valley stretching down. It looked as if they had left the city far behind, but the traffic was continuous. The bus struggled up the incline; the driver hooted as if to relieve his frustration with the weakness of his engine. A car swerved around them and overtook.

He had left his house just as the sun was rising over the water, a puddle of blood-orange spreading and rippling on the grey surface. He could hear a few noises emanating from Mariamma's backyard as he left through the back door. He hesitated for a moment, wondering if he should tell her, then decided against it. He did not intend to be away for very long: a few days, no more. From the road, he could not see the sea. Beyond the bank, he imagined the fishermen pulling in their boats. They would miss him at least, he thought; they would notice he was not there. But then this thought was immediately replaced by another: how could he be sure? He had been back only six months, not long enough even for a full cycle of the heat and rains. When he reached the end of the track, he arrived at the cluster of autorickshaws. No one acknowledged him, so used were they to his morning routine of striding towards the bridge over the backwaters to Junction. When he stopped in front of one, the driver stared at him blearily, then with surprise.

'Sir?'

'Bus station, please.'

He boarded the bus with many others and found a seat halfway down, which when a woman carrying a child boarded, just as the bus was pulling out, he relinquished. For the first half of the journey, nearly two hours, he remained standing, the breeze from the windows scarcely reaching the humid centre of the vehicle. The bus swayed and shuddered; the driver cocooned in his cabin drove at speed but with a satisfying concentration and conscientiousness. An ornament hung down, glittering, from the rear-view mirror. Occasionally, Thomas caught a glimpse of his shirt reflected in the mirror, the strap of his bag across his chest. He was pressed against the other standing passengers similarly beheaded in the reflection, everyone swaying in time, in a rhythm, as the bus climbed and climbed, winding its way up the hills.

When his daughter had answered the phone last night, no matter that he had rehearsed his words, they failed him. When she had repeated '*Allô?*', and then, after the silence had extended, 'Pa?', he had finally spoken: 'Nina.'

She had said again, 'Pa?'

He had spoken in Malayalam, which he rarely did with her any more: *Ninamol, oru karyam.* And as he said them, he remembered that they had been Nimmy's last words, as if she could, in her dying moments, see ahead to the future, a future she would not be part of. To Thomas and Rani, their fates now sealed; to this conversation he would hold with their daughter. That's quite a story, his daughter had said finally, to which he could only reply: yes, yes it is, *mol.*

She was quiet again for a long time, and he could not break into the silence. When she spoke again, her voice was soft, almost wondrous.

'I always thought you would go and get married or something,' she said. 'I mean, I thought you always intended to remarry, and that's why you went back. I think that's partly why I was upset. Because I felt you weren't being more open about it.'

'Nina . . .' He wanted to contradict her; he had never thought in those terms. But then who was he to say what his intentions had been when he had returned? Here he was, still unsure of how he had arrived where he was.

'So if you're worried about how I would feel about you marrying again,' she was saying, 'you needn't be. In some ways, I've already dealt with all that. I would rather you weren't alone for the rest of your life.'

Then she had paused, and he could hear her catch her breath. 'But *this*, Pa? I mean, will you be *happy*?'

The sweetness of her voice, her concern, brought tears of relief to his eyes. He choked on his words, and he could hear her gasp, and then she was laughing and sobbing at the same time until he laughed a little as well. When they had ended the call, he was as always, the phone beside him, sitting on his own, on his bed in his room. But he felt that he was not, however, alone. Nina knew; the others did not matter.

The bus deposited him on the small strip of earth that composed the village street. He looked around. Some signs were familiar, but there were many more stalls than when he had last been here, he calculated, nearly ten years ago. When he had come back to India with Nimmy, it was her family that absorbed their time and attention. There was no one left in Vazhakulam who really wanted to see Thomas: no parents, no brother. Only a smattering of cousins who were scattered enough and distant enough to not await his return.

But as he found the path that led away from the row of shops, up through the trees, he felt a sensation: his feet had not forgotten, his movements were one with this land. He was a son of these hills, these trees, this earth. He had settled near the sea in Cherai, but *that* now seemed like a dislocation. He had been in his teens when he had first seen the sea; he had known these hills since his birth. As he walked up, the shade from the trees a protection from the rays of the sun, the humidity as heavy as a blanket, his forehead beaded with perspiration, he looked around him. On such a rock he had sat with his brother, whittling at sticks to make a kite; he had tried to climb such a tree, falling off halfway up the trunk. He had lain on such a patch of earth, looking up at the canopy of leaves, dozing after school before his father had called for him.

He walked on and on, stopping only once to buy some fruit and some water from a roadside stall. The vendors were no one he recognised. Then he walked up the road, the steep incline which flattened out so that cresting the zenith you were presented with the view: a long, straight, red-dust road, narrow, with no markings. On either side, the audience of coconut trees whispering their welcome. And just visible ahead: the openness, the stillness, the paddy field which he had walked around, every day, to get to school and back. Before long the houses appeared on either side in a zigzag, small discreet bungalows set back from the road, a well, now disused, in front of each. He read the names: Kollaparambil, Philipose, Kuriacose. And then Imbalil: sold when his brother died with no heir, Thomas an ocean away, and his sister having denied all worldly possessions. He stood and looked at it from the road. He had not even been involved in the sale. Chechiamma had found a buyer, a local family who wanted another house for their younger son. The money had been divided: between Chechiamma's convent and Thomas, an inheritance which he had left untouched until he and Nimmy had decided to lay foundations in Cherai.

The front yard was well tended with pot plants and a clean patio area. There was no one in sight. He gazed and gazed. It had been changed, as nearly all the houses had since he had left India: gone was the front verandah, the house had crept around it to engulf it and fashion a living room, which when electricity and television arrived in Vazhakulam meant people wanted to stay indoors under the fans rather than risk being bitten by mosquitos in the dark. It was painted a light pink and there were net curtains in the windows: no sign of the old wooden louvred shutters. No sign of Amma, Uppan and their three children: one of the smallest families in the village, the others sprawling to eight or nine children. He turned and walked on, skirting the paddy field, drinking in the silence, absorbing the colours, the weight of the air.

He rounded the bend, just as he remembered, and saw the white church elegant against the blue sky. God, thank you for this land. The words came easily to his thoughts, as if by treading the ground of his youth, he could revisit the prayers of his childhood. There had been few moments in his life that he could remember when he had called on God, and even then the reasons had been laughably trivial: his calls had arisen from childish concerns. Most memorably had been that day, at age nine, when instead of returning directly to the house with the eggs he had collected from the family hen, he had stolen away and found refuge in a dell just like the one to his right. There, he had cracked each egg against his teeth, felt the slippery yolks slide into his throat, making him retch, but still he swallowed. He had been told by his friends that the most vicious, strongest martial arts experts that they all idolised did the same. After his crime, he had prayed to God: please let Amma believe me, and he had felt immense gratitude when his mother had exclaimed on hearing that he had fallen, crushed the eggs, but had not interrogated him. The memories were vividly clear: the colour of the eggs, the intimacy of the yolk in his mouth, the soft sound as the shell cracked at the merest touch. How easy, now that he was back here, among the same trees and earth that had watched him grow up, watched him move away, to remember.

To one side, from the bank to his right, among the trees he could hear voices, raucous laughter. A group of young men, hidden from view, the familiar sickly-sweet smell. One was beating a rhythm on some kind of drum, also familiar. What else was there to do in this beautiful land that, in its lushness, did not offer what many a young man craved? He turned away, forgot about them, and let his eyes rest on the church ahead, its slim white frame perched at the crest of the hill. The valley below a resplendent green, the wind rustling through the leaves of the thousands of coconut trees. There had been some kind of service, but now people were leaving, finding their footwear, slapping their chappals against the soles of their feet. The men tying their mundus above their knees, the women pushing down the pallu of their saris from their heads. Two children raced past him, brushing against him, reminding him that he was there, part of the vista, living, breathing, not just an onlooker. Everyone left within minutes, so that by the time he had skirted the entrance, walked around the building and stepped down the path, his feet finding their way, he was alone.

The graveyard was quiet; there was only the sun and the wind in the trees. He found his parents' graves with ease, looked on them, standing above at first, and then he unslung his bag from his shoulder, threw it on the ground and squatted beside it. The flat white slabs had a greenish tinge, unavoidable from the moss and the damp under the shade of the trees, but their names were clear, engraved on their own stone, side by side, as if they had died together, not six years apart. There lay his parents. As the youngest child, he had been his mother's favourite: a circumstance which was accepted and never challenged by his two older siblings. Chechiamma had been as indulgent of him as his mother: he had never wanted for his favourite snacks when he came home from school, and he had slept curled up against his mother with her smell of coconut oil and spices until he was seven. When she had died, before he was married, in his second year of college, he had spent some weeks staring listlessly at his books. Perhaps it had been then, his first foray into the lack of engagement that would dog him for the next years, his whole life even. He plucked at some grass by his feet, his thoughts fleetingly moving over Nimmy's small grave, in the crowded cemetery in Lambeth, the peaceful gardens.

He saw the other stone out of the corner of his eye but resisted for a few more minutes, delaying the movement as he felt the slow sadness creep up over him, it seemed from his ankles, over his groin, over his chest, as it always did. He turned his head: his brother's grave looked no newer than his parents'. In fact, he had died soon after, only just thirty, a handsome, laughing older brother, who had teased Thomas for marrying so young, attaching himself to one woman at such an early age. His brother had died unmarried, leaving no widow or children behind, only a trail of adventures, an adoring younger brother. The tears arrived, splashed on to his feet, and he cried for Nimmy too, who lay beneath the ground thousands of miles away, a different ground, alone and small: what had he been thinking?

The first blow caught him between his shoulder blades, more like a shove than a punch, sending him sprawling against his brother's stone as if his sibling had come to life and had started one of his rough tussles. Before he could straighten up, untangle his limbs, he felt an explosion in his ribs. Then came the smells: the sweet stench from their breath that made his stomach turn even as he was grabbing at the stone, his fingers clawing at the smoothness. The smell of sweat, of hair oil, the feel of hands over him.

They punched and they kicked him, gaining a methodical rhythm, first one then the other. Were there more than two, he could not tell. He could feel the metallic taste of blood between his teeth. Then they grabbed the collar of his shirt and yanked, once, twice, so that his head was jerked back and then forwards, until he heard a rip, the flap of material left hanging by his ear. Then, their hands running over his body, as intimate as a lover's, over his chest, then his waist. Over the backs of his legs and then into his groin. He heard a sound, realised that he had made it himself. But then, suddenly, no more.

Stillness followed. He lay on his brother's grave, his head on the earth beside it, his chest on the cool headstone. The wind rustled in the trees around him, a crow cawed. Minutes passed. When he stirred, he reached his hand out and to his astonishment he felt the strap of his bag. When he tried to open his eyes, he found only one responded, the other felt like a fist had erupted from his eyelids. He saw that the bag lay on its side, its contents spilled on to the ground. His extra shirt, a mundu, rolled now into a ball. He opened and closed his fingers, then tried to turn on his side; the pain was immense. He could hardly take a breath: a broken rib no doubt. His phone was gone, and his wallet, with it the photo of Nimmy and Nina. It was this that brought the fury to his chest, that they would be pored over, pawed at. He let himself shout out, only so that that he could hear his voice and know that he was alive. Then he lay back, his chest heaving, exhausted, spent, as if after a night of love, his body bruised and beaten.

What had he expected when he made this pilgrimage back to his village? That having heard that he was to take into his care a young girl and her unborn child, the trees, the earth, would rise to their feet on his arrival? That they would salute him, then bow down in admiration? That he would be celebrated as a true son of the land, his heroism lauded? What he had agreed to do was a small drop of water falling on a ground which was thirsty, parched. There were many more disappearables; he had only found one. He closed his eyes, but in doing so he could see. The beating: this was his applause.

There was a noise, a crackle on the ground, and he turned his head as quickly as he could, his shoulder ablaze with pain, his body tensed for more. His eyes tried to focus, the left eye now closed, only a blur from his right. They had not come back; it was a child.

A child wearing a frayed but clean buttoned blue shirt and brown shorts, standing and watching him, a stick in his hand. His large eyes, the thick eyelashes, not blinking. And from just behind a voice, carried over in the wind. A woman's voice, impatient, not anxious: '*Mon!* Where are you?'

The boy continued staring, motionless.

She shouted again, and without taking his eyes off Thomas the child suddenly opened his mouth, called back, his voice high with distress: 'Amma! Amma!'

A woman came running, and on seeing Thomas dropped her bag, pushed her son behind her.

'Who are you? What happened?'

He tried to sit up, but the pain in his side made him fall back. The woman stepped forward.

'Are you all right?'

'Yes.' His voice was thick, his lip swollen.

'Let me help you.'

She was thin but strong. Together, they manoeuvred his body into sitting position, his back against his brother's stone. He tentatively stretched out one leg, bent it, then the other. Miraculously, nothing was broken.

'*Vellum kudikke.*' She produced a bottle of water from her bag and held it to his mouth. Her hand against his cheek was cool, soothing.

'Thank you,' he said. 'Sorry to scare you.' He looked at the child, who was still standing a little apart. 'And your son.'

'No, no.' She sat back on her haunches, pulled the pallu of her sari around her. The boy came to stand behind her, laid his hands on her shoulders. They were close: he could reach out and touch them if he wanted to. The bell from the church rang once, then again, then stopped, as if it were being tested for the next service.

'Did they rob you?' she asked.

He nodded, gave her a weak smile, and she clicked her tongue in sympathy.

'These boys nowadays . . .' Then, 'You are from where?'

He smiled again. 'I was born here,' he said. 'I just came to visit . . .' he gestured to the gravestones, and she nodded in understanding.

He studied the woman, who was looking discreetly to one side. She seemed happy to wait with him until he felt ready to leave the graveyard. She would help him to his feet, he knew. They would find the priest, and he could call a cousin or even Nimmy's brother. It would be a chance for him to tell them of the new lease of life he was going to have. The thought made him laugh, and the ache in his ribs flared up as if chastising him for his levity. The woman was watching him curiously now, and he laid a hand on hers to reassure her, squeezed it. He had not been looking for applause, he realised, only a reminder that he was supposed to live. That he was to take a step forwards, a hand in his, and move into the light.

Acknowledgements

My deepest gratitude to my agent Stan, Alison Rae and all the team at Polygon, and Ailsa Bathgate.

My gratitude also to friends and readers for your encouragement; and to my family for giving me that unbreakable bond with Kerala.

To my two precious daughters: thank you, my sweethearts, from deep in my heart, for your love, support and companionship.

And to my husband: for everything you are to me, for always thinking the best of me.